# The Earl's Promised Bride

## One Night in Blackhaven
### Book 2

## MARY LANCASTER

DRAGONBLADE PUBLISHING, INC.

## ARE YOU SIGNED UP FOR DRAGONBLADE'S BLOG?

You'll get the latest news and information on exclusive giveaways, exclusive excerpts, coming releases, sales, free books, cover reveals and more.

Check out our complete list of authors, too!

No spam, no junk. That's a promise!

### Sign Up Here

www.dragonbladepublishing.com

*Dearest Reader;*

*Thank you for your support of a small press. At Dragonblade Publishing, we strive to bring you the highest quality Historical Romance from some of the best authors in the business. Without your support, there is no 'us', so we sincerely hope you adore these stories and find some new favorite authors along the way.*

*Happy Reading!*

*CEO, Dragonblade Publishing*

# Additional Dragonblade books by Author Mary Lancaster

**One Night in Blackhaven Series**
The Captain's Old Love (Book 1)
The Earl's Promised Bride (Book 2)

**The Duel Series**
Entangled (Book 1)
Captured (Book 2)
Deserted (Book 3)
Beloved (Book 4)

**Last Flame of Alba Series**
Rebellion's Fire (Book 1)
A Constant Blaze (Book 2)
Burning Embers (Book 3)

**Gentlemen of Pleasure Series**
The Devil and the Viscount (Book 1)
Temptation and the Artist (Book 2)
Sin and the Soldier (Book 3)
Debauchery and the Earl (Book 4)
Blue Skies (Novella)

**Pleasure Garden Series**
Unmasking the Hero (Book 1)
Unmasking Deception (Book 2)
Unmasking Sin (Book 3)
Unmasking the Duke (Book 4)
Unmasking the Thief (Book 5)

**Crime & Passion Series**

Mysterious Lover (Book 1)
Letters to a Lover (Book 2)
Dangerous Lover (Book 3)
Lost Lover (Book 4)
Merry Lover (Novella)
Ghostly Lover (Novella)

**The Husband Dilemma Series**
How to Fool a Duke (Book 1)

**Season of Scandal Series**
Pursued by the Rake (Book 1)
Abandoned to the Prodigal (Book 2)
Married to the Rogue (Book 3)
Unmasked by her Lover (Book 4)
Her Star from the East (Novella)

**Imperial Season Series**
Vienna Waltz (Book 1)
Vienna Woods (Book 2)
Vienna Dawn (Book 3)

**Blackhaven Brides Series**
The Wicked Baron (Book 1)
The Wicked Lady (Book 2)
The Wicked Rebel (Book 3)
The Wicked Husband (Book 4)
The Wicked Marquis (Book 5)
The Wicked Governess (Book 6)
The Wicked Spy (Book 7)
The Wicked Gypsy (Book 8)
The Wicked Wife (Book 9)
Wicked Christmas (Book 10)
The Wicked Waif (Book 11)
The Wicked Heir (Book 12)
The Wicked Captain (Book 13)
The Wicked Sister (Book 14)

**Unmarriageable Series**

The Deserted Heart (Book 1)
The Sinister Heart (Book 2)
The Vulgar Heart (Book 3)
The Broken Heart (Book 4)
The Weary Heart (Book 5)
The Secret Heart (Book 6)
Christmas Heart (Novella)

**The Lyon's Den Series**
Fed to the Lyon

**De Wolfe Pack: The Series**
The Wicked Wolfe
Vienna Wolfe

**Also from Mary Lancaster**
Madeleine (Novella)
The Others of Ochil (Novella)

# Prologue

THE VALE TWINS left their first family meeting with high hopes for Julius, their oldest brother. But as they made their way upstairs, leaving the others to plan their strategies, Leona found it was the youngest of her sisters who occupied her mind.

"If she focuses on Julius, perhaps she won't get up to mischief on her own," Leona said, following her twin into his bedchamber.

"I thought we *wanted* her to get up to mischief?" Lawrence said, leaving her to close the door. He understood she meant Lucy. "To help her decide whether or not she wants to marry Eddleston?"

"Well, that rather depends on Eddleston himself, doesn't it? And he hasn't written back to us."

"But he did write to Julius," Lawrence pointed out, "offering to come up in August."

"Yes, but we still don't know what he is *like*," Leona argued. "Lucy is convinced he is an unpleasant, dry, haughty old stick doing his late mother's bidding from duty, and it's true such a man would not do for any of our sisters."

"No, but Lucy's never met him either. From what I can tell, her judgments come solely from his name!"

"St. John Gore, Earl of Eddleston," Lucy recited. "I suppose it's the *Gore* that is so unfortunate. But you're right, it's no way to judge."

Laurence sprawled across the window seat, regarding her thoughtfully. "You're afraid that worrying she'll be tied to a horrid man by a childhood betrothal will make her do something foolish? Irrevocably foolish? She is not stupid, Leona."

"No," Leona agreed. "But she *is* impulsive and insatiably curious, and she does *not* like to feel hemmed in without a choice. Who does? I am afraid she will break out of her invisible bonds by doing something so outrageous that she takes her own choices away."

"Because neither Eddleston nor anyone else will have her if she sabotages her own reputation." Lawrence mulled it over, then glanced at her. "Deliberately, you think?"

"I don't know. She seems…withdrawn. In such a mood, I would not put it past her."

"Do we need to follow them into town on the night of the ball?" Lawrence wondered.

"We could," Leona said. "Or we could just emphasize to the others the importance of watching Lucy. Especially to Julius, thus making it easier to persuade him to go to the ball too."

"That's really rather brilliant," Lawrence said admiringly.

# Chapter One

FROM HER WALTZING partner's arms, Lucy gazed around her with a rising thrum of excitement. Everything delighted her, from the elegantly decorated ballroom to the butterfly-bright gowns of the ladies in their silks and muslins, and the way the extravagant candlelight caused jewels to sparkle and glint. Not that Lucy wore any jewels apart from the fine pearls at her throat—a gift from Julius, her oldest brother, for her first ball.

*This* was her first ball, even though she would be nineteen years old in a couple of months, and she had no intention of being limited in her acquaintance by four formidably tall brothers and two chaperoning sisters.

Accordingly, when the waltz came to a close and her partner—an amiable but somewhat over-talkative young gentleman—offered to return her to her sister, she replied, "Oh, my sisters have been dancing too. I believe I see them over there. Thank you, sir, I have enjoyed myself immensely!"

She smiled, and the young man, whose name she had forgotten in all the excitement of her first public waltz, looked gratifyingly dazzled.

"Perhaps you would like to dance again later?" he said hopefully.

"That would be lovely," she said, and hurried into the throngs milling off and on to the dance floor. With luck, her siblings would lose her.

Not that she planned any mischief, as such, but she did like to follow her own nose without the tedious formal introductions of her sisters, or the protective glowers of her brothers. Well, three of her brothers. Aubrey understood better her need for freedom.

Now that freedom seemed to fill her wings. She moved sedately among the couples and the chaperones, the young men both respectful and predatory, the older gentlemen often watching the women while they discussed politics or morality or the latest prize fight. She peeked into the card room, just a little warily, in case her sister Felicia was there—Felicia loved a game of cards—but although a few ladies were present, mostly watching, Fliss was not yet among them. Lucy allowed herself a brief glance around the faces of the players, a few of whom were only half paying attention. One had the serious, fevered concentration that boded ill for himself and his family.

Before her spurt of pity could cause her to intervene and make matters worse for everyone, she drifted away. In the gallery, the orchestra struck up a lively country dance that would probably have been fun, even with a brother. But she wasted no time on regret. It was hardly worth sacrificing her freedom for.

Instead, she examined the orchestra: the violinist going through the motions of tunes he had played a hundred times for people who never noticed him; the cellist who seemed not to be able to help the expressions flitting across his face as he played, his body swaying, and his feet tapping the floor. Those expressive players made her smile as her gaze swept on around the gallery and unexpectedly met that of a young man standing against the balustrade.

He stood perfectly still and yet somehow gave an impression of swift, restless energy. Perhaps it was the way the candlelight glinted and flickered across his shining, light brown hair. Something like shock jolted through her, no doubt because he was observing her as she observed everyone else. She tilted her chin but chose not to look away. For some reason, she felt that would have admitted she was in the wrong to be watching at all. Though if she was, so was he.

His lips quirked into a smile—not the arrogant or seductive smile she expected, that of a rake discovering a young lady examining him. Instead, it was almost shy, as though its owner hoped she was sharing in some joke no one else had seen. It was a rare, curiously attractive smile, but she hastily dragged her eyes free and walked on without appearing to notice him further.

However, a little frisson of interest shivered up her spine. Who was that man? One of the orchestra enjoying a break? Its leader, perhaps? Unlikely. He was too young. His coat had looked too fine and well fitted. His figure was slight but elegant, his face, despite its long, thin nose, almost delicate in its other features, like an artist's impression of aristocracy.

Perhaps he was just curious, like her.

She quickly found another distraction. Across the room, her brother Aubrey gazed at surely the most beautiful girl she had ever seen. More urgently, her eldest sister Delilah approached on a course that would intercept with Lucy's at any moment. Fortunately, Delilah had not yet seen her, so she slipped beneath the gallery into an open alcove. Through a half-open curtain, she glimpsed a set of stairs.

*Ah! These must lead to the gallery!* A childhood memory flashed into her mind—herself and the twins creeping up a different staircase to a different musicians' gallery to watch the gorgeous people dancing at embassy balls. Their late father, Sir George Vale, had been a highly respected diplomat, constantly traveling, and the family had always gone with him.

Before she knew it, Lucy was climbing the stairs in front of her. Well, she might like to talk to the musicians, or at least to applaud them. And if she came across the rudely staring gentleman with the smile, that might be interesting, too.

The stairs did indeed lead on to the gallery, where the lively music sounded just a bit louder and less well blended. She emerged into shadow, the only gallery lighting being around the orchestra and the more general light from the ballroom chandeliers, which penetrated only partially. Lucy was glad, since she did not really want to be seen up here by her family.

Keeping to the gloom, she moved closer to the musicians, trying not to dance her way across to the rhythm of their music. On the edges of the lighter area, she halted half behind a helpfully positioned pillar, and looked over what was visible of the ballroom. She could see half the dance sets and a large part of the seating area, including her family's table. Julius, her eldest brother, sat there alone, taking a nip from his flask. He looked…churned up, enough to both worry her and give her hope that whatever had quashed his zest for life was being breached.

She barely knew this brother, of course. He had only just retired from the Royal Navy, and for most of her life, he had been at sea. But she recalled enough fleeting visits to know that the twins were right to be concerned. He was not *meant* to be so passionless.

The hairs on the back of her neck prickled. She spun around, peering into the deeper shadows at the gallery wall.

The figure of a man shifted and detached itself from the gloom. The elegant stranger.

"You," she blurted, and could have kicked herself for admitting having noticed him before.

But only a very faint smile flickered on his lips.

"Me," he agreed.

Was he laughing at her? Impossible to tell.

"I don't suppose you were looking for me?" he asked, almost apologetically.

"Of course not!"

He sighed. "I thought not."

She glanced down into the ballroom once more. Julius appeared to be looking upward, so she took two hurried steps backward and hit something hard that immediately began to wobble as though it would fall.

As though *they* would fall. In the gloom, she made out a swaying tower of storage boxes, instrument cases, and even a tall hat someone had clearly abandoned on the top. Her instinct was to leap back and cover her ears—some accidents were simply inevitable—and hiss a desperate apology to the orchestra for the disruption.

But her companion leapt into unexpected action, throwing his arms around the tower, straightening one box in the middle, then grabbing a falling violin case with one hand and a flying guitar with the other. He dived forward, bending low, and the tumbling hat landed squarely on his head.

"Oh, well done!" Lucy said, torn between laughter and admiration. "I'd say I was sorry to put you to the trouble—and of course I should be—only I wouldn't have missed that for the world."

"I aim to please." The young man stepped around the now stable tower and propped the guitar and the violin case against the wall.

Lucy eyed the hat still on his head. "Do you suppose we could risk putting it back?"

He should have withered her with a stare at the very least, but instead he took off the hat and placed it carefully on top of the tower.

"Perfect," she said breathlessly, feeling the safety of the pillar at her shoulder once more. She placed one hand upon it to remind herself not to move again. "I was afraid the whole edifice would collapse with a crash, scaring the orchestra into a discordant cacophony or even silence, and everyone would stop dancing and look up here."

He moved forward to the other side of the pillar. "And your adventure would be over? Who *are* you seeking up here, then?"

"What makes you think I'm seeking anyone?"

He regarded her across the back of the pillar, and his eyes gleamed. "You appear to be more of a participant in life than an observer."

"On the contrary," she said with dignity, "despite that almost catastrophic accident, I am a *great* observer of life."

"And what or whom are you observing below?"

"My brother. Not that it is any of your business."

His gaze left her, moving beyond the pillar in the direction she had last been looking. "Captain Sir Julius Vale," he murmured. "And no, it is certainly none of my business."

"You know Julius?" She wasn't quite sure whether or not that pleased her. Julius was rising from the table and limping away, out of her line of vision unless she moved further into the light.

"Sadly not," the stranger replied. "I overheard someone mention his name. He is a striking man."

Instantly protective—for Julius had lost an eye and injured his leg in various sea battles—she flung the stranger a haughty glance. But he had moved on.

"Talk of striking, *that* is an astonishing headdress. One could hide puppies in there."

She couldn't help her surprised giggle, for the dowager's headdress in question was indeed a remarkable confection. "Wouldn't it be fun to try? Only, the puppies would be bound to chew it, and leap out, unraveling the whole thing."

He leaned his shoulder against the other side of her pillar. "Yes." He sounded awed. "But only think of the fun."

"I am," she admitted. "But sadly, I see no way to introduce even the tiniest puppy without being intimately acquainted with the lady. Which I am not."

"I'm sure you could contrive to be so with just a little effort."

"I probably could, but where, sir, would we find the puppy?"

"We will have to leave the building and seek out strays."

"*You* will have to," she corrected him. "I shall be too busy scraping an acquaintance with the lady."

"Of course you will. With regret, I shall have to give up on the idea."

"Why, are you afraid to brave the puppy alone?"

"No, I am reluctant to miss the pleasure of your all-too-brief company."

She frowned, for there was no polite flattery let alone flirtation in his voice. In fact, he sounded diffident, almost apologetic. "Why?"

Again, the smile flickered across his lips. He had expressive lips, only she wasn't quite sure *what* they expressed. "I sense a fellow mischievous soul."

Oddly, *she* sensed very little. This was rare. Since childhood she had been in the habit of gauging characters, not just the good from the bad, the friendly from the unfriendly, but things of a deeper nature. She still wasn't quite sure how she did it, but growing up, she had begun to realize it was a rare empathy, and to look upon it as a gift.

Her gift did not penetrate this man's character. She sensed only humor and a curiosity to match her own.

"Mischievous like an evil demon?" she asked.

Now he laughed outright. She liked the sound, soft and un-self-consciously musical, and so genuine that she had to smile in return. She amused him and found herself disproportionately pleased.

"Hardly," he said. "More like a seeker of amusement. Or a puppy trapped in a fabulous headdress."

This time it was Lucy surprised into laughter.

He watched her, the faintest smile playing on his lips. His expression was mild, but his eyes… His eyes were light, reflective, and unexpectedly, profoundly beautiful.

"Perhaps I could persuade you to dance?" He sounded unsure, almost apologetic, as though he did not really expect her to agree.

Which had the opposite effect of making her long to do so. Only, with a surge of regret, she knew that she could not. Otherwise, he would think she had come up here only for him. And that was neither quite true nor entirely false.

"I am not yet ready to go back down," she said. "Besides, the sets are all full."

"Not up here," he pointed out.

He took her gloved hand from the back of the pillar, as though to draw her back from observing eyes below, so she let him, and was spun suddenly around as though in one of the wilder Scottish dances. An instant of baffled exhilaration, and then he halted them both.

He still retained one hand to steady her. His eyes gleamed through the gloom, promising laughter, not seduction. "Five minutes. On the balcony," he murmured, dropped her hand, and sauntered to the stairs.

"Why?" she called after him.

"Reconnoitering for stray puppies, of course."

Again, laughter took her by surprise, and she didn't mind in the slightest. He most definitely intrigued her. She did not even mind his presumption in touching her, for it had been dancing and over, really, before it had begun. Moreover, she appreciated that he hadn't tried to persuade her to go with him now. Instead of making arrogant assumptions, he had simply accepted that he really was not who or what had drawn her up here in the first place.

So, while the sense of fun grew within her, she moved closer to the musicians. One or two of them glanced at her curiously while they played, as though aware of her and... *Good grief, I don't even know his name.*

She smiled at the musicians, listened, and watched for a minute or two, then raised her hands in silent applause before retreating back to the stairs. Only as she descended did some kind of common sense return. Reputation was all to a young, unmarried girl, and there were a thousand rules to protect her—and hem her in unbearably. All so that a husband who would neither love her nor think twice about betraying her would know she was pure. Someone like the unspeakable Earl of Eddleston, whose visit she dreaded like the plague.

Ignoring Eddleston—after all, they had ignored each other quite successfully since birth—she did not want to shame Julius or the rest of the family. On the other hand, she had so much of life still to experience, and there was something curiously attractive about the stranger, something elusive that she was curious to catch, or at least understand.

She waved to Felicia, who had spotted her from the card room door. The country dance ended just after that, so it was easy to lose herself in the throng. She found herself moving inexorably toward the open balcony door and forced herself to halt and think.

She was aware of the dangers surrounding apparently unprotected females. But this man knew Julius was her brother, and who would willingly annoy *him*? Besides, she was tired of safety, dull and predictable, and though the stranger's character was difficult to read, she sensed no threat from him.

Or did she? Despite his diffidence of manner, he was not *safe*, like her talkative waltz partner, whom she liked but whose name she could not recall. This man seemed to have no arrogance whatsoever, yet he radiated something that was daring and challenging and promised most beguilingly to be fun.

Still, one had one's pride.

Sighing and deliberately walking past the balcony doors without even glancing, she instead glimpsed the most serious of her brothers, Cornelius, deep in conversation with a very pretty young lady. Her eyes did not appear to have glazed over, so at least he was not talking about crop rotations. Cornelius was stewarding the Black Hill land for Julius, and he took his duties extremely seriously. However, the lady with him now was speaking animatedly back to him, and there was actually a faint smile on his lips.

That made Lucy smile too, because it was so rare. He worked too hard, relaxed too seldom, and yet he had such a good heart that he deserved to be appreciated by far more than his teasing family.

"What are you smiling at?"

She recognized his voice close behind her. It caused a flutter around her heart, but she did not turn. "Cornelius."

"Am I dismissed?" he asked ruefully.

"He is my brother."

"But it's not because of him you left me in pitiful solitude on the balcony."

"No, I decided it was improper."

"That," said the stranger, "is a whopper of gargantuan proportions."

She laughed, taken by surprise again, and glanced up at him. "Not entirely."

His eyes gleamed. "I found a pup."

"On the balcony?" she said in blatant disbelief.

"Hardly. Across the street. It might be a little too big, but we'd need to get it closer to the headdress to be sure."

"Hmm. Wait here while I look."

It seemed the perfect solution, though when she stepped through the balcony door, she was surprised to find a lady and gentleman already taking the air. Her heart lifted, because it seemed to prove that her odd acquaintance had really *not* been trying to inveigle her into a compromising situation.

Leaning her hands against the balustrade, she peered down into the street, as far along both sides as she could see without actually falling over the edge. Dark had fallen and the summer evening was chilly. A drizzle of fine rain landed on her neck.

A couple of well-dressed youths weaved along one side of the road, passing a flask between them. A carriage rattled past in the road, narrowly missing a crowd of young, working women, perhaps returning home. A cat slunk among the shadows, but she saw no dogs.

"It's gone," the stranger said, sounding disappointed as he leaned beside her.

"You did not wait," she accused.

"I was afraid you would vanish again."

She looked at him, trying to see behind the humor in his eyes. "No, you weren't. Why did you invite me?"

His lip twitched into a self-conscious smile. "I wanted to see if you would come."

"Ah. Honesty at last. Why does it matter?"

"Perhaps it doesn't. Shall we dance instead?"

# Chapter Two

THE OTHER COUPLE were retreating inside. Was that luck, or was the stranger actually looking out for her reputation?

"Very well," she said recklessly, and accompanied him back into the ballroom. Julius, who had clearly been looking for her, scowled from across the room, and she smiled radiantly back. The orchestra struck up a waltz, and the stranger took her hand and swept her into the dance.

For some reason, it took her utterly by surprise. She even stumbled slightly, for this was nothing like waltzing with the talkative boy, and she couldn't even put her finger on why. Just that her heart beat too fast and she seemed a little too breathless for the gentle movement of the waltz. She tried not to look at her feet. Felicia had been quite adamant about that.

"You needn't worry," her eternally surprising partner said, "you waltz delightfully."

"You notice my lack of practice," she said ruefully.

"Only because it surprises me. I had not imagined this was your first ball."

"Shocking, isn't it? And I am almost nineteen. My come-out was foiled by the death of my brother-in-law—my sister was to have presented me to the *ton*."

"Did you mind?"

"Not really. There was too much else to think about and to

do. In fact, my poor sister was at her wits' end when Julius took us all by surprise by retiring from the navy when they wanted to promote him, and whisking us all back up here to Blackhaven."

"And does Blackhaven please you?"

"What I know of it. There are some very interesting people here, though I tend to meet only the sick ones at the pump room."

"You suffer ill health?" he asked in clear disbelief.

She laughed. "Lord, no. My brother Aubrey, though he hates to talk about it. He was a delicate child."

"I sympathize. So was I."

"Have you come for the waters, too?"

"No, though perhaps I should try them out. Does your brother find them efficacious?"

"He is certainly better since we came here, though he claims the waters have nothing to do with it. What does bring you to the town, then? You are not a native, are you?"

"No, I'm not. I came on several errands, all of which are proving more complicated than I had imagined."

"I'm sure the man who rescued everything I sent flying will have no difficulty with a few complications."

"The trouble is, I do not have a disciplined brain. I am all too frequently distracted down irrelevant but much more amusing paths."

"Like your ridiculous puppy idea?"

"Among others," he agreed.

She eyed him with a touch of genuine unease. "You do know we can't *really* stuff a small dog inside someone's headdress, however ugly it is and however well I have become acquainted with the lady?"

"We don't actually have to *do* it. I just want to know if it's possible."

"Why?"

His eyes widened. "Why? Don't you?"

Her breath caught. "Well, yes, but I wouldn't actually *do* it!"

"Then neither shall I. Yet."

"Do you really have nothing better to do?" she asked curiously.

"Lots, though of course that depends on one's definition of better." The glint of mischief in his eyes died quite suddenly as he glanced aside to the couple waltzing sedately past them.

The male of the couple's eyes widened as though he were startled. Lucy's partner did not seem to notice, merely inclined his head to the lady—a tall woman in her early twenties, of pleasing rather than pretty features. Lucy smiled at her too, since she recognized her from the pump room.

It was all over in a passing moment.

"Do you know that couple?" her partner asked.

"No, though I have seen her in the pump room with an older lady I took to be her mother. He appeared surprised to see you here."

"Oh, he is mistaken if he thinks he knows me at all."

There was something very ambiguous in that statement. "Actually, *I* don't know you at all," she reminded him. "Not even your name."

He focused on her once more. "Tyler."

"Is that really your name?" she asked doubtfully.

"Sometimes. It is a good name."

"It certainly gives little away." Her breath caught. "Are you in *hiding*, Mr. Tyler?"

He smiled. "Your eyes positively dance at the prospect. It makes me sorry to disappoint you."

"Does it? Why were you in the orchestra gallery?"

"To see the whole of the ballroom better."

"Why? Were you looking for that man? Or the lady?"

His eyes smiled, so she knew she was wide of the mark. "No. But I found what I was looking for. I hope you did."

She thought about it. "I was certainly entertained, though I'm not quite sure how!"

"Escape," he said.

She thought about her life at Black Hill and was forced to admit, "I am not much imprisoned."

"Perhaps you are hemmed in by expectation. Or suitors."

"I have no suitors," she said, with an odd mingling of regret and impatience. Then, since she might have sounded rather pathetic, she added grandly, "In fact, I am already betrothed."

Was he disappointed? She had no reason to hope so.

"I trust he is a delightful young man."

"He is neither," Lucy said with relish. "He is old, rude, and neglectful, and yet insists on holding me to a promise I never made."

Mr. Tyler blinked. "What a monster! How can your family allow such a terrible match?"

She wrinkled her nose. "Honor and the word of gentlemen, I suppose, though from all I can gather it was women who urged the betrothal in the first place."

"Then surely women can break it. Get your sisters on your side. And any other female relatives you might recruit. I'm convinced they will beat down the males in no time."

She couldn't prevent her quick smile. "They probably would. But it is not quite so simple. You see, my betrothed is rich."

"That is certainly a great tragedy."

"It rather muddies the waters, since I have nothing else to contribute."

At this, he definitely looked startled.

She blushed hotly. "I have said far too much. Most of it is rubbish anyhow, so oblige me by forgetting I said anything at all. You must think me a blabbermouth of the first order, besides a whining ninnyhammer."

"No. I think…what you need is an adventure."

She smiled at him and heard his breath catch. "Oh, I do." And suddenly, she had never been happier, because it felt as if she had a friend.

HAROLD IRVING KNEW his nerves must be stretched when he began to imagine the features of his late wife on the face of a perfect stranger—a male stranger at that—and in Blackhaven, of all unlikely places.

There had just been something about the shape of the young man's face, the humorous set of his mouth, the depth of the rather fine eyes. But it was no more than a very superficial resemblance, only startling him, he supposed, because he was again contemplating matrimony. It was inevitable that Anne should lurk in his mind just now.

"Are you quite well, Harold?" Hester asked as the waltz finished. "You have turned very quiet and introspective."

God preserve him from perceptive females. Anne had been like that, too. It would undoubtedly be an annoyance in Miss Hester Poole when she was his wife, but he cheered himself with the thought that once they were married, he need go near her as seldom as he chose. In fact, he looked forward to the day when he was in charge of the relationship and had no need to fawn and agree with everything spouted by Hester or her old harridan of a mother.

"You bring me peace," he said humbly to Hester. "Dancing makes me think more frequently of my dear, departed wife. I was merely wondering to myself at the joy you have brought, banishing the sadness I inevitably felt at Anne's memory."

Hester looked slightly dubious. Perhaps it was a clumsy, if not tasteless, compliment. He blushed—which he could do at will— and smiled hopefully, like a dog looking for a bone.

Hester laughed, which, most irritatingly, she was given to doing when he had not the remotest idea why. Nor did he care particularly. She patted his hand and took her place beside her scowling mother. He doubted the old lady was really angry. Scowling just seemed to be her natural expression. Nor was she terribly old—fifty winters at most—but she cultivated the appearance in order to get away with blatant rudeness.

"May I fetch you refreshment, ladies?" he asked civilly. After all, he could do with the break. And a decent tot if it could be found in this benighted establishment.

Blackhaven, indeed! On the edge of nowhere, full of nobodies and quacks.

But at least, he thought, downing a large brandy before he bore the champagne back to his ladies, Blackhaven provided very little in the way of competition for Hester Poole's hand.

Or did it?

He almost stumbled as he realized a gentleman was standing beside Hester, in what appeared to be amusing conversation. That was a mere, minor irritation until the gentleman glanced up and Harold recognized the same man he had seen waltzing, who for some reason had reminded him so much of Anne.

Their eyes met, the younger man's mild and humorous. Harold wondered uneasily if he was part of Anne's family. It hardly mattered in his grand scheme, so he kept his amiable, gentleman-about-town expression pinned to his face, with an extra devoted smile for Hester as he presented her with a glass of champagne, and another for her mother.

Unlike her mother, who merely sniffed with a bare nod of thanks, Hester smiled back. "Oh, thank you, Mr. Irving! Mr. Irving is an old friend of the family. Harold, this is Miss Vale, whom we have often seen in the pump room while taking the waters, and Mr. Tyler."

Miss Vale, with whom Mr. Tyler had been dancing, was quite a fetching little thing—she must have been, for not everyone could make the old lady smile—and pretty, too, though far too lively for Harold's taste.

"Charmed, Miss Vale," Harold murmured, bowing. "Your servant. Mr. Tyler."

"Mr. Irving," Tyler returned. His bow was elegant, his manner a little shy but hardly overwhelmed. As though he were used to the best company, even if not the most sociable of men himself. "I think we must have met before?"

It was a very slight question, and Harold was happy to squash the pretension. There had been no Tylers among Anne's troop of cousins.

"I don't believe so, sir," he said. "I'm sure I would have remembered."

"Then I must be mistaken," Tyler said at once. He even looked slightly embarrassed, his smile verging on the apologetic. "I often am."

"Aren't we all, Mr. Tyler?" Hester said kindly. "Are you also a native of Blackhaven?"

"Sadly not. I merely have some matters to attend to in the area. But I find it rather charming, don't you?" He glanced from Hester to her mother to Harold.

"Utterly charming," Hester said. "In quite unexpected ways."

"It is well enough," the old lady allowed grudgingly.

"Quaint," Harold said, politely damning.

"Oh, Mr. Irving prefers London, of course," Hester said dismissively. "He fails to see any amusement so far from Town. But I think we are proving him wrong this evening!"

"My dear lady, you wrong me!" Harold protested. "Anywhere you are holds more than enough charm for me."

He glanced at Tyler as he spoke, to be sure he took the point and the warning. Hester was *his* heiress, and though he didn't fear the competition of a younger, more callow man, nor did he want the complication of rivalry. He wanted to be Hester's only option, for the sake of speed if nothing else.

Tyler understood perfectly. Harold saw it in his eyes. He hoped he didn't also see challenge there.

"Well, I am very glad to have met you," Miss Vale said to the ladies. "I shall look out for you in the pump room. Sir." She curtseyed, and Tyler bowed, obediently offering the girl his arm as they moved on.

Harold hoped she was enough to keep Tyler away from Hester.

"Vale," he murmured. "Have I heard that name before?"

"One of the local gentry families," Hester said. "Sir Julius Vale has land a few miles beyond the town. Retired Royal Navy captain. I suppose Miss Vale could be his daughter. Or a sister, perhaps."

So long as she had prospects enough to keep Tyler away from Hester Poole, Harold didn't much care.

"HE MIGHT NOT remember you," Lucy murmured to Mr. Tyler as they walked away, "but you know him, don't you?"

"Perhaps," he said vaguely. "If so, a long time ago." He glanced down at her. "What do you think of Miss Poole?"

"I like her. Though…"

"Though what?"

"I don't believe she is as fond of Mr. Irving as he thinks she is."

Mr. Tyler blinked. "That is a lot of presumption for a couple of minutes' acquaintance."

"I told you. I am a great observer."

"If so, you are much more formidable than you look."

"I wonder if I should be offended," Lucy said.

"Don't ladies wish to be formidable?"

"Depends on the lady. Delilah is formidable."

"I would have called her more sly."

Lucy stared at him, dropping his arm. "You cannot know my sister if you even imagine that of her!"

He blushed. "I didn't know it was your sister's name. I thought you were referring to the Biblical Delilah."

"Hmm. I always thought there was more to that story than the Bible reveals. But talking of my sisters, I need to make an appearance or they will surround me."

"Am I to escort you or am I dismissed?"

There was rueful humor in his eyes. He knew she meant the

latter and had fully expected it. It gave her pause, that assumption, not only because she didn't want to abandon him at all, and because it made him oddly vulnerable.

She almost took back his arm and dragged him with her. Only, for some reason, she needed to keep this new friendship to herself, not have it contaminated by sisterly curiosity and brotherly teasing.

"You should thank me for the dismissal," she said. "But you will remember me if you discover any further adventures in the ballroom?"

The smile dawned in his eyes. "It goes without saying."

*What if I never see him again?* She would not even have said goodbye.

She had known him barely an hour. She was being ridiculous, and if she never had anything else, she had to keep her pride. So, she cast him a dazzling smile and weaved around the dance floor away from him.

Despite her silly, disproportionate regret, Lucy did not find it hard to enjoy the ball. She was delighted to recognize an undercurrent of excitement in all her siblings—even Julius, who had not wanted to come, and whom she encountered walking around the ballroom with a rather beautiful lady.

She met the Countess of Braithwaite, with whom she was slightly acquainted already, and two of her sisters-in-law. She danced with several interesting gentlemen, including the handsome vicar and a mad Russian officer wearing his sword, who told her he was an English baron and made her laugh. Although the same Russian then introduced her to his wife, a delightful English lady with laughing eyes, and his sister, who turned out to be the extraordinarily beautiful girl she had noticed with Aubrey earlier in the evening.

Just as she was parting from the latter, she was whisked away, her hand held to a man's arm as he hurried her across the floor.

"Adventure," Mr. Tyler said with satisfaction. "Will you come?"

# Chapter Three

T HE ANSWER WAS never really in doubt.

"Where?" she asked, looking around.

"Outside."

"Not the puppy again?"

"No. My friend, Mr. Irving. I want to know where he has gone, and a couple is so much less suspicious than a solitary lurking male. Will your family miss you for half an hour?"

She suspected Julius had already gone, and she had surely lulled the others into a false sense of security.

"I'll wait for you at the door. You won't need your cloak."

And then he was gone, vanishing through the ballroom doors as casually as she had left him earlier in the evening.

*I will* need my cloak, she thought, torn between amusement and annoyance. *It's bound to be raining, and even if it isn't, it will be confoundedly cold!* This summer was barely worthy of the name.

She lingered only long enough to be sure none of her siblings were paying her attention, then sauntered out as though seeking the ladies' cloakroom. Taking Tyler at his word, she crossed the foyer, smiled at the astonished doorman, and sailed out into the night.

A cloak landed around her shoulders, light and silken and midnight blue in the lamplight.

"Is this a domino cloak?" she demanded.

"Of course it is. I found two of them lying around inside, no doubt from a previous masquerade."

"And no doubt because you left them there. You, Mr. Tyler, are up to something. I know the signs."

Tyler swung a black cloak around his person and offered his arm.

"Why are we following this man you're not even sure you know?" Lucy asked.

"To see if I am right. He escorted Mrs. and Miss Poole into the hotel, and I want to see if he comes out again."

"And if he doesn't?"

"I have no objections to a short midnight stroll without him."

Nor had Lucy. It was delightfully improper.

With his free hand, Tyler twitched the domino hood up to cover her head.

"I can't see," she complained, adjusting it.

"The aim is that others don't see and recognize you. Or me," he added, turning swiftly toward her as though amorously inclined. She had no time to feel more than astonished before she saw his reason.

Mr. Irving had not lingered in the hotel but had just emerged and was striding up the street toward them. At this time of night, there was no traffic to distract him. Tyler, smiling foolishly like a besotted and not entirely sober swain, took hold of Lucy's hood, murmuring something that didn't even seem to be words, in a quiet, slurred voice not remotely like his own.

Lucy giggled, partly because he was funny, and partly from embarrassment, but the sound seemed to please Tyler, who mumbled some more nonsense in a devoted voice. She was aware of Mr. Irving striding past without even glancing at them.

Tyler gave a loud sigh and let his mumblings trail off.

"Is that really how you court a young lady?" Lucy asked unsteadily.

"Why, does it work?" He sounded surprised.

Lucy snorted, while Tyler weaved them around in a large arc

and proceeded in the opposite direction, several yards behind Mr. Irving, who walked with all the briskness of a man who knew exactly where he was going.

"When I was at Oxford," Tyler said, "I saw a student regaling a girl just like that. She laughed like a drain and he took it for approval. He imagined he was making sense, poor soul—probably pouring out his heart, but it came out as pure gibberish."

"And you've been practicing ever since?" Lucy said wryly.

"No, it just came back to me. It's quite fun. The secret is to base it on actual words and alter them, with the odd gap."

"What did you actually say?" she asked, intrigued.

"Mostly nonsense," he replied.

"But he'll notice us now," Lucy said, nodding ahead toward Irving. "If he just glances back, he'll know we are following him."

"Why would such a thought enter his head? Even if he is up to mischief, he'll just assume I'm lost and dragging you with me."

"He might take it into his head to rescue me," Lucy said with some relish.

"Not he."

The words were careless, and yet the lightness seemed to have gone from his voice, causing Lucy to regard him more sharply. Unfortunately, they were between street lamps, and she could not make out his expression.

"You *do* know him, don't you?" she said. "Who is he?"

The next lamp cast a faint glow over his rueful smile. "My brother-in-law."

She stared. "And he does not recognize you?"

"He suspects some likeness, but in fairness, we have not met in about twelve years. I have changed more than he has."

"But your name…" she began, and trailed off. She frowned. "Tyler isn't your name at all, is it?"

"Sometimes. I like it best. He has turned right toward the market and the harbor."

"Perhaps he is fleeing the country. What has he done wrong?

Apart from court Miss Poole while he is married to your sister."

"Oh, he isn't married to my sister anymore. She died twelve years ago, so he is perfectly entitled to sit at Miss Poole's feet. She is a considerable heiress."

"And you don't wish him well? Are you acquainted with Miss Poole also?"

"Not until tonight." He raised his finger to his lips as they turned into the darker space between the high street and the lights of the harbor.

A light shone briefly from a building ahead of them as a door opened, releasing a blast of raucous noise and a miasma of tobacco smoke and alcohol. Irving walked inside and closed the door. The noise cut off, leaving only the fading stench.

Lucy walked faster, tugging Tyler's arm. "It looks very dark and dingy," she said, pleased. "He'll never see us watching him." Though, of course, they might have the same difficulty.

In any case, Tyler sped up even more, whisking her under the rusting tavern sign and straight past the door Irving had used.

"You can't go in there," he said firmly.

Lucy was disappointed in him. "Because it's unsuitable for a lady?" she said sweetly. "Like walking alone with a man not of her family, whose name she doesn't even know?"

Tyler closed his mouth. "That is a fair point. Call me a coward, but I would rather face your large and formidably heroic brother over taking you for a moonlight stroll than for taking you into an establishment like that."

She suspected it was his own conscience he feared more than Julius. Intrigued, she stopped pulling back and asked with awe, "Is it terribly wicked? It's just a tavern, isn't it?"

"An ale house or gin shop at best. But it has other…services, and any woman going in would be subjected to insult."

"Even with you?" she asked, disappointed.

"I'm not sure I would be much of a match for an entire room full of sailors."

It was true he was slight and looked more delicate than fierce, but even so, she suspected he was using the argument most likely to deter her.

"Then what are we going to do? Go tamely home without discovering what his business is and with whom?"

He rubbed his chin with the side of his forefinger. "We could see if we can peer in one of the back windows. If there are any."

Lucy was all in favor of that plan, although the thick, almost threatening darkness of the alley they turned into almost changed her mind. As though sensing her secret reluctance, he took her hand, and that felt better. She crept after him in single file, wary of piles of unidentifiable rubbish, and the ill-smelling dampness of the wall on either side.

Fortunately, the alley was not long, although the yard it widened into seemed equally dark at first. They paused, peering into the gloom. A few pinpricks of light revealed the existence of a back window, shuttered with worm-eaten wood on the inside. A solid door was also visible, and between them a number of barrels and casks piled against the wall, as much as three high.

Still holding her hand, Tyler moved forward and released her to pick up a small cask and place it in front of the window. He stepped onto it, almost ramming his nose against the dirty window and swaying until he could line his eye up with one of the larger holes in the shutter. He stilled and peered.

After some time of this, Lucy tugged impatiently at his cloak, and he turned his head.

"My turn," she whispered.

He stepped down, his breath sounding like laughter, and she took his place. She had to stand on tiptoe but eventually saw into the dingy room on the other side. Two gaudily dressed women in low-cut gowns shared a table and large mugs of ale with Mr. Irving and another man who was not so well dressed.

The women were laughing uproariously and one had her hand on Mr. Irving's thigh.

"Oh," Lucy uttered in sudden understanding. She jerked back too quickly, and the cask wobbled. It was just a step to the ground, but as she jumped free, Tyler caught her. For an instant, the strength in his arms surprised her, and the hardness of his lean body against her was unexpectedly pleasant, if shocking.

But the dull clatter of the cask must have been heard inside, for abruptly the back door swung open, allowing a feeble beam of light into the yard. A very large man stepped through, glowering.

"Run," Tyler breathed, releasing her and running for the yard wall away from the alley. Clearly, he wanted the large man to pursue him so that Lucy could bolt back down the alley. But before she could either obey or not, the man leapt with surprising speed for his size. He'd be on Tyler in an instant, and he was *huge*.

Lucy did not hesitate. She shoved the pile of barrels with her whole weight.

They were empty and flew in all directions. So did Lucy, falling forward with the force of her shove.

"Jump left!" she yelled to Tyler, just as a large barrel battered into the back of the big man's knees. He dropped beneath it while another, rolling in an impressive arc, headed directly for Tyler.

He turned at Lucy's warning, but instead of getting out of the way, he leapt on top of it. The big man stumbled to his feet and made a grab for him, but Tyler jerked forward, running on the barrel like some circus performer, and the barrel sailed past his attacker, picking up speed as it rolled toward the alley.

Lucy, bolting in the same direction, just made it into the alley first. Behind her, Tyler jumped, and the barrel crashed into the opposite wall. Lucy grabbed at his hand and pulled him along the alley, this time ignoring everything in favor of speed.

They broke into the street beyond. She pulled him toward the high street. Tyler pulled her in front of a slow-moving cart, and won by sheer brute strength, after which they flew along past the fishermen's cottages as though all the fiends in hell were after them.

In fact, no one was. The big man, having scared them off, clearly considered his work was done. Panting with laughter, Tyler slowed to a walk.

"How did you *do* that?" Lucy gasped with mirth. "With the barrel?"

"No idea," Tyler said unsteadily. "It just seemed like a good idea at the time."

Lucy laughed harder, and he grinned.

"I'm going to practice, though," he added.

"Oh, me too," she said fervently. "When not pursued by angry giants. Do you know where we are?"

He was guiding her up another street, away from the salty breeze of the sea. Her hand was still in his, and she liked the casual friendliness. It reminded her of childhood, and yet was entirely different. And improper. She would remove it. After just another few moments.

"Yes, I think so. We should come out behind the high street and be able to make our way back to the assembly rooms, still within the half-hour you specified."

"Really? It feels like *several* hours!"

"Ah, my scintillating company."

"You cram a lot into your half-hours," she pointed out.

"I would like to point out that it was you who upset the cask and attracted the giant's attention. And you pushed over the barrels."

"You should be grateful," she said sternly, and won a smile so dazzling that quite suddenly she couldn't breathe.

He was like quicksilver, his moods and expressions and actions tumbling after each other like so many barrels except somehow much more elegant. Yet he seemed quite without arrogance or any sense of entitlement. It was all quite wildly attractive. *He* was wildly attractive.

The awareness stuck her normally ready tongue to the roof of her mouth, so that when he pointed across the road and identified the old town hall, which now housed Blackhaven's gaol, she merely nodded. There seemed to be a good deal of activity around it. One man stood at the gate, scowling, while another two ran around from either side of the building.

Again, Tyler appeared to follow his nose, crossing the street, with Lucy once more holding his arm in a more decorous fashion. He had his domino pushed to one shoulder and looked quite dashing.

"Lost one?" he asked cheerfully.

The man's scowl deepened impossibly, while the other two men loped off in the direction of the harbor. "Not for long," he growled. "Sir," he added as an afterthought.

"Hope he's not too desperate a character."

"So do we," the man said with feeling.

"Good luck." Tyler touched the air where his hat should have been, and they walked on to the corner and turned left toward the high street. "I wonder how many prisoners they have?"

"Not many, I should think," Lucy replied. "It seems a very law-abiding town." Apart from the smugglers, of course.

"On the surface, I'm sure."

She glanced at him in some amusement. "Why, what do you imagine goes on here?"

He shrugged. "Poverty, like everywhere else. And that—" He broke off, gazing beyond her to the narrow street they were about to cross. His eyes began to dance.

Lucy looked too. A tiny puppy was gamboling toward them. Laughter surged up her throat. "How perfect!" Dropping his arm, she ran toward the puppy, who suddenly stopped dead then turned and trotted back the way it had come. Impossible to tell if it was playing or frightened.

Hoping it was the former, she followed, calling softly, "Here, little pup, he—"

"Lucy!" Tyler said sharply. His footsteps cracked hard on the cobbles, and she realized why.

The puppy had lunged into a doorway and sat on the boot of a shadowy man, pressing as close in as it could get.

Lucy stopped dead, and Tyler skidded to a halt beside her. The man, realizing he was seen, bent, scooped up the puppy, and stepped out of the doorway. He was not large or threatening, but in the streetlight he was clearly unshaven, and he looked ill. He muttered something and turned. The little dog peeped over his shoulder.

The man had only taken a step when Tyler said, "You've got some nasty bruises on your wrists."

The man froze. But he didn't turn back.

"Mr. Farmer?" Tyler asked.

Now the man spun around, shock and desperation in his eyes.

"Could you not have waited one more day?" Tyler asked, sounding more frustrated than angry.

"No," came the immediate reply. "What do you care? What do you want?"

"Thought you might like to know they're searching down toward the harbor."

"I thought they would." The man straightened. "Not that I care."

Lucy closed her dropping jaw and swallowed. *This* is the escaped prisoner? How did Tyler know his name?

"Someone to vouch for you," Tyler murmured, "would have had you out of there in a trice."

The escapee's lips curled in contempt. "Not for highway robbery, they wouldn't."

It seemed to be Tyler's turn to struggle for words.

"You're a highwayman?" Lucy asked. She'd never heard of a highwayman with a puppy before.

"*They* said I resembled him what held up two coaches south of Carlisle and banged me up until they could decide one way or the other."

Tyler stared at him. "Please tell me you didn't."

"Why, what's it to you?" the man said aggressively. "You going to yell for the law and get me hanged? While I'm standing right in front of you?"

His face and his voice were angry, but his hands held the little puppy with gentleness.

"If I had any sense, I would," Tyler said. In one swift motion, he swirled the domino cloak off his shoulder and swung it around the escaped prisoner.

The puppy bit it joyfully, but before Lucy could either laugh or demand to know what was going on, he snapped, "Pull up the hood," and, grasping the other man by the elbow, propelled him toward the high street. "Don't argue. We've made enough racket standing here. Play drunk and I'll hold you up. Otherwise, *you* can hold *me* up."

The escaped prisoner, hauled under the lamplight, puppy and all, looked as baffled as Lucy felt. "Who the devil *are* you?"

"Guess. You'll need somewhere to hide until morning."

The man peered at Tyler. So did Lucy.

"You're *him*," the fugitive said. "I thought you were just a story."

"A mere footnote, my friend." Tyler turned his gaze on Lucy, who was trotting along beside them. "I can only ask you to say nothing to anyone for now. I'll explain when I return to the ball, and then you must do as you think fit. Will you agree to that much?"

They were almost at the high street now. It hit Lucy like a deluge that she had no idea who Tyler was, what he had done, or what he was capable of. She had been utterly beguiled by his eccentric charm into this unwise expedition, and now he was asking her to protect an escaped prisoner of the law. The rueful understanding in his voice told her he knew it, too.

She glared at the highwayman. "Did you kill anyone?"

The fugitive glanced wildly at Tyler.

"Be truthful," Tyler commanded.

"Not recently," the fugitive said cautiously, which hardly comforted Lucy.

"He was a soldier," Tyler said. "Not a highwayman."

"Then you have until the end of the ball," Lucy said coldly, and swept left into the high street ahead of the others.

The assembly rooms were only fifty yards away, on the other side of the well-lit street, so she was quite surprised when Tyler fell into step beside her, appearing to hold up the impressively swaying fugitive on his other side. The puppy seemed to be asleep.

"You should go the other way," Lucy muttered to Tyler. "Fewer people."

"I'll see you back to the assembly rooms."

"There is no need. This is not London."

"There is every need."

So many questions and speculations swamped her that she had no idea how she would survive the frustration until he returned. *If* he returned.

The doorman stood outside the assembly rooms, gossiping with a passing crony. As they drew nearer, Tyler slowed.

"Go ahead now," he murmured.

Emotions crowded in on her. Pride compelled her to hurry forward without a word of farewell to either of them. She was afraid she had made so many mistakes tonight that she would never right them all.

The doorman stopped talking to bow her back inside the building. At the last moment, she glanced back up the street to where she had left Tyler and his companion. They were both still there, ambling pointlessly, but Tyler's gaze was directed straight at her. He really was making sure she returned safely to the ball.

For some reason, her anxieties dropped away, leaving her once more pleasantly curious, happy, and excited.

Until she walked into the foyer, sweeping off her domino cloak, and saw Roderick, her second-eldest brother.

He stood halfway to the ballroom, one smartly uniformed shoulder leaning against the wall, and he was quite definitely glaring at her.

She was in trouble.

# Chapter Four

L IKE JULIUS, RODERICK had been abroad for a large part of
Lucy's life, fighting first on the Peninsula, then in France and
at Waterloo. If Julius had lost his passion somewhere, Roderick
seemed to have a surfeit of it bubbling just below the surface. He
might have been more approachable than Julius, but right now he
didn't look any less formidable.

Still, brazening things out was what Lucy did best. She smiled
as though delighted to see him, abandoned the domino cloak
carelessly at the doorman's cubbyhole, and sailed forward to
meet him.

"Rod! Why aren't you dancing?"

"Because it's suppertime," Roderick said. "Where the *devil*
have you been?"

Lucy took his rigid arm. "Don't ask. I was only gone a few
minutes. I did nothing improper and nothing to be ashamed of."
She hoped. "And I am perfectly safe."

"Not from me, you're not. Or Julius."

She smiled and tugged his sleeve. "Don't be silly, Rod."

That disarmed him, as she had known it would, but an instant
later, his scowl re-formed and he changed direction, all but
striding toward the ladies' cloakroom instead. "Your hands are
filthy, and God knows what you've done to your shoes. Clean
yourself up."

He was quite right. And she could not entirely blame him for his threatening growl. "I shall wait right here."

Instead of trembling with fear, as she might have done before their father in a temper, she wanted to laugh. Fortunately, she managed to hold on to her contrite expression until inside the cloakroom, when a smile broke out. Roderick was quite right about her filthy hands—God knew what she had touched in the alley beside the tavern, or on the barrels. She was just glad she had taken off her gloves before then, and that the domino cloak had protected her ball gown.

She set about washing her hands and doing what she could about her spoiled dancing shoes. Her hair, so beautifully dressed and well pinned by Felicia, still looked fine. Only the color in her cheeks and the brightness of her eyes betrayed her excitement to the looking glass. She smiled at herself, just as two ladies came in. She turned her smile on them, fished her gloves from her reticule, and pulled them on.

Respectable again, she sallied forth to discover Roderick pacing up and down the foyer waiting for her. She went toward him immediately and again took his arm.

"Don't be angry with me, Rod. Truly, I did nothing wrong."

"I'm not angry with you. I'm angry with me for letting you go. Julius decamped about an hour ago, leaving me in charge."

"I'm not one of your soldiers, Rod," she pointed out.

"No, you're not, and you've no concept of danger either. You must *not* put yourself in danger, Lucy. No one is immune to predators and ruffians, and they don't all come with *scoundrel* written across their faces."

"I am good at reading character," she said, wondering if it was still true. Had she misread the enigmatic Mr. Tyler?

"You may not always get the time to do so," he snapped, then drew in his breath. "Sorry. You do not need to know such things, but you are my sister, and I would protect you."

He never spoke of his experiences in war, only of the funny moments, the interesting people, the beauty of the scenery or the buildings he had seen. She had a sense of lost camaraderie, of grief, pain, and anxiety roiling inside him, but she knew he would not speak of it, not to her.

"I'm sorry," she said, entirely genuine this time. "I won't cause you any more worry, I promise."

At that, he laughed, lightening his stern face immeasurably. "Don't be silly, Lucy, you can't possibly promise that. Just assure me for now that you will not leave the building again tonight."

"I won't," she vowed, then tugged his arm. "Did you say there was supper?"

AFTER SUPPER, SHE danced again with the talkative young man, and surreptitiously watched out for the return of Tyler. In the process, she caught sight of her remaining siblings, and had time to be pleased that they all looked happy. Even Roderick was *smiling*. She wished Julius had stayed, too.

Determined to be good, she had just returned to her family's table to sit out the final waltz, when she saw Tyler weaving through the forming couples. Since she had no desire to introduce him—certainly not to Roderick—at this stage in their acquaintance, she murmured something to Delilah about a promised dance, and hastened to meet him.

He was milling, as though disconsolately looking for a partner, although she was sure he knew exactly where she was. His eyes gleamed as soon as he saw her approach, though he bowed with perfect gravity.

"May I?" he asked, holding out his hand and looking more hopeful than certain.

She laid her hand in his. "You had better."

It won her a breath of laughter, which pleased her inordinately.

"I thought you weren't coming back," she admitted as he led

her onto the dance floor.

"What would you have done? Gone to the magistrate?"

"I danced with his son-in-law."

"You're avoiding the answer."

"I don't know the answer," she said. "Probably nothing until the morning."

He turned, stepping too close to her as if to avoid the couple behind, and, as the orchestra struck up the short introduction, embraced her. "Sorry," he murmured. "Do you mind being just a little too close? It's easier to talk without being overheard, and I will be otherwise the perfect gentleman. Though your excessively large brothers might call me out."

A clever riposte went clean out of her mind. Her body heated, and just for an instant she remembered Nick, Felicia's late husband, his hot breath and roaming hands, and shame almost made her tear free.

But Tyler wore gloves, and while he might have held her close enough for her skirts to swish against his legs and his thigh to brush hers as he stepped her backward into the waltz, his hold was light, his arm still at her back. Tyler, whatever and whoever he turned out to be, was a completely different man to Nick Maitland.

"Where is he?" she asked at once, mostly to distract herself.

"Safe for now."

"Who is he? What did he really do to be arrested, and what is he to you?"

"I'm not sure *exactly* what he did," Tyler admitted, so readily that she knew it was the truth. "But one of the reasons I came to Blackhaven was to extract him from prison. A friend asked it of me. Luke Farmer is a former soldier, returned after Waterloo, with a head full of perfectly justified grievances. He is a radical. Some might call him dangerous. Others might call him a benign force for necessary change."

"Which do you call him?"

"The latter. Or, at least, I did. That was why I came to argue him out of prison and into safety. He was not supposed to break out, which is almost an admission of guilt. Nor is he supposed to be charged with highway robbery, though that could simply be the bad luck of mistaken identity. I have a great deal to find out."

"All for a mere friend?" she said curiously.

"A friend and ally. We share a cause."

"A radical cause?"

A smile flickered across his face. "Yes. Lest you cast me off as lacking respectability, I shall assure you that the local member of Parliament, Mr. Hanson—who is also the brother-in-law of Lord Braithwaite, who owns that charming castle on the cliff—is another ally. I am not a guillotining revolutionary."

She thought about that. "And now that Mr. Farmer has spoiled your plan by getting *himself* out of prison, you feel guilty for not dealing with the matter today rather than preparing for the frivolity of a ball? Which is why you are now hiding Mr. Farmer."

"Something like that," he said with apparent relief. "But truthfully, I couldn't let a fellow hang on the strength of false identification and a few pamphlets—the law can be relentless, not to say unstoppable, in pursuit of the powerless."

She drew in her breath, forcing herself to think dispassionately. "It is an unlikely tale."

"But the truth. As I see it at this moment. Do you want to stop dancing now?"

"Are you trying to distract me?"

"No, I'm trying to find out if you are still uncomfortable."

"Still?" she asked, uncomprehending.

"You flinched when we first began to dance."

She flushed. "I was not thinking of you."

"I'm sure that should annihilate what is left of my pride."

"But it doesn't," she retorted.

"I am more concerned with your well-being."

Somewhere, the truth in his clear gaze soothed her. Mostly, she wanted to distract them both from her shame.

"There is no need to be. You really want to know if I will inform against Mr. Farmer."

"Will you?"

"How can I when I don't know where he is?"

A smile tugged at the side of his mouth and vanished. "You know where I am."

It was true he had aided the fugitive, but she chose a literal response. "Only at this moment. Not once the ball ends." Though she could hazard a guess. Ladies and gentlemen of quality stayed at the Blackhaven Hotel across the road.

"Thank you," he said quietly.

She did not want to be so quite so glad of his approval. She tilted her chin. "And if he turns out to be a highwayman, a thief, and a murderer?"

"Then I shall hand him into gaol myself."

He looked too elegant and much too delicate to take on a desperate ruffian, but somehow, she did not put it past him. He had not hesitated to run to her defense as soon as he spotted Farmer lurking in the doorway.

"Tell me about the magistrate," he said. "And the magistrate's son-in-law."

"Oh, Mr. Winslow seems quite amiable and fair-minded. Julius likes him. His wife is a little snobbish, but good-natured underneath. Lord Sylvester, the son-in-law, is amusing company. Apparently he was the wildest of the wild Tamar brothers, but he seems more interested in land husbandry to me. Of course, his wife is very agreeable—friendly, but in a quiet, unassuming sort of way."

"You really *are* quite an observer," he said. "I blush to think what you see in my character."

"You are too contradictory," she said honestly. "I would need to know you much better." As she realized how that might sound, her cheeks flamed, but he did not appear to notice.

"Perhaps it is as well you won't," he murmured.

Before she could work out what he meant by that, he turned

her in the dance, and they glided along the edge of the dance floor. The lady with the enormous, eye-catching headdress sailed past between them and the balcony doors.

"Oh, Tyler," Lucy breathed. "What did you do with the puppy?"

He snorted, and great waves of mirth surged up from her toes. Before it could erupt, he whisked her out on to the balcony, which was fortunately empty. They gave way to laughter until tears ran down their faces and Lucy was clutching her stomach with one hand and hanging on to Tyler's coat with the other.

When she sobered, he was gazing down at her, merriment slowly dying in his oddly beautiful eyes. "You really are rather wonderful, aren't you, Lucy Vale?" he said softly. "Would you mind very much if I kissed you?"

At that moment, she felt so close to him he could have done anything he liked, but the words somehow made it more real. Flame licked through her body. Butterflies gamboled in her stomach as she glanced instinctively at his parted lips, as shapely and elegant as the rest of him, quick to laugh and yet curiously vulnerable. And she wanted more than anything to feel them on hers.

She didn't mean to, but she tilted her head in invitation, and wasn't remotely sorry. His head dipped until his mouth covered hers—soft, gentle, incredibly sweet.

The pressure held for a moment, then he drew back. "I left him with Farmer, who seems to love him like a son. The poor little creature must have been skulking around the gaol yard for three days waiting for Farmer without eating more than the odd scrap."

"Then it would be a shame to separate them," she said hoarsely, and swallowed. Inside, the music was coming to a close. "Is Tyler your surname or Christian name?"

"Surname."

"Then your Christian name is…?"

His lips quirked. "Walter." Unexpectedly, he took her in his arms, holding her excitingly close against his body, and kissed her again, still with exquisite gentleness, but this time parting her lips and exploring, savoring. She reached up to his cheek in wonder and kissed him back.

He sighed into her mouth, and just as she began to understand what desire meant, he suddenly released her. "You deserve every happiness, Miss Vale. I'm glad we met."

And then he was gone.

*IF THAT HAD been my first kiss, perhaps I would not mind marrying Lord Eddleston.*

The thought came to Lucy as she sat in the carriage with Felicia and Roderick on the journey home to Black Hill. She had the impression that they were all happy, even excited, though Lucy was too full of her own amazing evening to interrogate her siblings about theirs. Felicia was chattering away about people she had met and a game of cards. In between, she asked questions about the others and castigated Julius *in absentia* for leaving early and surreptitiously. It struck Lucy that she was talking so much to avoid being questioned herself. Which was intriguing, but for another day. This evening, she was too tired, and her whole being seemed to be full of the man who might have been called Walter Tyler.

In the cold light of day, perhaps she would recognize this provision of a false name as too basically dishonest to deserve any trust. But he had been so blatant about it, and about hiding the escaped prisoner, that right now, she was far more intrigued than disgusted. She had to consciously stop herself touching her lips, where she could still feel the pressure of his mouth and the delicious turbulence his kisses had caused. An odd, mercurial man who somehow cast all others in the shade.

Yet she was uneasily aware that he had seemed to be saying farewell, as though he did not expect to meet her again. She hoped he was not leaving Blackhaven.

"You danced twice with young Ladburne," Felicia said.

"Did I?" she asked vaguely. She had danced twice with Tyler, too. Forcing herself, she blinked and said, "Oh, is Mr. Ladburne the talkative young man? Then yes, I did."

"He's Falworth's heir, you know. It would be a very decent match."

"I'm betrothed to Eddleston," Lucy said gloomily.

"Yes, but you'll never be held to it if you dislike it," Felicia said. "Will she, Rod?"

"What?" Roderick blinked, as though searching for the question rather than the answer, then said forcefully, "No. She will not."

"Is Ladburne rich, too?" Lucy asked. Perhaps he would be better than Eddleston. Perhaps he kissed like Tyler, though she doubted it. Beside Tyler, he seemed dull, though not quite the bugbear poor Eddleston had become in her imagination.

"Ladburne has prospects," Felicia said. "But that needn't concern you. We don't need money, Lucy."

You *do*, Lucy thought. Nicholas Maitland had left his widow with massive debts that she was paying off only gradually. But Lucy did not want to think about Nick. She wanted to think about Tyler—just for tonight. And then she would return to reality.

"Julius will never force this marriage or any other," Roderick said impatiently. "He's merely doing the honorable thing in allowing Eddleston this visit. Your wishes will be paramount, not Eddleston's."

"I can't think he would *want* to marry me," Lucy said.

"He's probably as annoyed with his parents about the betrothal as you are with yours," Felicia agreed. "I'm sure you may be comfortable about the whole thing. We are all behind you, Lucy."

*You would not be if you knew...* But Lucy would not think of that. She thought instead of Tyler catching the tower of boxes in the ballroom gallery, and the hat landing on his outstretched head. Of his reckless joy in running on the barrel away from the gigantic man at the tavern. Of his standing up for the fugitive, rightly or wrongly. And mostly, she thought of dancing in his arms, and of his kisses, tender and sweetly passionate…

She became aware that she was smiling and that Roderick's gaze was upon her. Hastily, she yawned and said vaguely, "It was a lovely evening. I'm so glad we went."

Her siblings did not disagree, not even Roderick, who was well aware she had been up to mischief of some kind. At least he did not know about the kisses.

# Chapter Five

THE GENTLEMAN WHO called himself Tyler was glad to have something to think about other than Lucy Vale. She made his heart ache, but she deserved more, better than he could offer. And his first priority had to be Luke Farmer.

He left the man at the King's Head inn, in Tyler's own room, together with the smuggled puppy, a cold dinner for each of them, and a lot of purloined cleaning cloths and water—he had dealt with puppies before. On the way out again, he told Trent, the innkeeper, that Farmer was a servant who should have joined him much earlier and whom he had dug out of the tavern this evening. He strongly advised against disturbing the man tonight, so far gone in his cups was he.

"I shall probably dismiss him tomorrow," he said in an irritated tone. "Tonight, I have spent too much time on the scoundrel already. I'm going back to the assembly rooms."

Later, returning to the inn once more with his head full of Lucy and regrets, he found Farmer asleep on the unmade truckle bed, covered by his coat and the spare blanket Tyler had taken from his own bed. The puppy was curled up at his master's chest, though it did spring up and wag its little tail when he entered.

Tyler considered removing it from the bed. He was fairly sure Mrs. Trent, the innkeeper's wife, would not approve of its being there, but he hadn't the heart. Both pup and master had had a rough few days. He almost changed his mind when he narrowly avoided treading on the pup's excrement next to his own bed, but he cleaned it up, put it with the human waste, and went to bed.

He did not dream of his late sister or the unspeakable Irving, of giant tapsters or barrels. He dreamed of dancing with Lucy Vale, and of considerably more than kissing her.

HE WOKE TO the sound of pattering feet, and something scraping on the floor. When he opened his eyes, the puppy was looking at him, wagging its tail, front legs bent in the invitation to play. Beyond him, Farmer, in his shirt sleeves, was mopping up a small puddle.

"I thought you might have scarpered," Tyler said to the latter.

"Thought about it," Farmer admitted. "But nowhere to go. They'll catch me if I try to leave Blackhaven."

Tyler struggled into a sitting position and forced himself to think. "Who identified you as this highwayman?"

"Rich lady at the hotel. Said I'd held her up ten miles south of Carlisle."

Tyler had to ask. "Did you?"

Farmer's eyes slid away.

Tyler straightened without meaning to and stared at him. "You did? Dear God, why?"

"People were about to be evicted, and I'd no money to help. Had to get it from somewhere."

"Who do you think you are?" Tyler demanded. "Robin bloody Hood?" He dragged his fingers through his hair. "I've a horrible feeling you're going to tell me this wasn't the first time you've committed highway robbery."

"Only once or twice before. In England."

"Scotland? Wales? Ireland?"

Farmer shook his head.

"Then I'll ignore anything but England," Tyler said, wondering why on earth he actually felt relieved. "Did you shoot anyone?"

Again, Farmer shook his head.

"That's something, then. What we have to do is get this rich woman to retract her identification of you, convince her she might have been mistaken."

"Not sure how you're going to do that," Farmer said gloomily.

"Neither am I," Tyler admitted. "Who is she? Does she have a name? Was there anyone in the coach with her when you held it up?"

Farmer frowned. "There was a younger woman with her, quieter but just as brave. And some blustering dandy trying to look good. Can't think of her name... Mrs. Waters? Waterson? No... Lake?" His face cleared. "Poole! It was a Mrs. Poole who identified me in the hotel."

*Poole...* Tyler's moment of hope began to fade. Mrs. Poole was the lady he had met at last night's ball, the mother of the heiress being pursued by Harold Irving. "I hesitate to ask, but what were you doing in the hotel?"

The puppy was scrabbling its paws against the side of the bed. Distractedly, Tyler reached down under its rear and boosted it onto the bed. It pounced on his shifting knees beneath the covers.

"Leaving some pamphlets," Farmer said. "I'd just dropped a few, casual-like, on the table near to where people sit and wait, and the old dear comes swanning through with her daughter and a few other people, including the squire—Mr. Winslow, who just happens to be the magistrate. I was quite relieved I wasn't still holding the pamphlets, only then the old dear sets up a screech—*That's the ruffian who held us up!*—and before I knew it, I was in the gaol."

"Then she was the only one who identified you? Did the daughter say nothing?"

"Actually, no, she looked more surprised. Uncertain, like."

"Well, that at least is good. What about the man from the coach? Was he there? Have you seen him since?"

"No. Is that not good, too?"

"Not really. I'm sure if we asked him, he'd identify you in a trice, if only to please the old lady. He wants to marry her daughter."

"She could do better."

"Indubitably. You're Lord Braithwaite's tenant, aren't you?"

"My father is."

"I thought well of Braithwaite. I can't imagine him evicting your father without very serious cause."

"Oh, it wasn't my father being evicted. It was Fred Gaffney over at Cloverfield. Land was sold to some mill owner a year or so ago, and he's a money-grubbing—"

"And this Gaffney is a friend of yours? Did he ask you to help?"

Farmer shuffled from one foot to another. "Not exactly. In fact, not at all. I just couldn't let him be evicted."

"And is he?"

"No." Farmer grinned. "He came into some money, found he could pay the rent after all, and the next quarter in advance. Harvest'll be rough again this year. Too much rain and no sun."

"Well. Let's hope no one sees the connection between your escapade on the high toby, and Mr. Gaffney's sudden wealth." He drummed his fingers on the bedclothes, and the puppy pounced on them.

Tyler laughed.

Farmer smiled. "He likes you."

"Hmm, well, he can't stay here, and neither can you. I'll have to dismiss you from my service. And find somewhere safer to hide you until we can sort this out."

Farmer regarded him with fascination. "You reckon it *can* be sorted out?"

"Perhaps." Tyler frowned. "I think I need to speak to Lord Braithwaite."

"Not Mrs. Poole?" Farmer sounded disappointed. "Or even this Irving character?"

"That's the whole point. If I go near Irving on your behalf, you'll hang. Someone else needs to approach him, someone of rank and standing." Tyler threw off the bedclothes. "Stand aside, if you please."

"Are you going to the castle now?" Farmer asked, backing away from his sudden motion.

"Definitely. I'll take your wretched canine with me. If the maid comes to clean, hide your face in the bed and groan a lot. Your head hurts like the devil from a spree in the tavern and my blistering scold."

THE EARL OF Braithwaite was no reactionary, but it took some time to convince him that hiding this particular highwayman was in fact beneficial to the country.

"Yes, but damn it, he can't just run around deciding to rob people just because a friend of his can't pay his rent!"

"No, he knows that now," Tyler said, crossing his fingers that it was true. "It was a moment of desperation. You have to understand how abandoned some of these soldiers feel. They risked their lives, accepted serious injury in many cases, spent years away from home fighting and defeating the French for their country. Then we don't need them anymore. They lose the army, the pay, and are let loose in a country that no longer seems like home. They can't get work; they have no means to live. The country they fought for won't help, and so they shift for themselves. Trust me, they see the injustices of life far more clearly than those of us who have such comfortable—"

"Yes, yes, there is no need to make speeches at me," Braithwaite said with a hint of amusement amidst his testiness. "I understand. Grant—the vicar—runs a soup kitchen to feed such men. He was a soldier himself, so he has some sympathy."

"Among the homeless is the first place the magistrate's men will look," Tyler pointed out.

"And Grant's house is far too busy." Braithwaite pulled thoughtfully at his lower lip, and Tyler's hopes rose.

"It would only be for a few days until I can prove it is a case of mistaken identity. In fact, you could help with that, too."

Braithwaite blinked at him. "If you were not a friend of mine, I'd kick you down the steps."

"If I were not a friend of yours, I wouldn't have climbed them in the first place. This is one of the many injustices we can actually help."

"You're in danger of speechifying again. And Michael Hanson truly vouches for this man?"

Hanson, the radical member of Parliament, was Braithwaite's brother-in-law. They disagreed on much, but there was a trust between them, a knowledge that each wanted the best.

"He asked me to sort it out," Tyler said. Of course, that was before the highway robbery had been mentioned, but there was no point in muddying the waters.

"And now you're asking me."

Tyler smiled winningly, and Braithwaite let out an abrupt laugh.

"Very well—bring the fellow up this afternoon. I know someone who's taking on injured soldiers and sailors. If I like your fellow, I'll introduce them. It's as much as I can do. He'd be too visible here."

"I know. Thank you. Are you by chance acquainted with a Mrs. and Miss Poole, staying at the hotel? And a Mr. Harold Irving?"

Braithwaite groaned.

TYLER'S NEXT TASK was to alter Farmer's appearance as far as he could. On the way back from the castle to the inn, he bought some new clothes, a comb, soap, and a decent razor, and presented them to the fugitive.

Farmer seemed particularly glad to see the razor, but Tyler snatched it out of his reach. "Not so fast. Were you clean-shaven when you held up the coach?

"Yes." Farmer looked baffled.

"And your hair brushed back like that under the hat?"

"Yes, but…"

Tyler had never tried his hand at barbering, but he set to with a will, smartening up the back and sides of Farmer's hair, but leaving the front longer to fall casually forward. It gave him a boyish look, while seeming to give his forehead a different shape.

Then he set to with the razor, leaving Farmer with long side-burns across his cheeks, and a rather smart, military mustache. As a final flourish, he scraped some of the arch from the man's eyebrows, making them appear straighter.

"By heck," Farmer said, awed, staring at himself in the glass. "My own mum won't know me."

"Don't go near your mum," Tyler warned. "Not till I tell you. Try the cap."

Obediently, Farmer reached for the headwear Tyler had just bought, and from habit crammed it on so that the hair was swept under it from his forehead. Tyler swiped it off again and plonked it on the back of his head. He looked a bit rakish, but smart enough.

"You'll do," Tyler said with satisfaction. "Just remember, *this* is how you look now. Keep to that. And avoid anyone you know. I'll be gone for a couple of days, and when I get back, I don't want to have to get you out of gaol again."

"I got myself out the last time," Farmer muttered, eyeing his new appearance with a mixture of doubt and surprise.

"So you did. Also, don't start any revolutions for the next few days."

Farmer wrinkled his nose. "Take a bit more than that," he said regretfully.

LORD BRAITHWAITE REUNITED Farmer with his ecstatic pup when they met some distance from the castle. After a few verbal exchanges with Farmer—mainly a plea not to let him down—the earl seemed satisfied enough to escort the man, the dog, and the bundle to his new residence.

"Thank you, Braithwaite," Tyler said.

"You owe me. I can't wait to collect this debt."

"A debt of goodness," Tyler said piously, and, with a quick grin, turned his horse and headed for Carlisle and the business he had neglected in coming first to Blackhaven.

HAROLD IRVING WAS very glad to be taking tea with the Poole ladies when the maid presented Mrs. Poole with a visiting card.

"The Earl of Braithwaite, ma'am," she said with considerable respect.

"Without the countess?" Mrs. Poole snapped.

"He says as it's a legal matter, ma'am. To do with when you was held up by the nasty highwayman."

"Well, I don't want him in here talking of that in front of my daughter."

"I was there, Mama," Hester said dryly. "He is hardly going to shock me. I am quite happy to go and speak to his lordship. Then your tea will be uninterrupted."

"You most assuredly will not. His lordship's mother is a very high stickler where propriety is concerned, and she'd ruin you without a second glance for being alone with him. I shall go down to speak to him. And you, Mr. Irving, will accompany me."

This suited Harold perfectly. His supporting the old witch would impress Hester, and he was more than happy to hobnob with a member of the aristocracy.

"I wonder what Lord Braithwaite has to do with the incident?" Hester said thoughtfully, as Harold offered his arm to her mother. "The magistrate is Mr. Winslow, and the culprit is already identified and locked up."

It was a fair point, and one Lord Braithwaite explained immediately. He was a tall, distinguished man, unexpectedly young when encountered close up. He awaited them in the empty coffee room and came forward to greet them at once with a civil bow.

"Mrs. Poole, forgive me for disturbing you. I have a difficult duty I am hoping you can help me with."

"Mr. Irving," she said, indicating Harold with a casual gesture he did not quite like.

Lord Braithwaite, however, looked pleased. "Excellent! How do you do, Mr. Irving? You were to be my next call, since I understand you were also in the coach that was held up near Carlisle?"

"Indeed." Harold bowed. "We identified the villain already. He is, I believe, under lock and key."

"He *was*," Braithwaite said. "Sadly, he seems to have escaped."

"How incompetent!" Harold exclaimed with annoyance.

"Indeed, I am somewhat annoyed myself," Braithwaite agreed. "But the escape has rather brought young Farmer to my attention, to the extent that he is causing me considerable difficulty! Which is why I ask for your help. The fellow turns out to be a tenant of mine, and I have his family and my own on my back to prove his innocence."

Braithwaite smiled and spread his hands in a gesture of helplessness. "They won't accept that a man can change after several years in the army. *We* may know better, but I am obliged to do my duty by the Farmers. Would you be so very kind as to help me by answering just a few questions, and then, perhaps, signing a paper I could use to show his family? And Winslow, of course, the magistrate."

"I should be happy to do so," Harold said at once. "Though I see no reason to distress Mrs. Poole—"

"Young man, I am not such a poor creature," Mrs. Poole said tartly.

Braithwaite bowed again. "I am very grateful for this. Be sure my wife will send you cards to our garden party next week. Sir, would you be so good as to wait in the foyer while I speak first to Mrs. Poole?"

Harold was not best pleased to be ejected when he wished to be seen as the old lady's support as she recalled such harrowing memories.

There was also the small matter that he could not actually remember a great deal. The villain had covered most of his face, and it had all happened so quickly. Besides, all Harold's attention had been on the wicked-looking gun. He was used to shooting at Manton's in London, and in similar places abroad, where he was considered something of a crack shot. However, facing the other side of the barrel had quite terrified him, if he was honest. He had no intention of being quite so honest with Lord Braithwaite. But he would have liked to hear what the old lady said so that it might jog his memory, at least.

However, Mrs. Poole waved him away, so there was nothing he could do except retreat with grace and kick his heels in the foyer for ten minutes. He could have been finishing his tea with Hester, softening her up enough for her to accept his offer of marriage.

It would have to be soon. There was no way he could even pay his own hotel bill, and the ladybirds at the tavern were not as cheap as they looked.

The coffee room door opened at last, and Lord Braithwaite bowed Mrs. Poole out with perfect courtesy.

"My thanks, ma'am. You have been very helpful. I look forward to renewing our acquaintance next week, if not before.

Good afternoon." When she had sailed past, with no opportunity for Harold to speak to her privately, the earl turned to him. "Mr. Irving, so good of you to wait…"

The little coffee room no longer looked quite so casual. Paper, pen, and ink were placed on one table, with a chair set on either side. For no good reason, Harold felt nervous. And Braithwaite was not even a magistrate—though no doubt he had the local fellow in his pocket.

"Please be seated, Mr. Irving. Now, tell me what you recall of the incident and the perpetrator."

"Oh, it was terribly sudden," Harold said. "I had actually nodded off in the coach and woke to shocking cries of 'stand and deliver.' A large pistol was thrust through the window, and this fellow on horseback was demanding money and jewels."

"Describe this fellow to me."

Since Harold could remember nothing about him whatsoever, he said, "Oh, he was a mean, paltry individual—the kind who is only brave behind the barrel of a gun, you know?"

Braithwaite nodded understandingly. "Indeed. What color was his hair?"

Harold frowned. "It was covered up by his hat and high collar."

"But you saw him again in the hotel when he was arrested and recognized him at once. Did he have his hat on then?"

"No… Yes." Harold floundered. Why would a man keep his hat on indoors? "Actually, his hair was thinning. But it was his voice I recognized."

"And his facial features?"

"Oh, they were covered by a scarf when he held us up, so there was little to recognize in the hotel, apart from his nasty little eyes."

"What color was the scarf he used to cover his face?"

"Black," Harold said, mainly because the whole incident was dark in his mind.

Lord Braithwaite began to write. For a man who must have

always been surrounded by secretaries and flunkies, he wrote very quickly. Then he set the pen in the stand and rose to look out of the window. "Just one more question, Mr. Irving. Do you see that man in between the liveried footmen in the street?"

Harold stood and looked in bewilderment. "Indeed."

"Do you recognize him at all?"

There could only be one reason for the question. They must have recaptured the escapee and be trying to identify him as the highwayman beyond doubt. The man's clothes were certainly different, and he looked quite strong rather than paltry, but still…

"He looks rather like our highwayman."

"You don't need to hear him speak to be sure?" Braithwaite asked.

"No, no. I saw him in the hotel later, remember?"

"I do remember," Braithwaite said. He sat down again, added a few more words, and pushed the paper across the table to Harold. "Is that what you told me and would be prepared to put your name to for the magistrate?"

Harold had to allow that the earl was accurate to the last detail. "That is *exactly* what I told you."

"Then be so good as to say so, sign and date the document, and then we may be clear, I trust, of the whole incident."

"I suppose," Harold said, hastily writing that this was his true account, "that none of our stolen property has been recovered?"

"Not that I know of. But I suppose he had time to sell it. It is most unfortunate. I am sorry you and the ladies have been so inconvenienced, to call it no worse."

"So am I," Harold said, signing his name with a flourish.

Lord Braithwaite took back the document, sanded it, and blew the sand back into the tray. He folded it neatly and stood to place it in a pocket inside his coat. Then he held out his hand with a smile.

"My thanks, Mr. Irving. I look forward to our next meeting."

TYLER RETURNED TO Blackhaven three days after the ball, and was striding up the high street, meaning to check with the hotel doorman whether Irving was still in residence there, when he saw Lucy Vale again.

He knew her even before he glimpsed her face, just by the way she moved, swift and graceful, almost as though she were dancing. His heart seemed to soar just at seeing her. She turned to the lady beside her, one of her sisters who had also attended the ball, talking animatedly, her piquant prettiness alight with fun, and it was all he could do not to stare.

Perhaps she was not conventionally beautiful. Perhaps her nose was a tad too long, her mouth too wide for the arbiters of fashion. But her shining hair, somewhere between dark blonde and pale brown, framed an unforgettable face, full of character, fun, and a deep, touching vulnerability.

Tyler halted, pretending to gaze into the draper's shop window until Lucy stepped into the waiting carriage and was swept away from him once more.

He did not like the way his heart ached. He didn't like it all.

# Chapter Six

LUCY HAD HAD a frustrating few days. Fortunately, her brothers and sisters seemed too preoccupied to pay a great deal of attention to her moods, so she did not need to explain why she jumped up to the window whenever she heard the sound of a horse or the wheels of a vehicle.

Her brothers and the twins were obsessed with a herd of horses that had crossed Black Hill, but formal visitors did not appear to interest them. At first, Lucy was afraid to go out in case Tyler called. She occupied her time at home by taking her turn with the garden work outdoors, and indoors, she scoured the local newspapers for mention of the escaped prisoner from the Blackhaven gaol.

It was while she searched the newest *Carlisle Journal* in vain for a mention of the escape that she came across an interesting report of a visiting stranger who had spoken at several workers' meetings in Carlisle. The report was enthusiastic—the newspaper being liberal in tone—and reported the visitor's speech as though it were verbatim. Although it was not what she had been looking for, she read it all and found it most interesting—just, informative, thought-provoking, and practical, compassionate without the usual condescension. It made her think of Tyler.

But then, most things made her think of Tyler.

Finally, she pulled herself together and decided *she* must look for *him*. Accordingly, she accompanied Aubrey to the pump room to drink his waters, made friends with the lady who had danced with Julius at the ball, and went shopping with her sisters. On no occasion did she catch even a glimpse of Tyler.

She even persuaded Delilah to have tea at the hotel one afternoon. And when Delilah availed herself of the cloakroom, she wandered about the foyer and approached the reception desk.

"I wonder if you might send a message to Mr. Tyler," she said boldly, "that the Misses Vale would be grateful for a moment of his time."

The clerk looked blank. "I'm sorry, ma'am. We have no Mr. Tyler staying at the hotel."

"Oh, perhaps he has gone already," she said, smiling to hide her unreasonable disappointment. "Thank you."

Of course, he had more or less admitted that Tyler was not his real name, so he *could* still be here. Even she could not bring herself to describe Tyler to the hotel staff, but she had not given up, and indeed did her best to persuade Delilah to stay longer in the town that day in the hope of running into him.

Delilah, however, insisted it was time to go home, and Lucy was distracted by the thought that her sister's feelings echoed her own. Was Delilah also hoping to see someone here, and annoyed with herself for even looking? Intriguing thought.

Having encountered Mrs. Macy, the lady Julius had danced with at the ball, she had already invited her to dinner tomorrow evening, along with the companions she was traveling with. So this evening, she innocently suggested expanding the dinner party to include other people.

"We could all choose someone we find congenial," she suggested. She carefully did not look at Delilah, but at Felicia, who, as the only married one among them, even if widowed, acted as hostess.

Lucy held her breath, for Felicia actually seemed to be considering the possibility.

"No," Felicia said with regret. "It would be rude to give so little notice, and the kitchen is not used to large dinner parties yet. Let us see how tomorrow goes, and then we might do a little more entertaining. If we are all in agreement."

Delilah shrugged, as if she did not care one way or the other, though Lucy rather suspected she did. Julius grunted. It was hard to tell whether he was excited or annoyed even by Mr. Macy's attendance tomorrow. The twins, however, smiled at her with approval, and neither Cornelius nor Aubrey objected.

Only Roderick watched her with any suspicion, so she avoided his gaze. However, after dinner, he followed her out onto the terrace she had been devoting her time to in order to make it a pretty place to sit—supposing the sun ever shone this summer.

"Who is it you are trying to invite to dinner?" he asked.

"As many interesting people as possible."

"Including the gentleman you danced with twice, who is *not* Lord Falworth's heir?"

"Why not?" she said breezily. "Do you know him?" She kept the question carefully casual, but she had no idea if she fooled him.

"What is his name?"

She hesitated, but only for a moment. She convinced herself she was not pursuing the man who so clearly had no further interest in her. She was merely solving mysteries. "He said it was Tyler, but I believe he was teasing me, only I can't quite work out how. Or why."

"Does he have a Christian name?" Roderick inquired.

"Walter. He said."

"Walter Tyler," Roderick repeated. "Wat Tyler was the leader of the Peasants' Revolt in the fourteenth century. I don't suppose that helps."

Lucy had the conflicting urges to laugh and to slap "Mr. Tyler."

"Yes," she said. "It does. I think he is a bit of a radical. So perhaps it is as well we shan't invite him. If he agitated Cornelius's workers, I would never hear the end of it."

Cornelius, who had stewarded other people's land in the past, was now Julius's land steward at Black Hill. He worked hard and conscientiously and took on every laborer with care. She had no idea what he paid them, nor what Felicia, nominally mistress of the household, allowed the servants.

On that thought, she resolved to visit the kitchen and discover for herself why Felicia thought they were not yet ready for large dinner parties.

"Lucy?" Roderick said as she turned to go in.

She paused and glanced back.

"Do you think," he said carefully, "that men who lie about their names for amusement, and who entice young ladies away from the safety of their families, should be trusted?"

Of course, she already knew the answer to that. But to say it was to acknowledge it, and then the adventure became somehow soiled.

"Not without good reason," she said, and hurried away before she could think too much about what that reason could be.

There had been nothing lover-like or seductive about Tyler's manner until the last dance, but she had no idea why he should have pursued Mr. Irving, nor taken her with him beyond the reason he had given at the time, that a couple strolling was less threatening, less suspicious, than a lone man.

The Vales did not yet have a full complement of servants. For example, there were no lady's maids or liveried footmen, only people to do the housework and cooking and open the front door. They had a man to look after the stables and one gardener to deal with the mammoth task of reviving the formal gardens surrounding the house. More outside workers were necessary, but Julius was hoping to take them on from the recovering soldiers and sailors currently in the hospital at Blackhaven.

Nevertheless, as she breezed into the kitchen, it seemed rather fuller than the last time she had been there. Although there was a servants' hall just behind the kitchen, the staff all sat around the large kitchen table, drinking tea and munching cake. Among those she already knew was the parlor maid, Betsy, but also a small kitchen maid she had never seen before and a couple of brawny men, one of whom looked vaguely familiar, so she supposed he was not new at all, though she couldn't think who he was.

It was Cook who saw her first. She had been Felicia's old cook in London, so Lucy wandering into her domain did not surprise her. In fact, Lucy was sure she jumped to her feet mainly to warn the other servants, who promptly shot out of their chairs and stood to attention like soldiers on parade.

"No, no, sit down and finish your cups of tea," Lucy said hastily. "I am sorry to disturb your short leisure time. Cook, I just wondered if my sister had spoken to you about dinner tomorrow evening? Do you have all the people you need?"

Having asked the question, she didn't hear the answer because her attention was suddenly caught by the brawny, oddly familiar man who was staring at her as though frozen in shock. As her eyes clashed with his, he hastily dropped back into his chair like his fellows and bent his head over his cup.

Lucy, moving away with Cook, racked her brain. Where *had* she seen him before? He had rather fine side whiskers and a military mustache. As she glanced back at him, he combed his fingers through his hair, dragging his fringe forward over his forehead.

"Thank you," she said to Cook, though she had no idea what the woman had just told her. "Who is the new man with the mustache?"

"Farm laborer," Cook said dismissively. "Rob Smith. Mr. Cornelius took him on the other day. He seems to be courting Betsy Gaffney," she added, nodding toward the parlor maid, who frowned with anxiety. "So I thought I'd look him over."

"Oh. Well, thank you, Cook. Sorry again to disturb you. Good night."

As she turned back toward the steps, Betsy the parlor maid was all but pushing her swain out of the kitchen door—and abruptly, his features made sense. She had only seen them in the dark and under the dim glow of street lights, but it was definitely Luke Farmer, the escaped prisoner accused of highway robbery.

LUCY RODE OUT alone the following morning in order to find Farmer. It took her almost until lunchtime before she discovered him repairing a stone wall between Black Hill and Braithwaite land.

He saw her coming and tugged his cap further down his forehead without stopping his work.

She reined in the mare beside him. He touched his cap, muttered something, and turned his back to reach for another stone.

"You can stop hiding," Lucy said. "I know perfectly well who you are. What are you doing here? Does my brother know who you are?"

Farmer sighed and straightened. "No, I don't think so. Lord Braithwaite suggested I might be useful, and Mr. Vale took me on, casual-like."

"Lord Braithwaite?" Lucy said in surprise. "Not Mr. Tyler?"

Farmer said nothing, although he shifted his feet like an uneasy man.

"Where *is* Mr. Tyler?" she asked mildly.

"Don't know, miss. Went away for a couple of days."

"To prove your innocence?"

"Maybe. Among other things—usually does lots of things at once."

Lucy leaned forward in the saddle to pat her horse's neck. "Does he? Is he coming back to Blackhaven?"

Farmer opened his mouth, then closed it again and tore off his cap. "Drat it, miss, don't ask me!"

"Is he in trouble with the law, too?" she asked, and was quite proud that her voice did not shake.

A gleam of humor lightened Farmer's scowling face. "More like to be the other way around. I don't fancy the law's chances."

Lucy wasted no more time. "What time are you seeing him?"

He stared at her, appalled. "Gawd, you're as bad as he is! How do you know—"

"I didn't, but I'm still waiting for an answer."

The possibility of defiance crossed his face, then he gave a reluctant smile. "Here at the wall, before midday."

Lucy glanced at the chained watch she wore on her riding habit—it had been her mother's—and then dismounted. "Excellent. My poor Millie needs a rest before we ride home."

Farmer groaned but made no effort to dissuade her.

Lucy, however, had sounded much more confident than she felt. Her heart might have beat a little too fast at the prospect of seeing Tyler again, but anxiety as to how he would greet her twisted her stomach.

She had come to the conclusion that his kiss had been one of farewell. He had no intention of seeing her again, and he had certainly made no effort to call at Black Hill, or to send her flowers, as other dancing partners had done.

She didn't like that this made her feel so alone. She knew she had built too much out of one evening's adventure in which, as Roderick had pointed out, Tyler had not behaved like a gentleman. Not that Lucy had much time for silly proprieties, but still, she had to doubt his respect for her.

Since she didn't know from which direction he would appear, she sat on the completed part of the wall, so that she was in profile from the tracks on either side of it. She didn't put it past him to bolt if he recognized her. And that made her angry. She wanted to think better of him.

Instead, she studied Farmer while he worked. He seemed to have some skill, and certainly put his back into it. A thought came to her.

"Since when have you been courting our Betsy?" she asked. "You can only have been with us three or four days at the most."

"Knew her before," Farmer said without looking up. "It was her dad couldn't pay his rent."

"I see…" She frowned and waved her arm to encompass the whole area toward the town. "Then this is your home? Doesn't everyone here know who you are? That you were the one taken up for highway robbery and then escaped?"

He straightened for a moment, then shrugged. "I'm Rob Smith here. Only Betsy knows otherwise. And you. I been away a long time." He looked beyond her, toward the Braithwaite side of the wall, and something changed in his face.

# Chapter Seven

HER HEART GAVE a tiny lunge. She knew Tyler was coming but refused to acknowledge it. She smiled at Farmer. "About Betsy, Cook is watching you."

Farmer grunted and bent back to his work.

She never knew exactly when Tyler discovered it was she who sat on the wall. The horse never changed its pace along the track. Nor, when she heard him dismount, did he betray any urge to bolt. He patted his horse and, leaving it beside hers, walked steadily toward her.

When he halted beside her, she finally turned her head and looked at him. "Mr. Tyler. What an unexpected pleasure."

His beautifully arched brows shot upward. "Is it? And here was I about to congratulate you on tracking me down."

He was no less attractive in riding dress, but his fine eyes were so veiled that she knew he was uncertain.

"I'm not perfectly sure that is a matter for congratulation," she drawled, in a decent imitation of Delilah in sarcastic set-down mood. "One grows to expect courtesy if not flowers."

Was that the faintest blush staining his cheeks?

"I have been remiss," he said.

"Oh, no, you have been busy. With peasants' revolts, I daresay."

His eyes lightened, not in shame or embarrassment, but

something very like pleasure in sharing the joke. His lips twitched into a smile. "I wondered how long it would take you to work out my name."

"I didn't," she said, incurably honest. "My brother Roderick did."

"Does he want to call me out?"

She raised her eyebrows. "For what?" she asked carelessly. "Unless you mean dropping Mr. Farmer upon us."

"I only just discovered he was here." He swung his apologetic gaze to the fugitive from justice who was still stolidly piling stones onto the wall. "How are you, Farmer?"

Farmer stepped back from the wall and met his gaze. "I'm well. Landed on my feet more than I deserve. My Betsy works at the house."

"And to think I didn't even know you had a Betsy." Tyler leaned one arm along the wall between Lucy and Farmer. "Well, you'll be pleased to know I have further good news. His lordship called on Mrs. Poole at the hotel. She described the man who held her up, giving him black hair and brows and a villainous expression. She said you were large and burly, and the kerchief over your face red. Mr. Irving, on the other hand, described you as a mean, undersized fellow with thinning hair and a black kerchief."

"Which color was it?" Lucy asked.

Farmer scratched his head. "Yellow and brown."

Tyler gave a lopsided smile. "Lord Braithwaite was so confused that he asked each of them to identify a man waiting outside the hotel. They, of course, could imagine only one reason for being asked such a question, and both answered that he was the highwayman who held them up. It was, in fact, one of Braithwaite's grooms, who couldn't possibly have committed the crime."

Farmer let out a bark of laughter. "Is the matter dropped, then? Or are they still after me?"

"I expect it will be dropped. Both Mrs. Poole and Irving gave his lordship permission to pass their statements to the magistrate, though Winslow might pursue the matter further himself. You had better lie low here a bit longer. Unless…" His gaze moved too swiftly to Lucy's, denying her the time to pretend she had been looking at something else entirely. "Unless Miss Vale objects to your presence."

"Mr. Smith's presence is of no interest to me," she said. "My brother Cornelius deals with the laborers."

"And what do you deal with?"

"Nothing. I potter in the garden in a mostly ladylike fashion."

The claim did not earn her the amused or condescending smile she expected. His gaze, though still veiled, seemed alarmingly perceptive.

Farmer said, "Well, I've been pottering with this wall since breakfast, so if you don't need me, I'll be joining the others in the kitchen."

"Go ahead," Lucy said, although he was already striding off in the direction of the house.

Tyler said nothing at all. Lucy fully expected him to leave, too, with or without an excuse. She wondered if her pride would be happier if she left first. While she debated the issue, he boosted himself onto the wall beside her.

"How are you?" he asked unexpectedly.

She blinked. "Do I appear unwell?"

He considered. "Disturbed. I hope you are not in some kind of trouble. And I hope I did not cause it."

"I expect the trouble to begin when Smith turns back into Farmer, and everyone wants to know why. Though he probably won't wish to stay on at Black Hill anyway."

"Who knows? But my question didn't really concern Farmer. What is spoiling your peace?"

*You are.* She drew in her breath. "Had I not sat here and waited, you would not have come near me, would you?"

He held her challenging gaze, though he looked a trifle rueful. "Probably not. I'm not terribly respectable just at the moment."

"Are you ever?"

"Probably not. I stir up trouble."

"You?" she said, and his lips twitched. "Or Mr. Tyler?"

"Mainly Mr. Tyler."

"What do you do? Agitate the workers to unrest and riot? Is that how you know Farmer? Do I have to warn Cornelius to keep an eye on him?"

"According to Braithwaite, your wages and rents are fair. The landlord's absence for so many years is to be deplored, but now that Sir Julius is home, things are apparently looking up for Black Hill's tenants and laborers." He leaned closer, nudging her gently with his elbow before straightening again. "You have a bright future."

"And you?" she asked.

"A checkered one."

"That is no reason not to be friends."

"Not for you," he said, a smile forming in his eyes.

With one of his sudden movements, he sprang off the wall and landed gracefully on the uneven ground. "Shall we walk a little?"

Before she could slither down by herself, he caught her by the waist and lifted her. His firm yet light hold caught at her breath. So did his closeness when he set her down, his hands still warm at her waist. There was a hint of rueful amusement on his mouth, but his eyes were much more turbulent.

"I kissed you," he said, and her skin burned beneath his gaze. "That is why we cannot be friends."

"You didn't like it," she blurted.

"Oh, I liked it. I liked it too much."

She frowned. "You think I expect you to marry me because we kissed? I am not quite so naïve and inexperienced as you imagine."

His eyes seemed to flare, and he released her, dragging her hand to his arm instead, and beginning to walk away from the horses. "Oh, are you not? Who else have you been kissing? Did *he* want to marry you?"

"God, no," she said, a little too fervently. "Nor did *I* wish to marry him, before you ask."

"But you let him kiss you? Did you like it?"

She shook her head impatiently, and before she meant to, she blurted, "He didn't *mean* it. I knew that. It was why I let him— Well, that and I was curious. I thought it would be harmless."

"It wasn't?" His eyes searched hers, as though he were trying to understand.

She dropped her gaze and shook his head. "Not to me. And not for the reasons you probably imagine. I discovered shortly after how much my sister loved him, and how hurt she would be by this *mere* kiss, which was nothing to either him or me." She raised her gaze defiantly. "He was my sister's husband and utterly foxed. If he even knew who I was, he had forgotten by morning. I knew he would. So my sister never knew. But she must have sensed some discomfort, for she sent me to Aunt Diana in Bath for a month before Aunt Diana sent me back. And then he died."

Part of her was appalled at having blurted this, her greatest secret, to a near-stranger. She wanted to close her eyes so that she need not see his disgust, but contented herself with glaring at him instead.

"I didn't forget," he said, so unexpectedly that the color surged back into her face. "I won't. That is why I stayed away. I doubt we can ever be merely friends. And you are already trying to shake off one unwanted betrothal."

"I expect he wouldn't want to marry me if he knew I'd kissed you."

"I wouldn't be so sure. You have an inner glow that is quite enchanting."

"That is by far the kindest thing anyone has ever said to me."

His smile was crooked. "It won't remain so for very long. I expect you already have a long line of eager suitors desperate for you to dismiss the unspeakable betrothed."

She sighed. "I probably won't. He is rich, you see."

"Unexpectedly materialistic," he pronounced.

"Isn't it?" she agreed. "But I have nothing else to contribute to my family."

Now he looked positively startled, although something closer to amusement quickly took its place. "I'm sure your family do not expect such a terrible sacrifice of you."

"Of course they don't *expect* it. Julius has told me that once I've met Edd—er…my betrothed—he will break the engagement if I want."

"Well, there you are, then," Tyler said.

She sighed. "Yes, but *should* I? Julius has put all of his prize money into Black Hill to make a home for us. I know Roderick has contributed. Cornelius stewards the land, because that is what he knows. Delilah and Felicia keep the house. I just use it and frazzle everyone's nerves with my occasional mad starts. Edd— that is, my betrothed's settlements are generously in our favor. Should I not grow up, and make him *my* contribution?"

At least Tyler considered, rather than laughing at her. "Do you think this *Edd* would wish to be merely a contribution to your family?"

"Since he has never troubled to meet me, I cannot think he greatly cares. A dry old stick of such haughtiness would not."

Tyler blinked. "What makes you think he is like that? Have you met him?"

She shook her head. "No, but it's in a letter of my mother's."

"Hmm. Perhaps I know him and could help?"

She almost told him. Her instinct as well as her curiosity urged her to that course, but honor won. She cast him a quick, unhappy smile. "I can't tell you that. I have made him sound so awful it would hardly be fair."

"I'll know anyway if the betrothal is announced."

"*If* it is," she said. "It's not that I do not trust your discretion— I have already bombarded you with confidences! It just would not be right."

He regarded her thoughtfully. "You're a funny little thing, aren't you?"

She wrinkled her nose. "I think you mean *horrid little thing*. What do you believe I should do?"

"About your betrothal? I think you should follow your heart as well as your head."

"Will *you*?" she asked.

For an instant he looked nonplussed. Then he said, "I hope so. Why?"

"I wondered about your interest in Miss Poole. And Mr. Irving. Did you tell her where he had been when he left the ball?"

"No, but then, I have not seen her. I don't want to marry Miss Poole, with or without her fortune."

To hide the embarrassment seeping into her cheeks, she glanced back over her shoulder to be sure the horses were not wandering off on their own, and found them right behind.

The mare snorted.

"Are your pockets stuffed with horse treats?" Lucy demanded.

"No. Sock just behaves more like a dog. He'd come inside and stand by the fire if I'd let him."

"He doesn't yet know your penchant for stuffing animals inside ladies' headdresses."

"Shh. He's very sensitive. Besides, I would never let him in. He'd block all the heat."

The nonsense conversation reminded her of the ball evening. "You are quite mad, aren't you?"

"Only in places." Idly, he patted his horse's nose. "I should go back to town. I suspect you should go home."

"I probably should. We have dinner guests tonight, and since it was my idea, I should probably be there to help."

He regarded her with some suspicion. "You haven't invited Irving and the Pooles, have you?"

"No, though now you come to mention it—"

"Don't," he said hastily. "I have a reasonable suspicion that

Irving is a very dangerous man."

She felt her eyes widen, more because of the seriousness in his voice than his actual words. "Many men go to places like the rooms behind the tavern. It might make them pitiable, but not necessarily evil."

"Now you are a worldly little creature. Who is coming to dinner?"

She gave in. "The lady Julius danced with at the ball—Mrs. Macy. And her friends Miss Talbot and Lord Linfield. Perhaps I will have Felicia ask you, next time."

He looked oddly thoughtful. "Perhaps I shall accept."

"Is that meant to frighten me?"

"It should certainly make you think, remembering the chaos that tends to follow me."

"Ah, but *you* haven't yet met my twin siblings."

"I look forward to it." He moved to the mare's stirrup and bent to offer his joined hands as a step to boost her into the saddle.

She accepted the reins, answering the smile in his eyes with one of her own. Her heart was beating fast, in a fluttering kind of way. It felt curiously warm. And happy. "Good day, Mr. Tyler."

He touched his hat. "Miss Vale."

# Chapter Eight

ALTHOUGH HE TRIED quite hard, Tyler could not regret running into Lucy Vale again.

Well, it was hardly accidental. Some fate had led Braithwaite to hide Farmer at Black Hill, where Lucy had inevitably recognized him and simply waited for Tyler to appear. He was flattered beyond belief that she would do so, even if only to scold him and indulge her curiosity.

Except, of course, it was more than that. He had deliberately befriended her at the ball, led her on an adventure merely because he thought she would find it fun, and topped his folly by kissing her. Which he certainly hadn't intended at the beginning of the evening. He had done his best to protect her reputation throughout, but it had never entered his head that he might hurt her feelings by ignoring her afterward.

As he rode back to Blackhaven, this filled him with alternate shame and triumph. She liked him. She had kissed him back. She had missed him in the intervening days, and not merely because of Farmer, or Irving. She tried to hide it, but he saw through her act. And instead of being appalled by her interest, he was excited.

He was in no position to take a wife. He was most certainly in no position to take Lucy Vale as his wife! And yet, for the first time in his life, he caught himself imagining marriage as fun.

Which was far, far too big a leap! Severely, he hauled his wild flights of fancy to the back of his mind, where they belonged. From there, he could consider them when he was less…happy. For now, he had far too many other things to attend to, not least of which, his brother-in-law.

He returned to the King's Head to change out of his riding clothes, and then strolled up to the hotel. It was time he made friends with Miss Hester Poole, the heiress whom his brother-in-law seemed about to marry. Blackhaven was far too close to the Scottish border for him to be comfortable with Irving's presence at her side.

Crossing the hotel foyer toward the reception desk, he nodded politely to two ladies he recalled seeing at the ball and took note of a scowling gentleman seated on the sofa nearest the desk. He was a stranger, and not particularly well dressed—his cravat was carelessly tied, and his coat showed signs of age, although the material and the cut were good. Behind the scowl, Tyler saw a good deal of character, possibly misdirected toward anger.

"Good afternoon," he said pleasantly to the sly-faced clerk. "I appear to have foolishly left my cards behind, but be so good as to take my name to Mrs. and Miss Poole with the message that I beg a moment of their time if they can spare it. I shall wait here."

"And your name, sir?" the clerk asked him superciliously.

"Tyler," he said, as if the clerk should already have known. He had no way of knowing, of course, but the attitude had the desired effect of flustering the man and sending him scuttling to obey.

Tyler arranged himself comfortably on the sofa perpendicular to that of the scowling man—whose scowl, if anything, had grown even fiercer, almost making a shelf of his brow. And he was glaring at Tyler.

"Good day," Tyler said politely. "Have we met, sir?"

"No." The single syllable was hardly encouraging, although at least the man had enough grace to look elsewhere. They sat in silence for a few moments, and then the man turned back to him with a glower. "I heard you ask for Miss Poole."

"And her mama, of course."

"Of course," the man said impatiently. He straightened. "I have also requested the pleasure of their company."

So much for a confidential chat. "How delightful." Tyler sat forward and offered his hand. "Tyler," he said amiably, although the intrusion of Tyler into his personal life was becoming an annoyance that would surely rebound on him before long. The trouble was, the Pooles had been introduced to him as Tyler already, and this was hardly the place for explanations. Particularly not if Harold Irving accompanied the ladies.

The man glared at Tyler's hand before taking it with clear reluctance. "Cairney."

"How do you do, Mr. Cairney? What is your preferred entertainment for the ladies, should they be available? A pleasant walk on the beach? An ice, perhaps? It is too early for tea, sadly."

Cairney looked him in the eye. "I haven't invited you."

"I haven't invited *you*," Tyler said with rising devilment. "Though if you stop scowling at me, I might. Seriously, you'll frighten Miss Poole back to London with that glower."

Cairney's lips curled. "She is not such a poor creature."

"No, but I can't imagine she chooses to be entertained by angry gentlemen. It cannot be pleasant."

Cairney's fists clenched. "Miss Poole is an old friend who knows my ways."

"Oh. I wondered if you were related to her mother."

Just for an instant, like cracked enamel, the light of an incipient smile began to split Cairney's face. At least the man could be amused, and he was clearly quick enough. And then Mrs. and Miss Poole appeared on the staircase, the older lady supported on the younger's patient arm, and Cairney leapt eagerly to his feet.

Harold Irving was not with them. Well there was still some good to be done here—at the very least, some amusement to be derived.

THE DINNER PARTY with Mrs. Macy, who was clearly someone of vital importance to Julius's past, went off very well. It turned out she was the companion rather than the friend of Miss Talbot, but one would not have known from the courtesy shown her. Of course, the twins interrogated Mrs. Macy, but she bore it very well. And both Lord Linfield and Miss Talbot had known the Vales' larger-than-life father and told some tales that seemed to soften even Julius's heart toward the old reprobate.

Flushed with the success of the dinner party, Lucy accompanied Felicia into town the following morning. Leaving her sister to make whatever calls she wished, Lucy claimed to have a few purchases to make at the market. In fact, she walked straight through the market toward the harbor and down to the beach, where, out of sight of the town, she ran barefoot through the sand, then sat on a rock and let feeling engulf her. She didn't try to analyze it, just let it be.

The first drop of rain reminded her to dust the sand off her feet, replace her shoes, and walk sedately back to town. There, she paused to consider the ice parlor. It would certainly be a pleasant place to wait out the shower, and no one would mind her being there unaccompanied. The customers were largely women, with a scattering of children. Among them were seated Mrs. and Miss Poole.

For Lucy, that settled it. She went inside, and a young lady showed her immediately to the small, vacant table beside the Pooles. They both glanced up as she passed, and she smiled with genuine pleasure.

"Good morning! Mrs. Poole, is it not? Miss Poole. I have just escaped the worst of the downpour!"

The old lady nodded curtly. Miss Poole's smile was more welcoming. "You are alone, Miss Vale? Won't you join us?"

"I would be delighted. I was on my way to meet my sister,

but I'm sure she too will be sheltering indoors until the wretched rain eases."

"Dreadful weather," the old lady pronounced. "Bound to reverse all the good of the waters."

"It is the same everywhere this summer," Miss Poole said soothingly. "London is wet and cold, too."

As she sat opposite Miss Poole, it struck Lucy that she looked tired and not terribly well. No doubt the old lady was exhausting, even depressing, but that did not account for the odd paleness around Hester Poole's mouth. Moreover, while Mrs. Poole's ice was more than half finished, Hester's was melting untouched in its dish.

"Please, don't wait for me," Lucy begged. "I'm sure my ice will just be a moment."

The old lady dived back into her treat. Hester picked up her dainty spoon and poked at the ice in front of her. Her face tightened, and nothing went into her mouth.

Concerned, Lucy awaited her moment. When Mrs. Poole was distracted in farewells to a departing acquaintance, Lucy leaned forward.

"Forgive me, Miss Poole," she murmured. "But are you quite well?"

Hester laid down her spoon. "No, not really. I feel a little sick, to be honest. I could never face sweet things so early in the morning."

"Then as soon as your mama finishes, we shall go," Lucy said decisively. Not that she believed Hester's reason, but she understood making light of illness. Her brother Aubrey had been doing it for years.

Perhaps it was not Mrs. Poole but Hester who needed the magic of the Blackhaven waters.

Lucy paid the bill quietly, and as soon as the old lady set down her spoon with considerable satisfaction, Lucy rose. "Look, the rain is almost off! Let me show you the bracelet I was talking about, Miss Poole. Ma'am," she added to the older lady, "would you care to accompany us, or rest here until it is dry? Perhaps you would like another ice?"

It was the perfect solution. The two younger women escaped, pointing the waiting girl to Mrs. Poole as they went.

Hester inhaled the cool air with long, slightly shaky breaths. Lucy took her arm, guiding her across the road and further along to a jeweler's shop window, out of sight from the ice parlor.

"Thank you," Hester said. "I can't think what came over me. I thought I would disgrace myself in there."

"Warn me if you are going to faint," Lucy said. "Lean on me and breathe normally."

After a few moments, a hint of color began to reappear in Hester's cheeks. The slightly green tinge had gone from around her mouth.

"Has this happened to you before?" Lucy asked gently.

"Once or twice," Hester admitted. "But it is nothing. I am better already."

"Have you consulted a physician? Everyone in Blackhaven speaks most highly of Dr. Lampton. My brother has consulted him and is doing very well."

"Thank you. I shall bear that in mind if I feel ill again. But the fresh air has worked wonders." She smiled at Lucy, quite a good effort. "Thank you for rescuing me!"

"It is my one talent," Lucy said. "I discreetly rescue my sisters from boredom and from over-persistent suitors. I rescue Aubrey from excessive coddling and the twins from scolds. It is a knack of which I am unworthily proud."

"*Worthily* proud," Hester argued. "Shall we walk a little? If you don't mind a drop of rain."

"I barely notice it," Lucy said truthfully.

They strolled in comfortable silence for a few moments. Hester was a very natural young lady, younger than Lucy had first judged, and oddly likeable.

Hester said, "At the ball, I met you in the company of Mr. Tyler, did I not?"

"Indeed." Lucy had to quell the fluttering of her heart just at the sound of his name. Ridiculous.

"Are you and he related, perhaps?"

"Goodness, no. Why did you think that?"

Hester smiled deprecatingly. "You seemed so comfortable together, but I suppose I hoped rather than suspected with any real evidence!"

Lucy regarded her with some fascination. "You *want* me to be related to Mr. Tyler?"

"So that I might learn about him."

Something twisted inside Lucy. It felt horribly like jealousy. "I'm afraid I know no more than you," she said, as lightly as she could manage. "I met him for the first time at the ball."

Hester looked disappointed, but merely shrugged. "He seems to upset Mr. Irving, and I cannot conceive why. I found him a most charming and unexceptionable young man."

This, on the other hand, was exactly why Lucy had been so glad to see the Pooles in the ice parlor. "How strange that he should upset Mr. Irving. In what way?"

"He tenses at the very sight of Mr. Tyler."

"Perhaps Mr. Irving does not care for levity?"

"No, that is true," Hester said, disappointment seeping into her tone. "But it seems to be a more personal dislike that I can find no reason for. And when I asked Mr. Tyler, he merely laughed and turned the subject."

Hating herself, Lucy said casually, "You saw Mr. Tyler yesterday?"

"He called in the afternoon, and we strolled around the harbor together."

*After he had spoken to me at Black Hill.* She had no reason for resentment. Tyler was indeed like quicksilver. It seemed he had slipped through her fingers and straight into the heiress's. She knew, of course, that Tyler had some ulterior motive and that it concerned Mr. Irving, yet still she did not like that he had sought Hester out. Lucy wanted to be special to him, and she didn't like that feeling. She didn't like it at all.

"Mama came, of course," Hester said. "And Mr. Cairney, whom we met in London. Are you acquainted with Mr. Cairney? He has just arrived in Blackhaven."

"No, I don't believe I have met him."

Hester's eyes smiled. "A grumpy Scot. He says little, and what he does say could annihilate armies. A forceful man, yet gentle as a lamb."

"Can the two go together?" Lucy asked skeptically.

"You must meet Mr. Cairney. In fact, speak of the devil…"

A stocky man had emerged from one of the narrow streets on the other side of the road and was crossing toward the hotel, nimbly skipping around an oncoming cart. Obviously, he caught sight of Miss Poole, for he paused and then veered toward her.

Hester performed the introductions. Mr. Cairney was perfectly civil, although Lucy could see the difference in his eyes when he looked at Hester, hear the changed tone of voice when he addressed her. Mr. Cairney was genuinely smitten.

Hester was not so easy to read, but it seemed to Lucy that she was not as indifferent as she pretended. And yet when Mr. Irving emerged from the hotel and swept toward them with delight, she all but elbowed Cairney aside in order to take Irving's arm. Was she using Cairney to make Irving jealous? Or was it the other way around?

Perhaps, being an heiress, she could spot a fortune hunter at a hundred yards and had no intention of accepting either of them. In which case, Tyler had no need to worry about Hester marrying his one-time brother-in-law.

AROUND THE SAME time, Tyler was strolling past the picturesque Church of St. Andrew in Blackhaven, deep in thought. Watching Cairney's tongue-tied, glowering courting of Miss Poole yesterday had made him think of Lucy.

Well, everything made him think of Lucy. And he had rather ruined his chances there, with lies far more than neglect. His one chance was to own the truth, it seemed, but then she would merely send him away in disgust.

She liked him, it was true. But in two short meetings, she could hardly be in love! Her feelings could not possibly be strong enough to overcome his deceptions. *But…*

What if he wooed her and won her love? She was a loyal and passionate young woman. She might hit him, but surely she would forgive? A plan began to form in his head, where too many plans already existed.

He became aware quite slowly of being watched from the railings around the churchyard. Blinking, he observed a boy and a girl, dazzlingly blond and alike. The boy wore loose breeches and a coat that was slightly too big for him, both in a light fawn color. The girl, who was almost exactly the same height, wore her hair down and her skirt hems up. He put them at about fourteen or fifteen years old. But their similarity gave him an idea. As if he had conjured them up from his own thoughts about Lucy.

He stopped and regarded them through the railings. He touched his hat brim. "Am I by chance addressing a Miss Vale and Master Vale?"

"I'm Lawrence," said the boy. "This is Leona."

"My name is Tyler."

"We know," the girl replied. "The man with the red hair told us."

"Man with the…" Tyler's mind cleared. "Cairney?"

"He went that way," Lawrence said, pointing toward the high street. "But he saw you coming from over there."

"And he pointed me out?" Tyler said uneasily. "Why?"

"We asked him if he knew Mr. Tyler—he looked around, then pointed to you."

Tyler closed his mouth. He couldn't work out whether the children were unnerving or amusing. "Dare I ask why you wanted to know?"

"Lucy mentioned you. So did Roderick, so we wanted to see for ourselves."

This required thought. And study. He eased himself onto the low wall beneath the railings and lifted one foot so that he could still face the Vale twins. At once, they sat on the wall, too, both twisted around to face him.

"Is Lucy angry with me?"

"We thought you'd be more worried about Roderick," Leona said.

Tyler sighed. "I probably should be, if he is angry."

"He's more likely to blame Lucy, so long as you didn't actually hurt her, and since she still likes you, we don't think you did."

"She does?" The world seemed suddenly brighter again, and everything worth the risk. "And thank you, though I don't see how you can tell."

"Lucy can," Lawrence said. "She nearly always knows what you're thinking, or at least feeling, and she's nearly always right."

"Are you warning me?" Tyler asked, impressed.

"I don't think I need to."

"And if we're wrong," Leona added, "we have a lot of large brothers. Even Lawrence is quite strong now."

"I can see that," Tyler agreed. "And I appreciate that Lucy has so many people looking out for her. Um… Was there anything in particular you wanted to say to me?"

"Well, yes," Leona said, idly pleating the fabric of her dress without looking at it. "Lucy has a problem. His name is Lord Eddleston."

"St. John Gore, Earl of Eddleston," Lawrence added, lest there be any doubt.

"Ah," Tyler said. "The betrothed."

"Lucy told you about him?" Leona looked pleased. "Her mother and Eddleston's made the betrothal when Lucy was a baby, solely on the grounds that they were best friends and their children had the same birthdays. Lucy's mother was a little silly."

"Lucy's mother is not your mother?" Tyler asked, distracted from the main point.

"Oh, no," Lawrence said. "We are illegitimate, although our mother was a countess. Do you mind?"

Tyler's eyebrows flew up of their own accord. "Nothing I could do about it if I did. Besides, some of my best friends are illegitimate." Probably half the family too, if the truth were known.

"Did you really peer in the back window of the tavern and run on a barrel out of the yard, with a giant chasing you?" Lawrence asked, grinning.

Tyler couldn't help smiling back. "Did Lucy tell you that?"

"And that you wanted to fit a puppy inside a lady's ridiculous headdress," said Leona.

"I only wanted to see if it would go."

Lawrence laughed. "Who wouldn't? And you caught all the things Lucy knocked over that were about to clatter on the floor and scare the orchestra into a violent discord."

"I don't know about the orchestra, but it certainly scared me," Tyler admitted.

Leona regarded him with something serious behind the humor in her eyes. "You're quite fun, aren't you?"

"From time to time," Tyler said modestly. "I hope."

"Lucy needs someone who is fun. Which is the problem with Lord Eddleston."

"Perhaps he is also fun."

They cast him a skeptical glance.

"We wrote to him," Lawrence said. "He did not reply. That is not fun."

"It's rude," Tyler allowed, "but not proof of his nature."

"Do you *know* him?" Leona asked.

"Slightly."

"And you want him to marry Lucy?" Lawrence asked incredulously.

"We wondered if *you* wanted to marry her," Leona added.

Tyler closed his mouth. This was dangerous territory. Very dangerous indeed. "I think the question we should all be asking," he said at last, "is who, if anyone, Lucy wants to marry."

"True," Leona agreed.

"But he has to want to marry her too," Lawrence argued.

"Actually," Tyler interrupted, "I can't imagine anyone would *not* want to marry Lucy. Apart from the problem of meddlesome siblings, of course."

"Of course," the twins murmured appreciatively.

"So what are you going to do about it?" Lawrence asked. "Are you going to call on us?"

"I think Lucy might enjoy an assignation more," Leona said seriously.

"That's just what I was thinking," Tyler said before he could help himself. He looked uneasily from twin to twin. "How many other gentlemen have you invited to make assignations with your sister?"

"None!" Lawrence said, clearly shocked. "For one thing, she wouldn't go. For another, we would never endanger her or her reputation."

"With respect," Tyler pointed out, "you don't know me from Adam. Or Lucifer, come to that."

"Lucy likes you," Leona said, and that appeared to be the end of the argument.

# Chapter Nine

WHEN LUCY WENT to bed that night, she had a great deal to think about.

Tomorrow, she would go to Blackhaven again, and explain to Tyler what she had found out. Of course, *finding* Tyler might be problematic, but it had come to her earlier in the day that if he was not staying at the hotel, he was most likely at the King's Head, which was a much cheaper place to put up than the hotel, and far more respectable than the tavern. She could at least ask at the inn.

She sat back against the pillows, not yet ready to blow out the last candle and go to sleep. Did she really have anything to tell him? It was really all impressions, gained from watching the interplay of Hester Poole, Mr. Cairney, and Mr. Irving. And, of course, the conversation with Hester after they had all walked up to the ice parlor to retrieve Mrs. Poole and returned to the hotel.

Hester had seemed reluctant to part with Lucy, and so she had taken tea with them in her private sitting room. That had been uncomfortable because it was Hester asking questions about Tyler, and his past with Mr. Irving.

"Yes," Lucy had answered. "I believe they knew each other when Mr. Tyler was a boy."

"How?" Hester had pressed.

Though Lucy liked Hester and wished to be truthful, it was

not her place to say that the two men were brothers-in-law. She did not know what Tyler's plans toward Irving were, or whether he wanted to be recognized. And she did not know Hester well enough to swear her to secrecy.

"I couldn't say," Lucy had managed.

"I wondered if perhaps Mr. Tyler knew Mrs. Irving."

Lucy had stopped stirring her tea, using a moment's thought to lay down the spoon and pick up the cup and saucer. "Why should you want to know that?"

Hester had hesitated, then said bluntly, "I am expecting Mr. Irving to make me an offer of marriage. He speaks much of his late wife, and yet I know nothing about her."

Lucy had met her gaze. "You have doubts," she said, with equal candor. "I feel one should not marry with doubts about one's husband. I have doubts about my betrothed—mostly because I have never met him! I certainly won't commit myself to marriage until they are resolved."

"Sound advice. Although you are younger than I, and time is not so pressing." Hester had then smiled. "How is it you have never met your betrothed?"

Thinking of her betrothed now—St. John Gore, fourth Earl of Eddleston—Lucy felt a considerable revulsion that she knew was unfair. She wanted to do her duty and ease Julius's financial burden. She wanted to make it possible for Felicia to pay her husband's debts, for Aubrey to travel for his health, Cornelius to take on staff to ease his burden, to give Delilah the freedom she craved, and secure the twins' future with a dowry for Leona and a university education for Lawrence...

She wanted all those things very badly. Yet over them all now hung the image of Mr. Tyler, a man who seemed to have several purposes but no reliable name. She had told him things she had never told anyone and never should. Even though she could not see him as clearly as she saw most people... It did not seem to matter. She trusted him anyway. She wanted him nearby, to discover, to adventure with, to kiss...

Her body flamed with memory. She turned her face into the pillow and wallowed for a little. Kisses were…delightful. At least, Tyler's were. She wondered if Lord Eddleston kissed like that. Or like Nick Maitland, Felicia's selfish, hedonistic husband.

Banishing Nick, she sat up, and was about to blow out the candle when something tapped against the window, like a bird beak or a twig in the breeze. Perhaps the wind was rising and there would be a storm. She listened for the sound of it rushing among the nearby trees or whining in the chimney.

A sharper tap sounded on the window pane, this time followed a second later by a soft thud on the ground below.

*The twins,* she thought in quick alarm. In the past she and they had attracted each other's attention by throwing small stones at their bedchamber windows. But now was a bad time for any of them to be out alone. Julius was in pursuit of horse thieves, at least one of whom was still hanging around the area and had threatened Mrs. Macy and her little boy.

Lucy leapt out of bed and ran to the window. She had not closed the shutters and usually left a gap in the curtains to let in the morning light when it came. Tugging the curtain back fully, she pulled up the window sash and peered down below.

A male figure detached itself from the shadows of the house.

"Lawrie?" she whispered.

"No. It's me."

Her breath stopped. It could not be—

"Want an adventure?"

She knew then for certain, and emotions tumbled through her—intense delight because he had sought her out, excitement, laughter, a spurt of alarm, too easily overcome. Rushing across the room, she tore off her nightgown and threw on the gown she had just taken off. Without waiting to wrestle with the fastenings, she merely swung her cloak around her and shoved her bare feet into half-boots. Then she seized the bedside candle and crept out of her bedchamber on tiptoe.

The house was in darkness, and everything seemed very

quiet. Lucy was aware of every creak of the stairs, every faint rustle of her dress or tap of her boot, even her breath, which sounded too quick and too loud.

She eased back the bolts on the side door and closed it softly behind her. The breeze immediately blew out her candle, leaving her in darkness, so she abandoned it at the door and waited for her eyes to adjust to seeing without it. Fortunately, the day's clouds had cleared, and despite the waning of the moon, there was enough pale starlight for her to creep around the house in search of Tyler.

As she approached the side of the house where she had last seen him, he stepped out of the shadows. His teeth gleamed and he strode toward her, one hand held out. Without thought, she hurried forward and took his hand, her heart hammering, especially when she felt his warm skin beneath her fingers. Neither of them wore gloves, making the gesture oddly intimate. But there was no time for either awkwardness or tenderness—he was already drawing her toward the cover of the trees at the edge of the overgrown side of the garden.

She ran with him, hand in hand, letting the thrill and the pleasure wash over her. Neither of them spoke until they were in the shelter of the trees, when they both paused to catch their breath, smiling at each other like naughty children.

"What are you doing here, you madman?" she demanded at last. "We have dangerous horse thieves—or something—on the loose, and my brothers are itching to catch them. What if they catch you instead?"

"I imagine they'll thrash me or call me out, or both."

"Don't you mind?" she asked, annoyed by the levity of his tone.

"I'm sure I will if it happens, but at least I'll know I deserve it for making assignations with their sister."

"You didn't make an assignation," she objected. "You just *appeared*."

"So did you."

"You threw stones at my window!" She frowned, peering at him as he picked his way along the track. It was darker here, and they were moving more by feel than sight. Branches caught at her cloak and hood. Abruptly, she tugged her hand free, and when he turned his head, she glared at him. "How did you know which window is mine?"

"The twins told me."

She closed her mouth, and when he took her hand again, she didn't object, mainly through surprise. "You've met the twins?"

"They accosted me outside the church this afternoon—I think to discover what my intentions were."

A breath of laughter caught in Lucy's throat. "Julius may think he is head of the family, but we all know it is really the twins."

"They are very anxious that you don't marry Lord Eddleston."

She sighed. "They told you his name, too. Well, they have heard me rail against the idea often enough."

"Did you know they had written to him?"

Her feet stumbled. "No. I did not know that."

"Apparently, he didn't write back."

"No, but he did write to Julius," she said. "*That* is why he is coming here. The twins brought about the very outcome they were trying to avoid for my sake."

"*Should* it be avoided?" he asked. "Is it not better to meet him and decide once and for all whether or not you can thole him? Then you can either send the poor man about his business or teach him to be a decent husband."

She frowned at him, slightly surprised that she could see him so well. "You have a very odd idea of a woman's power in marriage."

"Legal power and actual power are not necessarily the same. As I see it, it depends very much on the couple concerned."

"I suppose that is true, only—" She broke off as something thudded softly close by. A breath across her hair made her squeak in alarm.

"Don't worry," Tyler said. "It's only old Sock." Releasing her hand, he reached over her and patted the nose of the waiting horse beside her. A lantern hung from a nearby tree branch. Tyler reached up and retrieved it.

"You think of everything," she murmured. "I suspect you have done this before."

He strapped the lantern to the saddle, then mounted without fuss and held down his hand to Lucy.

She frowned at it, common sense making a brief appearance in her mind. "Where are we going?"

"Wherever you like," he said at once. "Midnight gallop in the moonlight?"

"Among the horse thieves?" she said, but already she had taken his hand, set her foot over his in the stirrup, and found herself swung up before him in the saddle. She flung her leg over to ride astride, as she'd done as a child, and hastily covered her rucked-up skirts with the cloak.

He shifted behind the saddle, and his arms enclosed her as he tightened the loose reins.

"You should let me have the reins," she said, oddly breathless.

"In a while," he said. "When Sock is used to you."

She suspected Sock made his own way through the trees without much, if any, guidance. To distract herself from his closeness behind her, the brush of his arms against her, she thought about what she had intended to tell him the next time she saw him.

"I met Miss Poole today, along with your Mr. Irving. And a Mr. Cairney."

He seemed to be very still behind her. His hands on the reins didn't move. "Did you indeed?"

"I like her. Miss Poole. And I am worried about her."

"Because of Irving?"

"Partly... She asked me about you. She has the impression Irving knows you and asked me how. She wonders if it has anything to do with Mr. Irving's late wife."

His breath whispered against her neck as he exhaled. "Did you tell her?"

"No. I told her *any* doubt should prevent her marrying him."

"What a very tactful answer."

"I thought so, but I'm not sure how much it will weigh with her. She talked about running out of time, and she is not old, you know, less than five and twenty, I am sure, so she has many childbearing years to come."

She broke off, unsure how to continue without being unfair to Hester. But Tyler seemed to grasp her meaning.

"You are afraid that, feeling time is short, she may rush into marriage with Irving, despite her doubts?"

Lucy nodded.

"Why would she do that?" he mused. "Why would she think that?"

"I am afraid she is ill," Lucy blurted. "She was taken unwell in the ice parlor, and I have the feeling it happens quite often. I told her to see Dr. Lampton, but I'm not sure she will."

"So she wishes to rush into marriage and have a child to whom to leave her fortune in case she dies prematurely?"

"Put like that, it sounds a little far-fetched," Lucy admitted. "It needn't be true. Just what she thinks. Though I hope she does not. I shall call again, perhaps contrive to introduce her to Dr. Lampton. Do you suppose he will be at the Braithwaites' garden party?"

"I have no idea."

"Well, you obviously have the earl's ear, so you could make sure he invites Lampton and the Pooles."

"You overestimate my influence. I'm sure we can manage such a meeting without involving the Braithwaites. Besides, I wouldn't be surprised if Irving didn't have a rival for Miss Poole's affections."

"Mr. Cairney," Lucy said with approval. "I like him. More to the point, I think Hester does, too. Her feelings for Mr. Irving seem more…ambivalent. We should encourage Cairney to propose."

"Leave them be," Tyler said uneasily. "No good ever comes of meddling. Look at your twins and Eddleston."

"Hmm." She was not entirely convinced. After all, who was he to scold *her* for meddling? But they were emerging from the trees onto the long meadow that led to the ruin.

"Which way?" he asked.

"Right, if you want to gallop. There shouldn't be rabbit holes, either."

She glanced over her shoulder and saw the flash of his smile, and then Sock took off.

The speed of the gallop was doubly thrilling with her back pressed to Tyler's chest, his arms like solid bands on either side. Once, she twisted to glance up at him, laughing with pure exhilaration, and knew he shared it.

But poor Sock was carrying both of them, so she didn't object when Tyler pulled up at the old church ruin. A pale beam of moonlight lent the ancient stones a silvery glow that looked oddly magical.

Tyler sprang down from the saddle and caught her as she jumped down to join him. She didn't know why his strength should move her, but it did. Everything about him moved her in ways she didn't completely understand.

Leaving the horse loose to crop the vegetation growing around the ruin, she led Tyler to the fallen stone against one half-wall that had served her as a seat in the past.

"Rod remembers coming here with Julius and Delilah some-times, when they were at home. My father was a diplomat and traveled a good deal."

"Then you have seen much of the world?"

She told him something of her life with her father and which-ever siblings were around. Julius had been at sea for most of her life, though he occasionally appeared at some embassy or other looking so bronzed and dashing that all the ladies fussed over him. As a hero of Trafalgar, he had been—and still was!—much admired.

"I basked in reflected glory," she recalled, "and then he went away again, and I felt quite lonely. I felt the same when Roderick went to join Wellington on the Peninsula, and Cornelius, and then Aubrey went away to school, and Felicia got married. But I was lucky. I always had Delilah and the twins. Then my father died, and it felt as if the world had ended."

His arm folded around her shoulders, and she accepted it in the comforting spirit it was offered. She even leaned into it.

"So we came home and stayed with Felicia, who had great plans to introduce me to the *ton*. Then Nick died and she discovered his massive debts. We had no idea what to do. Then Julius came home too, and we knew everything would be fine, so long as Roderick came back from Waterloo.

"He did, and Julius decided we should all come home to Black Hill. It was the perfect solution, and we were finally all together again."

"And yet I think you are still lonely," he said unexpectedly.

She shook her head. "Not lonely." She frowned, trying to find the words. "Just...excluded? The others regard me as a child in many ways, like the twins, to be looked after rather than allowed to be part of the family endeavors."

"And that is why you are seriously considering Lord Eddleston's offer? Should he make one."

"I've seen the way men look at me. I could probably induce him to offer for me."

She glanced at him, to make sure he was not disgusted.

"You probably could," he agreed. "Only you mustn't, if you don't want him."

"I won't want him," she said with sudden, tragic understanding. "The question becomes, could I bear him? Could he bear me?"

"No," he said fiercely, pushing up her chin with one finger. "*Never* marry for such a reason."

"Why not?" she countered. "Felicia married for love, and Nick made her miserable. I have heard of fond couples who married to oblige their families and found happiness together. It seems to me it is a gamble either way."

"If you wished only to oblige your family, you would not be so disturbed by the imminent visitation of your wealthy betrothed."

She wanted to look away, but he held her chin steady between finger and thumb. She hoped he could not see her blush in the dim light from the stars and the lantern. "I-I wanted an adventure first. A taste of something *I* choose."

His eyes changed in some indefinable way, devouring hers. "Am I to be your adventure, Lucy Vale?"

"Would you like to be?" she asked hoarsely.

His gaze dropped to her mouth, and the butterflies in her stomach soared and dipped. He leaned closer, and she parted her lips, her heart hammering with anticipation.

"I would," he whispered. "Oh, I would..." His lips curved into a smile, at once tender and voracious. "Only, though I might forget it occasionally, I *am* a gentleman."

He sprang to his feet in one sudden movement and held down his hand to her.

She took it and rose a little more slowly. "I like *this* adventure," she said.

He swallowed. "So do I. Shall we track down my poor old Sock?"

She was relieved that he took her hand again. Her fingers curled around his quite naturally, and she felt both soothed and thrilled by the intimacy.

Sock was munching grass and some scrubby leaves, but he seemed happy to leave his meal and amble back to his master without even being summoned.

"What is it you fear for Hester Poole if she marries Irving?" Lucy said suddenly. "Why do you dislike him so? Was he cruel to your sister?"

His body jerked. For a moment she thought he was pulling away from her, and she cursed her unruly tongue. That she confided in him did not mean he was ready to tolerate her demand for confidences. But instead, his fingers tightened on her before he deliberately relaxed them.

"I think he probably was." The words sounded as if they were forced out of him. "It was covered up at the time, but I am afraid… I believe…that she killed herself."

She halted, staring up at him. Then she put both arms around him. "Dear God. I am so sorry."

Slowly, his arms came up to hold her. His head dropped so that he was speaking into her hair. "I think he drove her to it by making people believe she was mad and threatening her with a lunatic asylum. He had spent all her fortune by that stage and couldn't get at her dowry, thanks to the way my father had tied it up. So he needed rid of her. Then he went abroad for some years. Now he's back, a gazetted fortune hunter, and Hester Poole is in his sights. It has been twelve years. No one will remember the irregularities around my sister's death."

She felt a slight pressure on her hair—had he kissed her?—and then he drew away, taking back her hand instead.

"So that is the real reason you came to Blackhaven?" she asked.

"It was one of my reasons, when I heard he was escorting the Pooles. And then, on the journey, I agreed to do what I could for Farmer to oblige a friend. And here I am." With his free hand he petted Sock's nose and neck, then gave the animal a mangled piece of apple from his pocket.

Lucy said, "Could you be wrong? I don't believe one ever knows, let alone understands, what goes on in people's marriages."

"I could be wrong," he agreed. "But I knew my sister and I saw what she had become under his supposed care. I have no proof, only the suspicion of a twelve-year-old boy… But should I allow Hester Poole to take that chance?"

Lucy shivered. "I shall befriend her."

"Stay away from Irving," he warned. "Don't get in his way and don't let him connect you any further with me."

"You have no faith in me," she said lightly.

"I have every faith in you to follow your impulses, which, like mine, are not necessarily wise! Into the saddle with you." He boosted her up and handed her the reins before he mounted behind her once more.

"Is Sock up to another gallop?" she asked.

"What do you think?"

Whatever Sock wanted, Lucy thought it was exactly what Tyler needed after she had raked up the tragedy of his sister. He might remember, and even act upon his memories, but he would not wallow.

So she tightened her legs and kicked Sock into a gallop. Tyler's arms came around her waist, and that made everything joyous and wonderful. Even the terrible fate of his sister took second place to the happiness of this growing closeness between them. He had trusted her, let her see his pain, and now he held her as *more* than a friend. As a man who was at least as aware of her as she was of him.

Perhaps the adventure was good for both of them.

At any rate, she galloped Sock along past the wood, meaning to take the direct path back to the house, only she had forgotten about the gate that was always opened for her, and the wall.

For a horrible moment, she thought Sock was going to jump the gate, which he surely couldn't do with both of them on his back! She wheeled him rather wildly around, clinging to his mane, while Tyler clung to her. Fortunately, Sock answered her instructions, though so crazily that the riders found themselves leaning so far to one side that they almost fell off.

Tyler hurled himself to the other side, dragging her with him, and Sock straightened up, snorting. Behind her, Tyler was snorting, too—with laughter, she could only presume—as she finally reined the horse in.

Sock turned his head, his expression so apparently reproachful that Lucy began to laugh too. Tyler slid his leg over the beast's back and jumped down. As soon as he held up his arms, she leapt into them and was spun around in an exuberant, laughing twirl.

There was no time to recover before she was pulled hard against him and his mouth seized hers.

Lucy gasped, not so much in surprise as in welcome, in fierce, sweet delight. *This* was what she had dreamed of with longing but without real understanding—the instinctive surge of passion that flamed from a deep recognition and swept all before it. An impetuous, totally overwhelming kiss, pleasurable, invasive, unbearably arousing.

She clung to his neck, her mouth fused to his, not merely in surrender but in eager response. Tyler kissed her not just with his whole mouth—his lips and tongue, even his teeth—but with his whole body, which moved so sweetly against hers, showing her his desire, absorbing her own.

She was lost in wonder, in hot, delicious weakness, and she wanted it to go on forever. She loved the softness of his hair, the rough stubble of his cheek beneath her exploring fingertips. She rejoiced in the quickness of his breath, the slow gentling of his mouth as it grew more sensual, kissing from her lips to her jaw and the side of her neck, while his fingers caressed her nape. She couldn't understand how she could feel such attentions so much lower down her body, too...

His mouth found hers again in a long, aching kiss.

"Lucy Vale," he whispered, "you kiss like my own private, beautiful demon sent to undo me."

"Is that bad?" she asked before she could stop herself.

He pressed his cheek to hers, and his shaky laughter winnowed through her hair. "Only for my self-discipline."

"Is this not meant to happen at assignations?"

"I don't know. I've never had one like this before." As though he understood her sudden anxiety, he raised his head and fluttered kisses across her eyelids, her nose, and, very softly, the corners of her mouth. "You are unique and sweet and passionate and very, very wonderful. Will you make another assignation with me?"

"Yes."

He hugged her closer for that. "Dare we risk a daylight assignation? I would like to walk with you hand in hand along the beach, although I suppose that risks discovery."

"Do you mind?"

"Not in the least," he said. "I have the means to avert any incipient scandal."

"Why do I believe you when I know you're talking nonsense?"

"My nonsense always makes sense in the end. How far are we from the house?"

She pointed to the gate. "Two minutes' walk, and perfectly safe."

"Then tell me where and when you will meet me again."

His eyes gleamed with an eagerness that she might have thought boyish, had she not felt the naked desire in his lips and hands. Her body flushed all over again, and it was an effort to think ahead. She didn't want him to go.

"Tomorrow," he urged.

Reluctantly, she shook her head. "I owe the garden some work. Unless we say the evening?"

"No, let us say the day after," he said ruefully. His arms were still loosely around her. "Midday?"

She nodded and raised her face for his kiss, which was long and tender.

"Until Friday," he whispered against her lips, and slowly released her.

She might have felt cold had it not been for the burning happiness inside. Beyond his shoulder, she caught a movement in the darkness. A horse-shaped shadow ambling downhill. "Tyler! Sock is going without you!"

With an exclamation, Tyler hurtled off after him. Lucy was

sure the slightest call would have brought the horse to him, but he ran anyway, caught the reins, and all but vaulted into the saddle.

When he raised one hand, Lucy, laughing silently, waved back, then climbed over the gate and walked up the path to the side of the house. She turned once and looked downhill. Silhouetted against the sky, a horse and rider waited. Tyler, still watching to be sure she got safely back to the house.

Fresh warmth closed about her heart. She lifted her hand again, and he returned the salute before she turned, picked up her abandoned candle, and slipped back into the house.

She more than half expected Roderick to be waiting for her—or worse, Julius. But all was still and quiet. She slid the bolts home, then felt in the darkness for the flint on the table by the door. She managed to relight her candle, then crept back toward the stairs. The twins were not sitting there as they often were. In fact, she made it back to her bedchamber as if she had never left it.

And yet everything had changed. Everything. Because of one eccentric, erratic, elusive, deadly serious young man who was nevertheless constantly in search of fun.

*I love him.*

# Chapter Ten

H AROLD IRVING DID not like Blackhaven. It was cold, wet, and in the middle of nowhere, and the normal rules of Society barely applied. For example, single ladies went out alone, unaccompanied by chaperone, gentleman, or servant. In particular, Hester Poole had taken to doing so—like some East India Company functionary taking up the customs of the natives.

Not that Harold particularly wanted to walk the mean little streets just to look at the sea or eat ices that were bound to be inferior to Gunter's. But such independence made him uneasy. He had escorted the Poole ladies all the way up here in order to make himself indispensable. And up until a couple of days ago, he had been sure that Hester would marry him.

Encountering that fellow, Tyler, at the ball—the one who looked so like his late wife that he might have been her brother— had been a shock, of course. As had the man's continued presence in Blackhaven, and the fact that Hester had noticed him and asked about him. But then she noticed that damned Scotsman as well. Harold could almost feel her slipping through his fingers. And he would not allow it.

Accordingly, he put up with it grudgingly when, from his bedchamber window, he saw her leave the hotel alone and stroll along the high street in the direction of the harbor. He even sat by the window, pretending to read the London newspapers from two days ago, to watch for her return. She might enjoy a luncheon at the hotel, although he supposed he would be obliged to tolerate her mother. Only when she did return, he was infuriated to see she was escorted by Cairney, the damned Scotsman.

And she was laughing up at him as though teasing him. He did not appear to mind in the slightest. There was not a scowl to be seen on the man's rugged features.

Harold hurled his newspaper to the floor and stamped across the room, throwing the door wide and slamming it behind him. However, he knew he had to control his temper, and as he sought to do so, the perfect idea came to mind. Accordingly, he changed direction and marched up to the Pooles' suite, where he knocked gently on the door.

It was opened by the middle-aged maid who was, he had discovered, unbribable. It hardly mattered for present purposes.

"Is Mrs. Poole 'at home'? I was hoping I might take her to luncheon in the dining room."

"Mrs. Poole has already gone down, sir. She was going to wait for Miss Hester at their table."

This damnable independence appeared to be catching. Before they had come here, Mrs. Poole would never have contemplated going to a public place without a female companion and a male escort. But it did not ruin his plan. Nodding curtly to the maid— he owed her no more when the ladies were not there to appreciate his courtesy—he hurried on to the servants' staircase, which led to the side of the dining room. He bolted down the steps two at a time, narrowly avoiding a catastrophic crash with a footman bearing a loaded tray, and landed heavily at the bottom of the stairs.

A quick glance toward the foyer showed him Hester was still there. He smiled as he straightened his coat and sailed into the dining room.

"Mrs. Poole?" he demanded of the first servant he came to, but in fact he could already see her at the table that had become familiar over the last few days. He moved straight toward her. For once, she was not scowling. In fact, she was almost smiling. Thank God, he was winning her over at last.

He smiled back. "You will allow me to join you?" he said before he even reached her. He was in a hurry, after all, to appear established here before Hester joined them, with or without her blasted Scotsman.

The old lady blinked at him in surprise, and, too late, he realized she had not been smiling at him at all, but at the gentleman opposite her.

Tyler rose to his feet, bowing not to him but to Hester and Cairney, who had come up behind him. Only after he had held Hester's chair for her did he deign to glance at Harold. "You will join us, of course?" he asked pleasantly, the perfectly courteous host.

Such a little thing, and yet the wind was taken out of Harold's sails so effectively that he wanted very much to punch the smiling face that might so easily have been his late wife's.

"Do you come from a large family, Mr. Tyler?" Hester asked some time later. They had been discussing Lord Braithwaite, whose much-anticipated garden party was to be held the day after tomorrow, and who was the proud possessor of five sisters, three of whom were now married.

"Sadly, I am all that is left of my immediate family," Tyler replied, not noticeably upset by the fact. "My only sister died some years ago. What of you, Irving? Don't you have brothers?"

Harold froze. How did Tyler know he had brothers? He was almost sure he had never mentioned them. In truth, he barely thought of them.

*My sister died some years ago...*

Harold stared at him. It had been twelve years since Anne's

death. This annoying young man would be about the same age, surely, as her schoolboy brother would be now. The eyes… An unpleasant chill passed over him.

The man's name was Tyler. He could be no possible relation, except distantly, and Harold had no fear of such creatures. He had no fear of anyone. Anne's family had cooperated fully to have her death declared accidental. As he had known they would. Even the mother, with her clever, suspicious eyes, was long dead. He had to stop seeing those eyes in other people.

"Brothers?" he repeated, pulling himself together. "A mere two, hardly enough to compete with his lordship for siblings."

"Or the Vales," Hester said. "There are *nine* of them, I believe."

"Most of them are on the wrong side of the blanket," Mrs. Poole pronounced.

"Mama!" Hester protested. "Even if that were true, it is hardly their fault."

"I knew a Major Roderick Vale in the army," Cairney said. "I believe he hailed from this direction. Told me once he was almost Scottish."

"There is a Roderick, is there not?" Hester said, glancing at Tyler.

Harold recalled that at the ball, Tyler had been accompanied by a Miss Vale.

"I have heard the name," Tyler said, "but I have never met him."

Cairney grunted and returned to his plate. Conversation returned to the Braithwaites' garden party. Harold had been invited, along with the Pooles, and so, apparently, had the annoying Tyler.

"Will you be there, Mr. Cairney?" Hester asked, making Harold fume internally.

"I don't care for such things," Cairney said, not quite rudely.

Harold smiled. "Not been invited, old fellow?" As soon as the words were out, he knew it was a mistake. Hester had seen the sneer and the spite he couldn't quite hold back.

"You should come anyway," she said, totally ignoring any lack of invitation. "I expect you'll discover Major Vale is there, too." She looked around the company. "Do you know, I feel like a drive out into the country this afternoon? There is a fortress, and a ruined abbey I have not yet seen. Would anyone else enjoy such an excursion?"

"Sounds dull," Mrs. Poole pronounced, "but I'll come. It's a change from drinking the wretched water."

"We'll take water with us," Hester promised with a touch of inappropriate humor.

"Actually, I wouldn't this afternoon," Tyler said. "I think there's a storm coming."

Before Harold could rejoice in avoiding the tedium of such a trip, Cairney rose abruptly to his feet.

"Excuse me," he barked. "I have matters requiring my attention. Thank you for luncheon, Tyler. Ladies, good afternoon." He pushed in his chair and walked off.

Harold would have rejoiced again, only he glimpsed Hester's face, and just for an instant, she looked positively miserable.

LUCY FOUND THE twins watching the rising storm from the sitting room they euphemistically called the schoolroom.

"Julius is out there," Leona said. A smile flickered across her face. "Mrs. Macy is with him."

"Is she indeed?" Lucy said, pleased. She rather liked Antonia Macy. More to the point, she seemed to be humanizing Julius again.

"He meant to show her the ship he's borrowed from Captain Alban," Lawrence added. "But I hope they're on the way back or they'll get caught in the storm."

"If anyone knows the sea, it's Julius," Lucy said. She sat on the window seat, facing them. "I believe I have you two to thank for arranging assignations for me."

"It was only a suggestion," Leona said, grinning. "Will you go?"

"I already have."

Lawrence whistled. "That wasn't what we suggested. We said tonight, when we could watch out for you!" He frowned austerely. "I'm not sure I approve of his going behind our backs."

Lucy's lips twitched, but she didn't laugh, even though she still felt so happy she could burst into song.

"Well, I suspect the storm will put paid to any assignations tonight," Leona said. She glanced at Lucy. "Do you still like him?"

Lucy nodded. She wasn't sure of the words, and she had this idea that she should say them first to Tyler in any case. Just not yet. Her need to see him again was a joy and an ache.

When she came in, she had meant to scold the twins for writing to Lord Eddleston behind her back. But it came to her now that there was no point. She did need to talk to him, although the idea of marrying him to help the family was both more appalling and more distant. As for the twins' interference, one might as well forbid them to breathe. Meddling was what they did. It was probably good for them to discover that Tyler, at least, was one step ahead of them!

Their plans for Julius seemed to be working well.

Thunder was rumbling in the distance when she found Farmer's pup, now rather impudently called Toby—after "high toby"—scrabbling to get in at the kitchen door. Another rumble made him cower, so she picked him up and took him inside.

"Miss Lucy, I'll have no animals in my kitchen!" Cook said at once.

"You let the cat stay," Betsy said.

Cook glared. "The cat catches the mice. This scrap will steal from the table! Have you seen how high he bounces?"

Farmer loomed out of his seat at the table. "I'll take him back to the stable, miss," he said, and Toby jumped joyfully from her arms to his.

"He's frightened of the thunder," Lucy said. "That's why I brought him inside."

Cook, marching up to Farmer and his pup, glared at the animal, who sprang up and licked her nose. She laughed, and Lucy crept quietly from the room.

THE STORM WAS spectacular. Julius came home before dark, bringing with him Mrs. Macy and her lively little boy, whom everyone made a fuss over. They were soaked to the skin, and it was decided the visitors should stay overnight. Lucy, glancing from Julius to Antonia Macy, was pleased. Something was going on between them, brightening them both, bringing the old Julius back and fusing him with the new. She was glad she liked Antonia. Everyone did, except perhaps Delilah, who knew more of their past relationship.

Whatever the twins knew, they were clearly happy, too.

In the morning, the storm had blown itself out, leaving the ground soaked and muddy, and a few young trees damaged. Cornelius rode out early to assess the damage to land and buildings. Mrs. Macy and little Edward returned to Blackhaven, and Lucy, having arranged to go into the town with Cook, ran up to her room to change.

She wanted to look her best for her assignation. She wanted Tyler to look at her in the daylight with the delight he had shown in the dark. She wanted him to kiss her, and see his face, his eyes, when he did.

*Foolish…*

She didn't listen to the faint, warning voice in her head. Her happiness was too new, too intense and all-consuming.

None of her dresses were this year's fashion, nor even last, but she chose a favorite morning gown of pale cambric, which had a matching pelisse, and with which she could even blend her best bonnet.

"Don't you look pretty as a picture?" Cook beamed at her as she climbed up onto the kitchen trap beside her.

Relieved, Lucy smiled back. Her siblings had all appeared scattered and busy, so she had merely left a note in the hall to say where she had gone.

Cook had no time to waste, so they traveled as quickly as the pony allowed. As a result, by the time they parted near the market, Lucy was still too early for her assignation with Tyler. So she strolled down the high street to the hotel, where she asked for Miss Poole.

After a short wait, a maid came and conducted her to Hester's sitting room.

Hester was looking a little wan and pale, though she welcomed Lucy with genuine pleasure. "Just the person I need to cheer me up! The storm was wild yesterday, was it not? I hope there has not been much damage."

"So do I! Are you unwell again?"

"No, no. I felt a little delicate earlier, but I am quite recovered. Did you want to do a little shopping, or shall we just enjoy a gossip and a cup of tea?"

"Tea would be delightful," replied Lucy, who had no money to spend on fripperies. "Will you be at Lady Braithwaite's garden party tomorrow?"

"Indeed, yes, I am looking forward to it, if only to see what measures her ladyship takes to combat the inevitable rain. I can't imagine the weather will spare even a countess for an entire day."

"It is a shocking summer, is it not? Cornelius is worried about the crops. I expect most of the country is, which will make more hardship."

"Mr. Cairney said something similar. I shall have to pay more attention to my charities and less to frivolity like this." She lifted a book from the table and pushed it toward Lucy. "Utter drivel, but so amusing because one can spot the real people her characters are based on. Have you read it?"

Lucy picked it up. *"Glenarvon."*

"It has set London by the ears because it's quite clearly by Lady Caroline Lamb, and she spares no one, least of all Lord Byron. Of course, as unmarried ladies we are not meant to know about such affairs. But it does make me laugh."

Lucy genuinely didn't know, so only smiled. "Then it cannot be bad."

While they drank tea and nibbled fresh scones, they spoke of many things, including the propriety of friends using each other's first names, but Hester seemed strangely brittle, distracted despite her easy chatter.

"Forgive me," Lucy said at last. "But are you *sad*, Hester?"

Hester blinked. She smiled, clearly about to deny it, only tears started to her eyes and she gasped.

"Oh, Hester!" Distressed for her, Lucy crossed to the sofa and hugged her friend. "What is it? What has upset you so? Is it love?"

Hester nodded, wiping at her eyes with a tiny wisp of handkerchief that was clearly not up to the task. Lucy passed over her own as support, while continuing to hold her.

"Whom do you love?" she whispered into Hester's hair. *Don't say Irving. Please don't say Irving…*

Hester could say nothing, for her tears only came faster.

"Is it Mr. Cairney?" Lucy asked.

A gasp and then a nod answered her. With an effort, Hester sat up and, endearingly like a child, wiped her eyes on her sleeve. "I am so sorry." She gulped. "I loathe watering pots, but I don't seem able to help it." She drew in a shaky breath. "You find it odd that I should lo—*like* Mr. Cairney?"

"No," Lucy said at once.

"He is gruff and brutally honest and has few social graces beyond basic politeness, but his heart is good. I know that."

"Then why do you cry?" Lucy asked. "I have seen the way he looks at you, and I could swear your affection is returned. I am rarely wrong," she added with a hint of anxiety, as this news failed to brighten Hester's unhappy expression.

"Because he will not offer for me," Hester said, and blew her nose defiantly on Lucy's handkerchief.

"Perhaps he does not have the means to support a wife," Lucy suggested delicately.

"He is not particularly wealthy, but he can easily manage that. The problem is not his wealth. It is mine."

"Ah…" Thoughtfully, Lucy poured them more tea, although it was likely to be a little too cold. "He is afraid you think he only wants your fortune?"

Hester nodded.

"I don't believe he does," Lucy said. "Not for a moment."

"*He* would not court me for such a reason."

Lucy regarded her carefully. "Does someone else court you for your fortune?"

Hester looked at her as though she were a slow child. "Everyone does."

"I don't believe that either. I meant someone in particular."

"Harold. Mr. Irving."

Lucy frowned. "Then why do you let him near you? Why did you let him escort you to Blackhaven? Did you not know before?"

"Of course I knew," Hester said impatiently. "Bringing him was Mama's idea—it *is* more comfortable to travel with a gentleman—and I didn't dissuade her. But I did not know then that Mr. Cairney would be here."

"And now you are trying to make Mr. Cairney jealous by occasionally favoring Mr. Irving?"

Hester nodded. "It doesn't work."

"It probably does," Lucy argued. "Just not with the outcome you want."

"I feel a little like you with your betrothed, though of course I am not engaged to either—torn by duty when your heart is elsewhere."

Heat burned Lucy's cheeks. "I don't recall telling you my heart was engaged."

Hester laughed, a rather watery effort but genuine enough. "My dear, it is quite obvious in the way you speak of Mr. Tyler. In fact, if it were not for the infuriating Mr. Cairney, I might set myself up as a rival for Mr. Tyler's affections. Oh, don't look at me like that. I could not win there. Not with twice my benighted fortune. *He* does not like Harold."

"No," Lucy agreed.

"Harold does not like him either, and I don't know why."

Lucy took a deep breath. "I think there is too much you don't know about Mr. Irving. If I were you, I would give him his congé and have a severe talk with Mr. Cairney."

Hester met her gaze. "And are you going to give your betrothed his congé?"

Lucy's stomach twisted. Duty was a terrible thing. "Our cases are different."

"They are." Hester's shoulders slumped.

"You owe no duty to Mr. Irving," Lucy said, pressing her point.

Hester flapped one arm, dismissing such an irrelevance. "You have all the time in the world, Lucy. I don't."

"Why do you keep saying that? You are four and twenty, not four and seventy! Hester, are you *ill*?"

Hester stared at her, expressions darting through her eyes so quickly that even Lucy could not read them. Her smile was oddly tragic. "Perhaps. In a way."

She did not sound as if she were at death's door. Unrequited love, Lucy decided, was making her ill. She had thought that only happened in books, but when she thought about the changes in Julius since he had met Antonia Macy again, she began to believe there was a basis in truth.

"Do nothing rash," she instructed, suddenly realizing that the clock on the mantel was approaching midday. "I must go. But I will speak to Mr. Cairney and leave him in no doubt of his foolishness."

It came to her that she was meddling, just like the twins, but Hester was so unhappy that something had to be done. She struggled into her pelisse, deep in thoughts of Hester and Cairney and Irving, and yet desperate to get to the beach and to Tyler.

# Chapter Eleven

H E SAT ON a rock, making the most of a post-storm blink of sunshine. He had removed his coat, which he'd dropped casually on the rock beside him, and, in shirt sleeves and waistcoat, was throwing pebbles into the sea so that they skimmed and bounced.

Lucy's heart fluttered, just at the sight of him. The sun made his brown hair golden, like a halo around the fine-drawn features of his face. She had never thought of men as beautiful before.

He was concentrating on his pebbles, cheering himself when they bounced, so he did not see her picking her away across the sand toward him. After the storm, the beach was strewn with seaweed and driftwood and far more stones than usual, making it look massively untidy. Which might have explained why she and Tyler seemed to have most of the beach to themselves.

Tyler ran out of pebbles and reached down to grab some more from the sand at his feet. Catching sight of Lucy, he straightened, a spontaneous smile curving his lips. He sprang off the rock and strode to meet her.

"It's maddening," he said, his eyes devouring her. "I can't greet you as I wish."

Since his intense gaze seemed locked to her mouth, she had no difficulty understanding him. For once, she could think of no reply, so she merely stretched out her hand to him. She meant it to appear as the sophisticated bestowing of a favor, but in fact, it seemed more of a plea.

His fingers, still a trifle sandy, closed around her gloved hand. He bowed with perfect courtesy, but his eyes were warm enough to burn. Last night had not been merely about the darkness.

"Shall we walk?" she said breathlessly.

He glanced up toward the road, where someone was driving a shaggy pony toward the town. A woman with two children was hurrying in the other direction. Nobody seemed to be paying them any attention, but he dropped her hand at once and returned to the rock, where he shrugged into his coat and then offered her his arm.

"I missed you," he said.

Pleasure streamed through her, not unmixed with relief. She had been so afraid that he did not feel the intensity she did. She was still afraid, but she hugged his words to her heart, and reveled in the feel of his arm beneath her hand, his body moving so close to hers—his very presence.

"What have you been doing since I saw you last?" he asked, before she could decide whether or not she should admit to missing him.

"Oh, it has been quite exciting. Julius had been out rowing with Mrs. Macy and her little boy when the storm sprang up. They arrived back at Black Hill soaked to the skin. They had to stay the night, and I am convinced she cares for Julius. He is so good with Edward!"

"You are matchmaking," he said, amused.

"No, no, it was the twins who wanted him to go to the ball, so you must blame them, but I think it is working out very well for him."

"And for you?"

She glanced up at him, heat seeping into her cheeks. "I am very glad to have met you," she said, her words ridiculously formal for the turbulence of her heart—and the breathlessness of her voice. He smiled as though he understood, setting off a whole new set of feelings within her.

Could this be her future? With this unpredictable, delightful man whose true name she didn't even know? The thought was both frightening and sobering.

To cover her confusion, she rattled on. "I called on Miss Poole this morning, too. Irving is curious about you. I'm sure she does not want to marry him, but Mr. Cairney has scruples about her fortune. I'm hoping he will be at Lady Braithwaite's garden party tomorrow, but if you see him, you might speak to him."

For the first time that she could recall, Tyler actually looked alarmed. "Dash it, Lucy, a man's scruples—and his marriage!— are his own affair."

"You don't say that about Mr. Irving."

"That's different. I genuinely believe he is a danger to Miss Poole."

"So is Cairney, in a different way. He is making her ill."

Tyler frowned, then his brow cleared and the harassed look seemed to fall off him like a discarded cloak. "I'll think about it later. For now, I would rather concentrate my attention on you."

"I am perfectly fine."

His smile was devastating. "I know."

She laughed. "Stop trying to flatter me and tell me what you have been doing since we last met."

"Annoying Irving. Writing political articles and speeches –"

"Seriously?" she interrupted, staring at him.

"Oh, I can be terribly serious."

"I know," she said, thinking of his determination to help Farmer. "Farmer said he was arrested while distributing pamphlets in the hotel. Did you write them?"

"I might have had a hand in them. Do you really want to know what Mr. Tyler does? It might make a difference to how you regard him."

"Then you had better tell me."

He guided her around a rock that looked particularly slippery with seaweed. "Where do I begin? With political and social injustice?"

"Let us take that as understood. What is your part in it?"

"I don't want to perpetuate it. But like most people, nor do I want revolution like in France. Yet in fear of that revolution that no one wants, the authorities clamp down on *any* calls for change. And so nothing changes, and people with nothing, even hope, get angrier. If they don't get angry, nothing changes. And if they do get angry, the law crucifies them."

"That doesn't appear to leave much room for hope."

He nodded. "That's what I thought. So… I formed a society."

"A secret society?"

"Of necessity. With the aim of pushing for change—better wages and working conditions, expanded voting rights, universal education, those kinds of things—only as hard as we can without causing riots or anything that will bring only further oppression. People die when soldiers are brought in to quell riots. They also die when they have nothing to eat and are too weak to work—when there is any work."

"Then surely it is an impossible balance to maintain."

"Difficult," he said, "but not impossible. Educating those with power to understand what they must do, and those without obvious power to understand how to use what they have. Occasionally, it goes wrong and someone is arrested, so we have a network of people to help free them, one way or another. That's what I thought had happened to Farmer. It never entered our heads they had arrested him for highway robbery."

"But you helped him anyway."

"I know. I probably shouldn't, but he is a good man." He sighed. "You are right, of course. People can't run around committing crimes just because life has been unfair to them. And I'm sure he frightened the Poole ladies, besides stealing from them. But I think he has realized all he could have lost."

"All he still might lose," Lucy pointed out. "To say nothing of my family for harboring him and Lord Braithwaite for bringing him to Cornelius. Besides, he can't live in hiding forever. His own family are a mere few miles away."

"No, he will have to come out of hiding and be formally released by the magistrate. With the statements Braithwaite extracted I'm sure it can be done, but Winslow may well want Irving and the Poole ladies to look at him again." He kicked a large pebble out of her path, then caught and held her gaze. "That is one case, and not at all typical. The bigger question to me right now is whether you can live with what I do."

"What exactly *is* it that you do?" she asked. "You've told me your aims, not the things you do to accomplish them. Though I'm guessing it includes pamphlets and speeches. That was you addressing the meetings in Carlisle, was it not? As reported in the *Carlisle Journal*."

To her surprise, color seeped along the blade of his cheekbone. He looked almost sheepish. "It was. Mostly, I just talk to people. Not everyone can read my words of wisdom. Meetings are good because you can reach so many listeners at once, but we have to be careful of numbers, so often it's just a matter of talking in taverns and alehouses, visiting factories and mills, spreading the word to workers and owners, tenants and landlords, members of Parliament, aristocrats with influence. They are all represented in our society."

After several thoughtful moments, she realized he was watching her with some anxiety.

She let out her breath in a rush. "It must be a huge undertaking."

"It is."

"Does it work?"

His eyes lit with a smile. "So far. And slowly. We can't keep track of every grievance, so occasionally riots pop up without us being aware, with tragic consequences, like in Ely earlier this summer. It is something of a tightrope, but we have done some good."

"Do you break the law?" she asked.

He considered. "Stretch it," he replied at last. "But I am unlikely to be carted off to gaol."

"Wat Tyler," she mused. "You are not leading a peasants' revolt, are you? You're trying to avoid one."

"Oh, I want the revolt," he argued. "I just want it to be peaceful."

The tide was going out. They could clamber over the rocks to the Black Cove, where it was usually quieter. Out at sea, a couple of ships were sailing slowly southward. The breeze stirred her hair, while above her, the gulls cried and circled. She held on to Tyler's arm. He brought a cause as well as fun. And not a little danger.

She said, "What can I do to help?"

*"WHAT CAN I do to help?"*

Tyler had hoped merely not to appall her. He knew she loved excitement, but even in his wildest dreams he had not imagined her offering to help. That came from sympathy, from belief. He wanted to hug her.

He contented himself with covering her hand and drawing her subtly closer. "You are wonderful, Lucy Vale."

She blushed—he loved making her blush—but shook her head. "No. I barely noticed the things you speak about. I like to help people when I can, but I never looked beyond what was in front of my face." She seemed about to say more, then smiled, an elusive, secretive smile, and shook her head. "Shall we go over the rocks? Or wait ten minutes for the tide to recede?"

In his exuberance, Tyler wanted to jump over the whole ridge of rocks like a horse. Instead, he stepped up, scuffed at the rocks to test for slipperiness, then leaned down, scooped Lucy up by the waist, and set her down on the sand on the other side.

Then he jumped down to join her and, seeing they had the beach to themselves, took her hand and swung it high in the air.

"Thank you," he said. "You make me very happy."

"I'm happy, too," she said in a rush.

"Lucy, my Lucy." He drew her in the shelter of the rocks, and though he had meant to be good today after his liberties of the night at Black Hill, he couldn't resist turning her lovely face up to his and kissing her—gently at first, and then, when she returned his embrace, with increasing passion. Her skin was so soft, her mouth so warm and inviting... He drew her closer, adoring all her feminine curves as they fitted against his larger, lustier person. She would be a wonderful lover, not just for her beauty but for the passion he sensed within her. When Lucy gave herself, it would be completely and forever, and that was both thrilling and shocking.

*Forever.*

He had known this girl a week. It was hardly enough to fall in love, never mind plan forever, And yet... Happiness raged through him.

He was already courting her. "Forever" had been acknowledged the night he chose quite deliberately to seek her out at Black Hill. Knowing who she was and who he was. And knowing she might not forgive him the latter. He still was not sure of that.

So he kissed her neck and her ear and whispered, "I should make myself known to your brother, Sir Julius."

"You will meet him tomorrow, at Lady Braithwaite's garden party," she said, breathless from his kisses. "We are going early."

"Then so will I."

His gaze was riveted to the pulse dancing so wildly at the base of her throat. He bent his head to kiss it, and with a gasp of laughter, she broke free. She was right, though everything physical in him objected. This was not the time or the place to take everything, nor even to give it.

"A skimming contest," she called over her shoulder, then bent and picked up a pebble, which she threw expertly into the sea. It bounced twice before vanishing under a wave.

It was a perfect afternoon, for the most part undisturbed by other people. A couple of children from the town did join in their "skimming" competition before remembering they were meant to be home and scurrying off again.

They walked barefoot in the sand, raced each other, built sand mountains rather than castles, paddled in the sea, and talked of everything, both funny and serious. Banter flowed between them, light and natural, and yet beneath it hummed an excitement he had never known before in any aspect of his life.

During a companionable silence as they sat on a rock, close together, gazing out to sea, he said, "You never ask me my real name."

A smile flickered on her lips. "You will always be Tyler to me."

"Then you don't care if I'm a duke or the thirteenth son of the coalman?"

"No."

He slipped his arm around her waist—perhaps to stop her running. His heart beat uncomfortably hard. "Lucy, my name is—"

But she sprang up suddenly. "Goodness, what is the time? I must get home before dinner, or they will all come and look for me and I'll never hear the end of it. I'd better take a hired carriage from the hotel."

Torn between frustration and amusement, he recognized that the moment for revelation had passed. He concentrated on helping her dust off her sandy, elegant little feet—she wore no stockings—and return them to her boots. Then, tying on her bonnet strings, he kissed her quickly, placed her hand decorously in his arm, and marched back to town with her.

In front of the hotel, he helped her into a carriage, paid the driver in advance, and bowed a civil goodbye. Only her eyes, warm and shining, told him he was not the merest acquaintance. But that look made him the most deliriously happy man alive.

God help him.

And her.

HAROLD IRVING GREW increasingly worried. Hester maintained a distance that was almost cold, considering he had abandoned the pleasures of London to escort her all the way to this godforsaken backwater. The trouble was, Blackhaven was not quite as empty of company as he had imagined. From the Braithwaites at the castle to the vicar's wife, many of the natives appeared to have claims to the aristocracy and the *ton*, and Hester was not short of callers or confidantes, should she want them.

The wretched Vale girl had been again, and Harold was beginning to think her a malign influence, and not just because he had first met her in the company of the blasted Tyler.

Still, every instinct pointed to Tyler rather than Cairney as his main enemy. Cairney was too damned stiff. Hester might prefer him, but he would never stoop to be thought a fortune hunter. Fool.

Tyler, on the other hand, was clearly a sly dog and as indifferent as he was to Society's opinion. They both wanted their hands on Hester's money, and Harold recognized a worthy opponent. Hester already laughed with him as she never did with Harold. Well, it was time to eject him from the scene and close the deal with Hester. Only, how best to proceed?

He knew nothing about the man. He could not ever remember hearing of a Tyler family, and none of his casual inquiries had borne fruit. The man wasn't staying at the hotel, nor did he drink at the tavern or frequent its other services. He did not seem to be the guest of the local gentry. He could have taken a private house for a month or two, of course, in which case Harold would have to follow him to find out.

More likely, Harold thought, was the local inn, which he had only just heard of. The King's Head was cheaper than the hotel and considerably more respectable than the tavern—just the place for a gentleman of limited means to set up camp while hunting the heiress.

Harold set off that afternoon with high hopes. If Tyler was not in, he could ask questions freely of the staff, even get a quick peek around his room. If he *was* in, then Harold could get him drunk—preferably at his own expense—and get the truth out of him that way. Before deciding how best to scare him off.

For once, the rain stayed off and Harold found the walk not unpleasant. He had almost forgotten that his original reason for disliking Tyler was his likeness to Anne, and Anne's snot-nosed brother. But the thought was still there at the back of his mind.

He strolled into the inn with all the condescension of a great man deigning to bestow his custom. The main room was quiet, although he could hear the sounds of children close by. A pretty, smiling young woman greeted him politely.

"Yes, sir, how can we help you?"

"A pint of your best ale, if you please, since it is such a pleasant day. And perhaps you might inform my friend, Mr. Tyler, that I am here and would be glad if he would join me."

"Mr. Tyler, sir?" she repeated, standing aside to let another man pour the ale. "I don't believe we have anyone of that name here."

"Really?" Damn, had he rented a house after all? "Tall gentleman and well dressed. Light brown hair and extraordinary eyes. Walks like a da—" He coughed, remembering his manners for now. "A dancer," he finished, not quite able to hide his contempt.

"Oh, you must mean Mr. Gore. Most elegant man and such fine eyes..." She trailed off, looking quite alarmed, no doubt by Harold's expression.

His ears seemed to be singing. "What name did you say?" he got out.

"Gore, sir. Mr. Gore."

Harold sat down too quickly and reached for his ale like a drowning man for a lifeline. He had been right all along. The man didn't need the money. He only wanted Hester to annoy Harold.

The "why" of that was for another day. For now, the first priority had to be to get rid of him. How?

Blind panic faded slowly, until, finally, he could think again. Some of Mrs. Poole's infernal chatter came back to him. In her opinion, Tyler—Gore—was in pursuit of the Vale girl.

Vale… Now he could dredge up older memories. And the thoroughly amusing realization that Lucy Vale had no idea who Tyler was. None of them had. And no one—least of all Hester—liked a liar.

Harold's enemy was as good as routed.

# Chapter Twelve

THROUGH HER OWN euphoria, Lucy was vaguely aware that all was not well either with Julius or Delilah. Of course, Julius was still pursuing his horse thieves, who had turned out to be something much more sinister—which might have accounted for his distraction, but not for the *lost* look she had glimpsed in his face when they passed on the stairs. Delilah would not talk to her about it either. She could be too close-mouthed when she chose.

Lucy resolved to keep an eye on them both at the Braithwaites' garden party, to where she traveled in the carriage with the twins and Aubrey.

"What ails Julius?" she asked the twins.

"We're not sure yet," Leona replied. "But it's something to do with Antonia Macy."

"What?" Lucy demanded.

Opposite her, Aubrey shifted restlessly. "Leave it alone, Lucy. You are as bad as they are. Meddling makes everything worse. And Julius is as entitled to his privacy as anyone else—including you."

Lucy looked at him. "What do you mean by that?"

"I mean *you* are up to something you don't want anyone else to know about."

"And you are not?" Lucy retorted, more from habit than any real suspicion.

To her surprise, an intriguing hint of color crept along Aubrey's prominent cheekbones. "None of your business, is it?" he challenged.

"No," she admitted, resolving to have another chat with the twins in private. "But you'll know mine soon enough anyway."

"I'll try to look forward to it," Aubrey said, yawning ostentatiously.

She stuck her tongue out at him and let her mind dwell where it wanted, on Tyler, who would surely be at the party all afternoon and into the early evening… Her heart skipped a beat. She would introduce him to Julius, to everyone. Even Aubrey.

"Do you suppose there will be anyone else our age at the party?" Lawrence asked, no doubt to change the subject. "Felicia said the earl's family only has small children."

"I suppose we could practice being adults," Leona said with such doubt that Lucy and Aubrey both laughed.

The castle was a magnificent edifice, which they had only seen from a distance before. Parts of it were medieval, but there were splendid wings and façades built in the last hundred years or so, to make, no doubt, for a much more comfortable home. The surrounding grounds were breathtaking—formal and terraced gardens and extensive lawns, all blending into slightly wilder scenery beyond.

A large marquee had been erected on the lawn—no doubt in case of rain. Elsewhere, a lively game of pall mall was in progress, with players making the most of the current blink of sunshine. But the doors to the great hall had been flung open, and from there, the lovely young Countess of Braithwaite assured them, they could access all manner of other entertainments, from musical performances to poetry readings and an exhibition of paintings.

"We had hoped to have the poet Simon Sacheverill join us today," the countess said, indicating to her footman to serve her guests glasses of punch, "but sadly, that fell through. My sister-in-law will be reading his latest work instead." She turned to the twins. "Come with me, and we shall go in search of the Launcetons. They are about your age, I think, and I'm sure you can get up to splendid mischief together…"

Beside her, Lucy was only vaguely aware of Aubrey's suppressed excitement. She was too busy searching for anyone who might be Tyler. By the marquee, Hester Poole waved to her.

"Happy?" Aubrey said, clearly anxious to pursue his own interests.

"Yes, yes, run along," she said grandly, and he grinned as he strolled off, leaving her to join Miss Poole.

She was glad to see Harold Irving was not part of the group surrounding Hester, although nor was Mr. Cairney. As she drew closer, she saw the pall mall players more clearly, and her heart gave a funny little twist, for one of them moved very like Tyler.

It was his turn to strike the ball, and everyone was laughing, moving well away from him. The aim was to hit the ball through the next hoop set in the ground, but Tyler actually swung his mallet right back and smacked the ball so hard that it flew over several hoops and landed just before the last, where it trickled slowly in.

"Huzzah!" he exclaimed, throwing up his arms as though in triumph and resting the mallet against his shoulder.

Everyone else was laughing and declaring him disqualified, at which he grinned and collected what looked to be bank notes from some of his fellow players. Clearly, this had been a wager. Though it might have lost him the game, it had won him some money and a good deal of merriment.

Lucy could not help smiling, but, remembering her decorum, she went first to Hester, still hoping Tyler had seen her arrival.

Hester looked better than yesterday, with a little color in her cheeks, and greeted Lucy with evident pleasure. "Do you all know Miss Lucy Vale?" she asked her companions.

"Sir Julius's sister?" asked the youngest of the ladies present. "I believe our brothers are thick as thieves over something or other."

"Lady Maria Hanson," Hester said to Lucy, "who is the earl's sister. And Mr. Hanson, the local member of Parliament. And Lady Torridon, also the earl's sister."

Lucy curtseyed, regarding all her new acquaintances with interest. Especially Mr. Hanson—was that not the name of the person who had asked Tyler to intervene in Farmer's arrest? Was he also part of Tyler's secret society?

As they chatted, she noticed Tyler surrendering his mallet amidst much mirth and then strolling, surely in her direction. In the other direction, she was less pleased to see Mr. Irving emerge from the hall with a tall, distinguished man she recognized as the Earl of Braithwaite himself. She had seen him in church with his family, although they had never spoken. Whether from Lady Torridon's wave or their own intention, they too walked toward Lucy's group.

They could do without Irving, Lucy thought. And where was Mr. Cairney? Really, she needed to speak to him severely about his quite unnecessary scruples. Mostly, though, she was so aware of Tyler's approach that she could not concentrate on the conversation and merely fixed a smile on her lips to look amiable. She could feel the blush of anticipation rising to her cheeks, the delight of just seeing him, of being in his company…

"Come and meet Miss Lucy Vale," Lady Torridon was saying to her brother.

Lucy hastily forced herself to greet the earl in proper fashion. She curtseyed, and he bowed over her hand, saying something about Julius and Cornelius and Felicia, whom he already knew.

"Oh, there are lots more of us still," Lucy said humorously. Her neck prickled, and from the corner of her eye, she saw Tyler saunter past their group. His gaze was on her, inviting, summoning, and her breath caught with pleasure. Her infinitesimal nod was to tell him that in just a moment, she would excuse herself.

Tyler would have strolled on, but too late, Lucy realized that Irving had been watching them.

Irving half turned toward Tyler, deliberately including them in the group. "And are you all acquainted with Lord Eddleston?" he asked loudly.

It took a moment to penetrate her love-sodden brain, to realize that Irving wasn't making a foolish mistake or introducing someone else entirely.

"Oh, Eddleston and I are old friends—and old combatants," Braithwaite said amiably, though his voice seemed to come from very far away, muffled in the shocked ringing of Lucy's ears.

St. John Gore, Earl of Eddleston, her betrothed. Her lying, deceiving betrothed, who had deliberately made a fool of her.

Tyler—or Edd, as he was more commonly known to his friends—was not a violent man, but he could cheerfully have punched Harold Irving full in his spiteful mouth.

This was more than merely showing off newfound recognition. This was being as damaging as possible, making sure to wreck Lucy's trust in her Tyler as well as to secure Hester for himself. He could read the triumph in Irving's eyes, and all the old, helpless rage he had felt as a child, when he first realized that Anne's husband liked to hurt, surged like a tide.

And then there was only Lucy's shocked face, all the warm, delicate color seeping away. All the vulnerability he had sensed hidden beneath her fun was now on naked display—along with the accusation. He had deceived her, and more than that, she thought it had been a joke.

His fury melted into simple need to ease her hurt. And he couldn't, not in this company. God, there was even one of her brothers and a sister approaching. He had no chance of speaking to her alone as he needed to.

Then she turned away from him, and he realized with dismay that there was nothing he could say now to make it better.

"I thought your name was Tyler," Hester Poole said, half

amused.

"My foolish joke," he said, barely aware what he was saying. "Miss Vale will explain." He spoke her name to make her look at him so that she would understand he loved her, but she was already hurrying away as though to join her siblings. "Or Mr. Hanson, perhaps."

"Oh, Eddleston is that peculiarity that should not exist," Hanson said with friendly mockery. "The radical peer. So any similarity between him and Wat Tyler of peasant revolt fame is obviously delusional."

Everyone laughed, Irving loudest of all. *He* was delighted with his day's work. Even the arrival of Mr. Cairney obviously could not dampen his high spirits.

What an epic failure of Eddleston's much-vaunted sensitivity and powers of calculation, as seen in his careful balancing of protest and calm. He had known yesterday at the beach that he had withheld the truth too long. And yet he had let the moment go. If he had told her then, in his own words, he could surely have saved her this hurt.

Certainly in public. But perhaps she wouldn't have forgiven him anyway.

"What's going on?" Hanson murmured, drawing him away from the group to walk vaguely in the direction of the football being played by some small children further down the hill.

"My stupidity has just met a little private vengeance, and someone else is hurt."

"Can I help?"

Edd managed a smile, because somewhere he was grateful. "Thank you. Be sure I'll let you know."

"I haven't thanked you yet for rescuing Luke Farmer. Please tell me he wasn't involved in highway robbery."

"I wish I could. For what it's worth, it seems to have been a moment of angry desperation, and I don't believe he'll do it again. Braithwaite spoke to the witnesses, who are, fortunately, useless. I was hoping Winslow would then drop it, but it hasn't turned out quite so simply."

"Where is Farmer?"

"Working for the Vales. Er—I'm afraid I got Braithwaite to help hide him, and he took him to Black Hill."

"I know. He's dubious about the whole thing, but he trusts you."

"God knows why," Eddleston said with rare gloom.

It was half an hour later when he came face to face with Irving. They met unexpectedly in the gallery, where some pictures were being exhibited, most notably those by Braithwaite's talented brother-in-law, Lord Tamar. Eddleston swung around to leave in search of Lucy once more, and almost ran into Irving.

That Harold looked just as surprised as he was little comfort.

"St. John," Harold said with all the condescension of an adult for a troublesome child. "Without your ladylove, I see."

With an effort, Eddleston kept his face bland. He even managed a social smile. "Not very brotherly of you, Harold," he replied. "Trying to come between a man and his betrothed."

"You mean succeeding," Harold corrected him, "where you failed to come between me and mine."

Eddleston laughed. "Do you think so?" Somehow, he kept the savagery from his voice as he nodded over the balustrade to the hall below, where Hester was deep in conversation with Cairney.

Without even glancing at Harold's reaction, he sauntered away along the gallery and down the stairs.

LUCY, HAVING FLED the unbearable like a dog trying to escape the crash of thunder all around him, somehow danced straight past Roderick and Felicia with an airy wave and proceeded to stride around the garden at breakneck speed.

She could not deal with the hurt and the disillusion here. It would take months, maybe years. She could not endure even thinking about the lost, foolish happiness running off her like rain into a puddle. All she had left was pride, and the determination to use it.

She had never felt so fragile, so brittle. But she would not break. As she marched back to join the throngs gracing the countess's party, her rising anger took her by surprise. It helped with the pride and the determination, so she hung on to it.

So, now he was revealed, the unspeakable St. John Gore, Earl of Eddleston, whom she had always disliked, even without any justification. Well, now she had cause! What would hurt *him* most?

To have made no difference. Not even to be ignored, but to never have mattered. As she had clearly never mattered to him.

And there, in front of her, was her first ally, his face lighting up at the sight of her. The talkative young man she had danced with at the ball—what was his name? Ah yes—Mr. Ladburne, the heir of Lord Falworth.

She bestowed her most dazzling smile upon him and was fiercely glad of its effect. He came to her at once, like an eager puppy. Since the first drops of inevitable rain were forming, she allowed him to escort her into the castle, where there were officers to flirt with and Mr. Cairney to tease. After all, she still had her duty to Hester.

Dismissing Mr. Ladburne to find her some lemonade, she took Cairney's arm instead. Of course, she had misjudged Tyler—*Eddleston*—so badly that she had lost faith in herself, but if Hester wanted Cairney so badly that it made her ill, then unless he were a serial bigamist or beat his children, she should have him.

"Mr. Cairney," she began, "you must allow me to be blunt. You are making a cake of yourself. More to the point, you are making a cake of Miss Poole."

The man stiffened and cast her a disdainful glance that should have shriveled her back to a schoolgirl.

Lucy smiled and patted his arm. "Do you wish to marry her or not?"

Color flooded into his face. He jerked as though to withdraw his arm, and she hung on, as if to remind him of the talk such a gesture might cause.

"That is none of your business, Miss Vale," he said between his teeth.

"Of course it is," Lucy replied. "Hester is my friend. She has many suitors, of course, so she need not wait for you forever. I have to say, I don't rate any of the others much above the level of fortune hunter. Especially Mr. Irving, I'm afraid. But if you wish such misery upon her, I don't really know why I am trying to change your mind."

All the color drained from his face so quickly that she was afraid he might faint. Hastily, she tugged him down beside her onto a vacant sofa. "You think I am being brutal, Mr. Cairney? Can you imagine what is like for any woman, let alone a warm and honest lady like Hester, to be married for her money, neglected and at the mercy of such a man? Do you understand the sheer powerlessness of a woman in marriage? You may think that right and proper—being, I had thought, a very decent man yourself. But there are very different men out there, and a good many of them want to marry Miss Poole."

Mr. Cairney opened his mouth to speak, but no sound came out.

"You have scruples," Lucy went on relentlessly. "Admirable. But should anyone else's happiness be sacrificed to your pride? And it *is* pride. If you and she understand why you are marrying, what business is it of the world's to believe you a fortune hunter? Do you care? *Should* you care? I had thought you a better man."

"I…" Mr. Cairney cleared his throat. "I have no reason to believe she would accept my suit."

She stared at him. "And that is a reason not to try? Mr. Cairney, do I really need to tell you that faint heart never won fair lady?"

He tore his gaze free of hers, as though searching for Hester. He raked his fingers through his short hair, making it stand up alarmingly until he dragged them back in the opposite direction, making it almost flat again.

"You make it sound as though I would be rescuing her," he said at last.

She beamed at him. "Exactly, Mr. Cairney. And consider her dignity instead of your own."

He blinked, then uttered a short, harsh laugh. "You are a devastating critic for so young a lady. I know several terrifying schoolteachers who could learn from you."

She bestowed a brilliant smile upon him and rose to her feet. "If you like, you may escort me to the poetry reading. I happen to know we shall find Hester there, at least for the next five minutes."

Poetry, however, proved a little too much for Lucy's careful façade. Something about Sacheverill's words, read with feeling by one of Lord Braithwaite's sisters, was too poignant to hear. So, abandoning Mr. Cairney at Hester's side, she crept from the room. To her surprise, she noticed Cornelius seated alone in the corner, his eyes riveted to the reader. A sudden memory came back to her, of Cornelius in an embassy garden, a book of poetry on his knee while Roderick teased him.

For some reason, that seemed sad, too. Everything was sad today.

Before emotion broke through, she fled.

"Phew," said a male voice behind her. "Horrible stuff, isn't it?"

She turned to find a complete stranger grinning at her with boyish charm. "Oh, I'm fond of poetry normally, but I'm not in a sad mood." *Ha!*

"I'm the opposite. It makes me laugh, and my wife sends me out of the room. Shall we find something more amusing?"

He presented her with a welcome glass of wine, and they ate a few tasty morsels while listening to the music in the hall. However, the music made Lucy restless too, so they strolled along the covered walkway to the marquee, where the children were dancing. The twins were having a whale of a time, each dancing exuberantly with a much smaller child.

Lucy was laughing and applauding with everyone else when she saw Tyler—*Eddleston*—nearby, watching her. She refused to be moved by the misery or the plea she read in his eyes. She had been so wrong about him before. That first encounter in the assembly ballroom gallery, when she had noticed how little she could sense from him, should have warned her he was hiding, and for a reason.

So she flung him a careless nod of recognition, waved to the twins, laughed up at her congenial companion, and tugged him back toward the castle. Halfway there, they met Mr. Ladburne, who was clearly looking for her, and who walked back the way he had come on her other side, glaring at the other man. Lucy smiled and took his arm, too.

After tea, there was dancing. Lucy, besieged by partners, had no difficulty avoiding Eddleston, whom she saw dancing with the countess, and with the extraordinarily beautiful girl she had last seen Aubrey pursuing. She danced with her poetry-hating admirer, whom other people called Dax, then with Ladburne, and a dashing army officer, and then with Dax again.

*Surely it is almost time to go home?* she thought as she whirled off the dance floor and almost bumped into Roderick.

"A stroll with your lonely brother," he said amiably.

Dax grinned, saluted, and sauntered off.

"Not an advisable connection, Luce," Roderick murmured.

"Don't lecture me," she warned.

"He's a rake of the first order, and he is married."

"I know he is married, and therefore quite safe to flirt with." Even as she said the words, she remembered Felicia's husband. Nick had been safe. "Drat you, Rod, he is amusing. Can't I laugh now and again?"

"If you tell me what the devil is the matter."

She laughed, a short, brittle sound that was a hairsbreadth from tears. "Nothing, silly. I am enjoying myself hugely." And before he could ask further, she darted off into the waiting company of Ladburne and two army officers. She could not even see Tyler. *Eddleston.*

# Chapter Thirteen

L ORD EDDLESTON—WHO WISHED more than anything right
now to be merely Tyler—was, in fact, cornered by the Vale
twins as he walked through the rain toward the castle stables.

They came up on either side and jostled him under a sheltering oak tree.

"What have you done to Lucy?" Lawrence demanded.

Edd sighed. "I'm not the man she thought I was. The man I
said I was."

"Then who are you?" Leona asked.

"Eddleston."

The twins exchanged appalled glances.

"St. John Gore, Earl of Eddleston?" Leona asked carefully.

"The very same," Edd said, sketching a mockery of a bow,
but if he expected shock and the scolding he undoubtedly
deserved, he was disappointed.

The twins were looking at each other again.

"We should have guessed that," Leona said.

"We should," Lawrence agreed. He frowned at Edd. "You
didn't ignore our letter at all, did you?"

"Not even a little. It made me think. I rarely thought about
the wretched betrothal, and when I did, it was always as
something that could be dealt with sometime in the future. It
never seemed urgent, because I was in no hurry to marry, and

because I never thought of it from Lucy's point of view."

"So why make her acquaintance incognito?" Lawrence asked.

"I wanted to learn what *she* wanted. I didn't want to meet her at some formal occasion where she would say what she thought she ought with her family looking on, even forcing her. An unwilling marriage would be hell for both of us." His lips quirked. "I thought a quick conversation, perhaps a dance, would tell me all I needed to know. It didn't. But the more time I spent with her, the more I realized it was no longer about merely learning her wishes. It was…"

*It was about winning her. God help me, it still is.* But he could not say those words to her siblings.

"And now she knows," Lawrence said. "And she doesn't like that you lied to her."

"She thinks it was all lies. She no longer trusts me." Ironic, really. It was the stranger at the beginning she should not have trusted. Now he was at her feet.

"Have you explained all this to her?" Lawrence asked.

Edd shook his head. "I can't. Not today."

"She is in no state to listen," Leona said, frowning at the rain. She glanced at Edd. "Are you giving up on her?"

"God no," he said fervently, and only as he said the words did he realize just how true they were. He would never give up. He refocused his gaze on the twins. "Are we no longer friends?"

They turned identical frowns on him.

"We want Lucy to be happy," Leona said.

"So do I." He had never meant anything so much in life. Even his causes, his successes and failures, had never inspired this powerful a need. He drew in a breath. "If I can't make it right, if she still wants me to go, I will. But I will always stand her friend."

That was true too, even though the thought of leaving her sank him deep in desperate misery.

"Look after her," he said abruptly, and walked back out into the rain.

"I AM WORRIED about Lucy Vale," Hester murmured to Mr. Cairney. She had danced twice with Mr. Irving, and once with Lord Eddleston—*not* Mr. Tyler—but the final waltz of the garden party was the one she had almost given up hope of.

"I shouldn't worry about that young lady," Mr. Cairney said dryly. "She is well able to look after herself. And everyone in her orbit."

"Do you think so? Flirting quite so outrageously with the local regiment? To say nothing of *Daxton*."

"Oh, I think she has the measure of Lord Daxton. He is full of nonsense, but he never strays. He is devoted to Lady Dax."

She blinked at him in surprise. "How do you know that?"

Cairney blushed. "I stayed with them once. Knows a lot about sheep. And crop rotations."

Laughter caught in her throat. "That is what I like about you, sir! You always surprise me."

He smiled back. "Truly? Is that good?"

"Mostly," she said, feeling the blush rise to her cheeks.

"Shall we finish this dance, or would you care to walk on the covered terrace?"

Her heart beat too quickly. Trying not to expect too much, she allowed him to guide her out of the hall and through an empty room where the French doors stood open to a pretty terrace overlooking the gardens.

They were alone.

"Miss Poole," he said in a rush. "I hope you know how much I esteem you, the pleasure I take in your company."

"Likewise, sir," she said lightly, hardly overwhelmed by the depth of his passion.

He drew in a breath. "Only my morbid awareness of the difference in our fortunes has kept me silent until now, but I have been led to believe... That is, I have come to hope...that my scruples are…unimportant." He clutched his hair. "Oh, the devil! I am useless with words and speeches! Hester, would you consider marrying me?"

She wanted to laugh, just because her heart had begun to sing. "I might," she said breathlessly. "Under one condition."

"Name it." His eyes glowed with a warmth she wanted to bathe in.

"That you love me."

Which was when he snatched her into his arms and showed her, finally, the depth of passion she craved.

HAROLD'S PLEASURE IN destroying Eddleston's little scheme was, by the end of the garden party, somewhat lost in his own unease. Hester and Cairney seemed to have grown curiously close, and she barely looked at Harold during the short journey back into town.

Clearly, it behoved him to act quickly.

Accordingly, as soon as Cairney had left them at the hotel— like Eddleston, he was staying at the King's Head—he asked Hester for a private word.

"You may use my sitting room," Mrs. Poole said, betraying unprecedented discretion. "I have things to see to in my bed-chamber. I shall only be five minutes," she added, sailing through the inner door and closing it with a pronounced click.

Hester remained standing, so he walked up to her and took her hand. She withdrew it at once but did not turn away from him.

Instead, she looked at him directly. "No, don't speak, Harold. Let me tell you my news first. You have been a good friend to me, and I want you to be the first to know. I have not even told my mother, but perhaps I owe this to you for your kindness. I have agreed to marry William Cairney."

Harold wanted to gnash his teeth together. It was all he could do to muster a rather ghastly smile, but hopefully that would give her the impression of a broken heart.

"Then let me be the first to wish you happiness."

"Thank you, Harold," she said gently.

He did not want her thanks. He wanted her damned money. "I suppose this is not the time to warn you against impoverished Scottish fortune hunters, but please, do nothing quickly. Make the engagement a long one."

Her eyes fell. "I shall, of course, discuss such matters with Mr. Cairney."

He decided that now was not the moment to reason. He decided to impress her with the dignity of his grief. "Then I shall bid you goodnight. Know that I am still and always your friend."

When he held out his hand, she gave him hers, and he kissed her fingers with the greatest respect before turning and walking slowly from the room. He thought he did it rather well, though when he got to his own chamber, he hurled his hat at the wall in sheer fury.

Not that he had given up. Not by a long chalk. But he had to change his plans *again*. And he hated that.

THE MORNING AFTER the garden party, Lucy was at a loss as to what to do with herself. She maintained her cheerful aspect at breakfast, where the discussion was all about Julius's wretched horse thieves, whom he had already gone off to pursue, along with some corrupt official of the hospital that was the biggest recipient of his charity. Lucy pretended to be interested for five minutes, then fled alone to haul weeds from the still-neglected side of the garden.

Although she worked furiously so she did not have to think, the unspeakable Lord Eddleston kept intruding into her mind, with Tyler's smile, Tyler's kisses…

*I should have known.* Only now did she remember that the first night she met him, he had called her Lucy. She had not told him her name. But he knew hers because he had come to look her over as though she were a horse—in between his other adventures to secure the release of Farmer and discover the truth of his sister's death. She had been nothing, just a mild amusement between courses of a larger, more important feast.

Had he decided she would do as the earl's bride? Or had he intended to meet Julius and quietly break the contract by mutual agreement? Which was exactly what she had wanted at the outset.

With a groan of annoyance, she hurled a huge thistle into the bucket of garden rubbish and straightened, glaring at the rest of the garden.

Was she being entirely fair? She of all people should understand an impulse gone wrong. Letting her sister's husband kiss her, for example. And yesterday, after Irving had so maliciously blurted out Eddleston's identity, he had seemed miserable…

But then, he had *seemed* honorable and in love with her. She couldn't believe anything anymore, and that was his fault, too. She tore off her gardening gloves and tossed them on the ground before marching back to the house in search of a drink. She needed to speak to the twins.

When she passed through the front hall, a glass of fresh water in her hand, she found a bouquet of red roses on the table. They would be for Felicia or Delilah. Or from Mr. Ladburne—was he someone else she had to feel guilty about? She wanted to walk straight past them and not care, but inevitably she paused beside them, letting their scent drift into her nostrils.

She snatched up the card. It wasn't even signed, but it was definitely addressed to Miss Lucy Vale. Beneath her name was scrawled only one word. *Sorry.*

"Damn you," she whispered, dropping the card and rushing upstairs before the tears came again.

She needed to speak to the twins. But they were not in their schoolroom or in either of their bedchambers.

"Do you know where the twins are?" she asked the maid walking past with a bundle of towels.

"They went out, miss—into Blackhaven, I think, with the major."

"Thank you," she said, and turned away. She had no intention of going anywhere near Blackhaven. Let him come here. If he dared.

Her determination lasted into the afternoon, until, emerging from the dining room after a solitary luncheon, she made a rare sighting of Cornelius bolting through the house.

"Where is the fire?" she called, in a feeble attempt at humor.

He skidded to a halt. "Julius has gone after the gun smugglers, and they've got Antonia Macy. If you're coming, come now."

Lucy did not wait to grab more than her bonnet and the cloak that hung in the hall before haring after Julius. She clambered up onto the gig beside him, and Cornelius urged the horse into a quick trot.

Lucy's personal troubles had fled in the face of Julius's danger. "Gun smugglers?" she said. "I thought they were horse thieves!"

He cast her a sardonic glance. "You haven't been keeping up, have you?"

There was no time even for shame in that. "Where is Julius? Where is Antonia?"

"Julius is pursuing them by sea with the aid of Captain Alban and a revenue cutter. I believe Antonia has been abducted, but by whom and why I don't yet know. The twins are in Blackhaven, rounding everyone up to save her."

"For Julius," Lucy whispered. "But is Julius safe?"

"I don't know," Cornelius said harshly, and now that they were on the road, he commanded the horse to speed up.

AFTER CALLING ON Mr. Winslow, the magistrate, and failing to find him at home, Eddleston returned to the inn to plan his next move. In the coffee room, William Cairney sat in a comfortable chair with a newspaper he was clearly not reading. He looked so unusually relaxed that he caught Edd's erratic attention.

Cairney glanced up and smiled. "Greetings, my lord. Care to join me?"

Edd changed course and sat down on the other chair. "You look like a cat with the cream. Dare I hope you have good news?"

Cairney blushed. "You may wish me happy. Miss Poole has agreed to be my wife."

Edd thrust out his hand, grinning. "Heartiest congratulations."

Cairney gripped his hand strongly and released it. "Thank you. I am the happiest of men."

"You look it," Edd said. "How did this change in your fortunes come about?"

"Your Miss Vale," Cairney said, looking slightly sheepish. "She made me see my scruples were more selfish than honorable. She is disarmingly small, with all the force of a hurricane."

In spite of himself, Edd smiled. *That is my Lucy.*

Only she wasn't his.

He dragged his mind back to the matter in hand. "In any event, I am very glad for you, and for Miss Poole." He hesitated, then added, "Have you thought that your happiness has created a dangerous enemy?"

Cairney's lip curled. "If you mean Irving, I hardly consider him dangerous."

"Then you are wrong. The man is relentless in his own course. That you have won Miss Poole may not be the end of it in his eyes."

"What, do you think he will call me out?" Cairney said incredulously. "If so, I assure you, I would happily meet him."

"No, I very much doubt he would do anything so open and honorable," Edd said.

Cairney frowned for a moment or two, then leapt to his feet. "I believe I shall call on my betrothed."

"About time, slow-top," Edd replied. "Give me five minutes to change out of this riding dress and I'll walk with you. While you visit your betrothed, I believe I shall have a word with Mr. Irving."

Cairney's nostrils flared. "That is *my* task, Eddleston."

"No, I don't believe so," Edd said, walking away. "My quarrel predates yours by twelve years."

WHEN THEY ENTERED the hotel, Edd discovered why he had been unable to find Mr. Winslow. The magistrate appeared to be part of an exuberant party taking place in the tearoom. Through the open door, Edd saw it was dominated by Vales, including Lucy, who was leaning across the table to talk to a small boy, her piquant, beautiful face happy and laughing.

Pain and loss closed around his heart like a claw. She did not see him as he strode by with Cairney.

"Quite a tea party," Cairney said to the clerk at the desk, who smiled.

"I believe there is a betrothal involved, sir."

"Whose?" Eddleston got out, his voice hoarse with sudden, overwhelming fear. *Not Lucy, not Lucy.* Surely disappointment with him would not have pushed her into something so foolish… And yet she was a creature of impulse.

"Sir Julius and Mrs. Macy, I believe," the clerk confided. "Judging by the toasts."

Edd breathed again and discovered Cairney's curious gaze on him. Hastily, he smoothed his face and climbed the stairs ahead of the Scotsman. They separated on the first-floor landing, Cairney going toward the Pooles' suite and Edd directly to the door he had previously discovered was Irving's.

Only as he knocked did he realize he had not asked the clerk if Irving were even in. He realized he would rather be lurking in the foyer downstairs, waiting for a glimpse of Lucy, or even a chance to speak to her. She hadn't looked angry still. But then, she hadn't been addressing him.

The door flew open, taking him by surprise, and Irving stood there, scowling and impatient.

A short laugh issued from Irving's mocking mouth. "Why, St. John. Come for another family chat?"

"About old times?" Edd said blandly. "Why not?" As if taking it for invitation, he walked inside, leaving Irving to close the door, and settled himself in the armchair by the fireplace.

Glancing up, he found Irving gazing at him with widened eyes.

"*You* put Cairney up to it, didn't you?" Irving exclaimed.

"Up to what?"

"Offering for Hester Poole! Will he even marry her?"

Edd blinked. "I imagine so. He is, he assures me, the happiest of men."

"Is that what you came to tell me? To gloat about?"

"Lord, no. I wanted to clear the air between us."

Irving made a gesture of contempt with his hand and threw himself into the chair opposite Edd. "There has been plenty of air between us in the last twelve years. I have not seen you since you were a snot-nosed schoolboy."

"Oh, I saw you," Edd said conversationally. "In my mind, whenever I thought of my sister and what you did to her."

Irving's lip curled. "Your sister—my wife—was a tragically disturbed woman."

"She was after she married you. I have not come to debate details with you—though rest assured I have plenty—but to grant you a stay of execution."

Irving laughed. "A *what*?" he sneered. "Are you planning to murder me, little man?"

"You may address me as 'my lord.' And no, not unless I have

to. I thought I would let the law take its course."

Irving was still amused. "Unless…?" he said. "What?"

"Give up on Miss Poole. Leave her be, set your sights on some other rich female—"

"And you will let me go?" Irving interrupted in blatant disbelief. "You are as detached from reality as your poor, mad sister."

Eddleston's hand clenched in sudden pain, but he forced himself to relax, hopefully before Irving noticed.

"Oh no," he said. "I will expose you, and probably charge you so that you stand trial, just…not yet. *If* you step back from Miss Poole."

Irving actually laughed. "You mean to take her from Cairney? Good luck! Won't the Vale chit play after all? I don't imagine either lady likes a proven liar."

"They don't. My motives need not concern you. Just understand that is my only offer of any kind. When it expires, I will come for you." Edd rose unhurriedly from his chair.

"Behold me," Irving drawled, "shivering in my shoes."

"You should be but be a good fellow for once in your life and do it elsewhere. Sadly, however, we will meet again."

"Oh, I hope not," Irving said, doing his best to sound amused.

Edd let him have the last word. He had done his best for now, and his greater concern was to get to Lucy before she vanished again.

# Chapter Fourteen

T HERE HAD BEEN nothing for Lucy and Cornelius to do to help Julius or Antonia, except wait on the shore with the rest of the family and half the town for them to land. But whatever had been wrong with Julius over the last couple of days, it had clearly been rectified by his reunion with Antonia. Though unsurprised by the announcement of their engagement, she was highly delighted for them.

She had always liked Antonia, and she was genuinely thrilled that Julius would have a family of his own to share Black Hill with. A spouse to laugh and cry with, to be his friend, his partner, his lover. If she had longed for these things herself, even imagined for a few precious moments that she had found them, well, she had been wrong. And deep in her heart, she had always known she didn't deserve them.

And now she wouldn't even be able to contribute to the family by marrying Eddleston. Who, perhaps, had been all she deserved.

Refusing to think any more about herself, she set about making the hotel tea party as happy as it could be, chatting with everyone and playing with little Edward Macy, who was a delightful child. Only as their game spilled out into the foyer did she glimpse *him* at the foot of the staircase, watching her with a faint, wistful smile.

She straightened, her heart giving the silly lurch it always had at the sight of him. Her sense of loss was absolute, and yet she could not look away.

And she could not believe him. All the fun was gone. All the love…

He began to walk toward her, and in panic, she seized Edward by the hand. "Come, we had better go back to protect your mama from the wicked smugglers."

She walked away from him, the child swinging on the end of her arm. And this time it felt symbolic.

SHE TOLD JULIUS the following day.

She found him in his study, writing letters. Just for a moment, she allowed herself to enjoy the return of purpose and passion to his expression, to his every movement. It was as if he had been asleep since he left the sea, and Antonia had wakened him back to his old self.

She smiled because she couldn't help it, even though her own heart was in pieces.

He glanced up, his quick smile answering hers. "What? Have I an ink smudge on my nose?"

"Not yet." She came further into the room and sat on the chair near the other side of his desk. "I came to tell you of a decision I have made. I hope it won't inconvenience you too badly, but I have decided *not* to marry Lord Eddleston."

Julius put his pen in the stand and sat back, regarding her. "Then you know he is in Blackhaven? Did you meet him at the garden party?"

"Did you?" she countered.

"Someone told me he was there, but no, I didn't happen to meet him. I expect he will call at Black Hill. Do you not wish to put off your decision until then? I know he is earlier than we expected, but we did agree we owed him one visit at the very least."

"I—I have changed my mind."

Julius was nothing if not perceptive. He peered at her. "Is there someone else?"

"What makes you think that?"

"Something Rod said. And I know you're up to something. I've just been too preoccupied by my own affairs to investigate yours."

"There is nothing to investigate, Julius. There is no one. And I don't want even to *see* Lord Eddleston."

"Well, I'm afraid you will have to if he asks for you. I am happy to be there with you, if you like. Or one of your sisters, if you prefer. Devil take it, we can *all* accompany you, and that might well prevent him saying anything at all you don't want to hear. But it would only be courteous to acknowledge him. I did invite him here."

"Only after he had invited himself."

"Nevertheless. Why have you taken him in such violent dislike now?"

"I have merely decided I don't wish to be married. Ever."

He blinked. "Lucy, you are not yet nineteen years old. No one will make you marry anyone, but as a reason to dislike Eddleston, that answer is a whopper."

She shifted restlessly. "When will you and Antonia be married?"

"In about three weeks. As soon as the banns are read."

"Will you go away on a big wedding journey?"

"We might. But if Eddleston waits three weeks to call, I shall be surprised. Though he has not even written to say he is in Blackhaven."

"Perhaps he has changed his mind, too," Lucy said. Though knowing him as she did, she was aware he could just appear without warning. Or perhaps he would simply leave Blackhaven. That would be easiest, though for some reason it didn't make her any happier.

She stood to go, but paused to say, "I am glad for you and Antonia."

He grinned. She wasn't sure he didn't blush.

"You don't think she'll mind us all living here too?" she asked with sudden anxiety.

"I imagine she will enjoy it. Edward certainly will! In any case, you won't all be here forever. I've always known that. But it will always be a home to come back to."

As she left him, she tried to envision herself as a middle-aged spinster aunt, looking after Julius and Antonia's children, spoiling all her nieces and nephews with little treats. She would like to be a fun aunt. Only she felt too exhausted for fun right now. Instead, she had to be prepared to meet Lord Eddleston whenever he deigned to appear. She would be regal, casual, dismissive, yet perfectly courteous.

In the meantime, she went in search of Farmer—or Smith, as he was known at Black Hill. Walking across the stable yard, she met Jenks, who had once sailed under Julius and was now his head groom.

"Shall I saddle the mare for you, miss?" he asked, doubling back.

"No, thanks, I'll saddle her myself."

"It's no problem," he said, just a shade anxiously, and when she didn't change direction, he added, "To be honest, ma'am, a few of the lads are having a break, and it'll embarrass them if you catch them."

"Then they're too easily embarrassed. I've no intention of *catching* them."

But as soon as she crossed the threshold, she heard *his* voice. Lord Eddleston's voice.

"…a risk," he was saying. "But the alternative is to live in hiding or on the run until someone recognizes you as the escaped prisoner."

Involuntarily, Lucy pressed her hand over her lurching heart.

"You can't do that, Luke," Betsy the parlor maid said. "*We* can't do that. You got to take the chance and go to the magistrate."

"And if he bangs me up again?" Farmer demanded. "They'll hang me like as not if I go to trial."

"Not on the evidence they have," Eddleston said. He, Farmer, and Betsy were sitting on a pile of clean straw, so focused on their conversation that they didn't see Lucy. Eddleston looked surprisingly comfortable. As Tyler would have been. "Lord Braithwaite will speak for you. I have no guarantees, Farmer, but it is your best chance."

As though she were blind and deaf, Lucy continued walking toward the mare's stall. Suddenly, they all sprang to their feet, but still Lucy did not look.

"Carry on," she said, reaching up to stroke the mare's nose. "I'll be gone in a moment."

"Do you think he should go, miss?" Betsy asked.

"To the magistrate? It depends how he wants to live." Reluctantly, Lucy turned, seeking Farmer's gaze—*not* Eddleston's. "Do you want to stay here? In Blackhaven, I mean."

Farmer nodded once.

Betsy said, "There you are, then. And if they *do* bang you up, Mr. Tyler can get you out again."

Lucy curled her lip to show her contempt for "Tyler" and went to fetch the mare's saddle.

"I got to go back to work," Betsy muttered. It sounded as if she were dragging Farmer with her. "And so do you."

"Tomorrow," Eddleston called after them. He sounded too close, and an instant later, his hands closed over the saddle, lifting it for her. She only just managed to get her own hands out of the way in time.

"I can manage," she said coldly.

"I know. I was hoping we could talk while I help."

"I don't want your help or your talk." Lucy seized the bridle she wanted and marched past him to the mare. "I don't even want your presence, my lord. Be so good as to remove it."

"Lucy, nothing has changed!"

She had slid the bridle over the mare's nose, but now turned to stare at him. He stood in front of her, still holding the saddle.

"Nothing important," he amended.

"So lies are unimportant." Furiously, she fastened the bridle and led the horse out, forcing Eddleston to step back. "What do you want, my lord?"

He set the saddle on the mare's back and regarded her over the top, his brows raised. "To marry you."

"Oh, stop it! The joke is over." Everything was over, and she wanted to cry, only she would never give him the satisfaction. Furiously, she began to fasten the girths.

"Lucy, there was no joke," he said softly. A smile flickered across his lips. "Except the puppy. And the barrel."

"Enough!" The command should have been sharp, but it came out too hoarse. "You have spoiled the fun. You have spoiled everything. Because you deceived me. *You lied to me.*"

Unshed tears blurred her eyes, and she didn't see him move, but suddenly he was there beside her.

"I never lied to you. I just didn't tell you the whole truth. Yes, I should have told you sooner, but please don't hate me over a name."

She threw her head back. "I *despise* you over a name. *That* name."

She thought he might have whitened, and was fiercely glad to hurt him back.

He said, "Then you are even sillier than I am. Whatever my name, I love you."

Once, such a declaration would have cast her into transports of joy. Now she gasped to cover the surge of tears and loss. And without warning, his arms came around her and his mouth took hers.

Tyler's kiss, Tyler's lips... The feeling was the same. Her treacherous body still melted, and she could not bear it. She pushed him away in fury, and was surprised, even angry, when he let her. She jumped, hauling herself on to the mare's back and kicking her into motion. Somehow, she even remembered to duck to get out of the stable door, and then they galloped across the yard. Her one desire was to get away from him before he saw the tears, the hurt that could never be mended.

She might not believe that he loved her. But his words, his kiss, had prompted the terrible knowledge that whatever he had done, she still loved him.

EDD LET HER go, mostly because he realized her need for solitude—to lick the wounds he was ashamed of inflicting, and, hopefully, to begin the process of putting the shattered pieces of her happiness back together. As he gazed after her and the horse vanishing into the distance, he felt the first stirrings of hope. She could not have been so hurt without profound feeling for him, and just for a moment he had felt, *tasted*, that emotion in her kiss. There had been a moment of not mere yielding, but of desperate need that surely matched his own.

*Love?*

*God, I hope so…*

He couldn't recall ever making such a mess of anything before. Wrong steps had always been recoverable. But Lucy was no mere subject for study, no mischievous prank, or political plan gone wrong. She was a living, passionate, wonderful being, and he wanted her with his very soul. More than that, he wanted her to be happy. Just for a little, she had been happy with him…

He walked across the stable yard, nodding to the groom on his way, and found his way to the front of the house.

The door was opened by a manservant without livery. One empty sleeve was pinned neatly to his chest. It seemed to be true that the Vales were employing injured veterans of the late war.

"Good morning," he said cheerfully, presenting his card. "Is

Sir Julius at home?"

"If you'd step inside, sir, I'll inquire."

Edd, abandoned in a comfortable hallway that was a room in its own right—there was even a fireplace, as well as an upholstered settle, and a table with writing materials—looked around the scattering of pictures on the walls and listened. It was a quiet house, considering how many people lived here. Perhaps everyone was out. If the twins were at home, he was fairly sure they would be right in front of him.

The servant came back. "This way, my lord."

He was led to the passage on the other side of the hallway, and shown into a room to the left. It appeared to be a pleasant study, with a large bookcase and a couple of old-fashioned cabinets and two comfortable chairs near the empty fireplace. Captain Sir Julius Vale rose from behind a large desk and came toward him, stretching out his hand.

"Lord Eddleston. A pleasure to meet you at last. I'm Julius Vale. Glass of brandy? Or tea, perhaps?"

"Brandy might help," Edd said. "Thank you."

Vale cast him a humorous look as he went to the decanter and poured a splash of brandy into two glasses. "That bad, is it? I understand we almost met at the castle the other day, but I only heard afterward that you were there."

Edd accepted the offered glass with thanks and took the chair indicated by his host. "I confess I have been in Blackhaven rather longer. I arrived almost a fortnight ago."

"Then I imagine you had business in the town other than my sister."

It was said pleasantly enough, but Vale clearly would not overlook a neglect that amounted to disrespect and even rudeness.

"I did, as it happens, but I found your sister was my priority, which was why I attended the same assembly room ball you did."

Vale looked at him more closely. "Did I see you dancing with Lucy?"

"Probably. I certainly danced with her. Twice." Edd twisted his glass between his fingers. "This is the difficult part. I am sure you can understand my natural curiosity about a lady to whom I was betrothed and had never met. I hope you will also understand why I chose to meet her…incognito, as it were."

"Perhaps you should explain it to me."

Although there was no overt threat in the voice, Edd had to stop himself shifting in his chair. He felt like a midshipman summoned before the captain because he had failed in his duties. Or like the schoolboy he had once been, trying to explain to the headmaster exactly why it had been necessary to build a small aviary on the school roof.

"If I had done what I freely admit would have been the correct thing," he said slowly, "and waited upon her here, in company with you and the rest of her family, it would have been horribly formal, awkward, and unnatural. Strangers unjustly— even foolishly—engaged, by our parents. She would only have known me as such. And I would never have known for certain how she felt about me or the betrothal. She might have wanted to be a countess. She might have hated the whole idea but been prepared to do her duty. She might have had some romantic idea of a fairytale prince, which I most assuredly am not."

"I see the picture," Vale said. His face had not softened in the slightest.

"So did I. And I fully intended to do the honorable thing. Whatever that turned out to be."

Vale's brow twitched. "And what *did* it turn out to be?"

A sudden surge of laughter caught in Edd's throat. "Astonishing. I have never met anyone remotely like your sister before. So full of fun and kindness and a rather reckless impulsiveness that I'm afraid I recognize only too well."

He sipped his brandy. "For whatever it's worth to you, I came to realize that she was inclined to accept Eddleston's offer in order to do her duty by her family, but she did not like it."

Vale was scowling now. "*What* duty to her family?"

"One that she might have made up but seemed important to her. She felt she contributed nothing to your collective household, wealth, or well-being. And she wants to."

Vale's jaw dropped.

Edd smiled faintly. "You are a large family, all with great character and talents and determination. I knew this without having met any of you except Lucy. You may not know it."

"She felt…inferior?" Vale said in disbelief. "Useless? *Lucy?*"

"Oh, it's only a tiny part of her, I know. But I cannot imagine *you* would like to be married for such a reason."

Vale, who had just been celebrating his own betrothal, swallowed and raised his glass to his lips. "No indeed." He seemed deep in thought, perhaps recalling Lucy's moods and behavior in the last couple of weeks. His eyes refocused on Edd. "And what did you want, Eddleston? To wriggle out of it? To make her fall in love with you? To acquire a complaint wife?"

Edd blinked. "Compliant? Lucy?"

Vale let out a breath that might have been laughter, and then it vanished. "You have been meeting her clandestinely, behind my back."

"I have," Edd admitted.

"With what purpose?" Vale barked, and Edd took an instant to pity those failing midshipmen.

Edd helped himself to another sip of brandy. "At first, just to get to know her, to decide what to do, and then because she intrigued me and was delightful to be with. And then I stopped worrying about decisions because I think I had already made it. I want very much to marry Lucy. Only now she knows who I am, and she thinks I deceived her."

A brief look of illumination flashed across Vale's face, as though he finally understood Lucy's mood since the garden party. But he retorted, "You *did* deceive her. There is no doubt about that."

"Yes, but I didn't deceive her about anything that matters!" Edd sat forward to push his glass onto the table, every inch of him eager and passionate. "Yes, I'm Eddleston, but that's hardly the most important thing about me. It's not who I am inside. That is the man Lucy knows as Tyler, who gets into mischief but tries his very best to make a better world. I want that for Lucy, too. More than anything, I desire to make her happy, and God help me, I need that to be with me."

Vale stared at him. Edd could feel the blood burning in his face, but he held the older man's gaze without difficulty.

"And if Lucy doesn't want you?" Vale demanded.

Edd closed his eyes. "Then I'll leave. Of course, she may break the engagement and the contracts will be mutually dissolved." He forced his eyes open again. "I ask only the chance to make things right with her. She is angry with me just now, but I think…I *hope* that she still cares."

"Are you asking for my help?" Vale asked icily.

Edd shook his head. "Of course not. I am trying, belatedly, to do the right thing. I ask only that you don't forbid us from meeting."

Vale drew in his breath, then set down his glass and stood. It appeared the audience was over. "I don't, for now. But know the decision is Lucy's, as it would always have been. Know too that if one more lie crosses your lips, or you hurt her in any way, you will pay."

"I will," Edd agreed.

# Chapter Fifteen

LUCY HAD RIDDEN halfway to Blackhaven before she realized where she was. She decided to keep going and call on Hester. She longed to turn her mind to someone else's problems rather than letting it go round and round her own, achieving nothing.

She was even angry that Eddleston had not followed her to plead his case, even though she had no intention of listening, let alone believing him. She realized she should have made Aubrey come with her so that he would drink the waters that appeared to be so good for him. Mind you, she had not seen him this morning, so he could have been anywhere, even already in Blackhaven.

There was something soothing about the town with its mixture of busy, hardworking residents and idle visitors who could afford to consider nothing but their own minor health complaints.

Leaving the mare with the ostlers in the yard behind the main hotel building, she went inside and hurried straight up to Hester's rooms. As soon as she was admitted, she saw the difference in her friend.

Hester seemed to glow with some inner happiness.

Lucy stopped in her tracks as Hester rushed to meet her. "What has happened?" she demanded.

"Everything!" Hester exclaimed gaily. Her face was wreathed

in smiles. "I am engaged to marry Mr. Cairney."

"Oh, how wonderful!" Lucy seized her friend's hands and dragged her to the sofa. "Tell me all!"

Blushing and laughing, Hester described how Mr. Cairney had proposed during the garden party, and how she had immediately told Mr. Irving.

"How did he take it?" Lucy asked, feeling a sudden chill in her blood as she remembered what Tyler—*Eddleston*—believed about Irving and his sister.

"Surprisingly well," Hester replied. "I expected tantrums, to be frank, but he seems to be a greater gentleman than I gave him credit for."

*Or he has not given up.* Loath to spoil her friend's happiness, Lucy only smiled. "Well, I am very glad for you, and I think Mr. Cairney will make you the perfect husband! I know you will be very happy together."

"Do you know, I really think we will be?" Hester's expression changed suddenly. "But here am I rattling on about my own good fortune. What of you? Your Mr. Tyler is the Earl of Eddleston, your terrible betrothed!"

Lucy forced a laugh. "He was never *my* Mr. Tyler, and he certainly is not my earl. I told Julius this morning that I wanted him to break the contract once and for all."

"Did you?" A shadow of uncertainty passed over Hester's face. "Are you sure that is what you want? You'll forgive me, but you seemed somewhat smitten. And he—"

"Not in the least," Lucy said. "Oh, I'll not deny he was great fun. But I could never trust a liar. Someone who has deceived me without so much as a blink—and for more than a week…" She trailed off, catching something stricken in Hester's expression. "What? What did I say?" Hester forced a smile, but the sudden desperation in her eyes frightened Lucy. "Hester?"

Hester jumped up. "Shall we go for an ice? Or a walk, perhaps, to the harbor?"

"Perhaps a walk," Lucy said, indicating her riding habit. "I smell of horse and will hardly be welcome indoors! I shouldn't really have called here, only I was eager to know how things transpired with Mr. Cairney."

"He is a good man," Hester said with an incomprehensible air of wistfulness.

"He is," Lucy assured her. "Hester—"

"I'll fetch my cloak. Is it as chilly outside as it looks? At least it is not raining…"

BY THE TIME she waved Lucy off on her way back to Black Hill, in company with one of her numerous brothers encountered on their walk, Hester was exhausted from too much smiling and too much meaningless chatter, all of it her own. Lucy had looked increasingly perplexed but forbore to press her.

Once the Vales and their horses were lost among the high street traffic, Hester turned and walked swiftly past the hotel door and kept walking until she came to the King's Head inn. There, she sailed straight through the common room and up the stairs. She knew which room was his, for he had described it incidentally during some story that had amused her at the time.

If he was not in, she would ask him to call at the hotel during the hour her mother generally napped. But the door opened almost as soon as knocked, and the astonished, beloved features of Will Cairney met her desperate gaze.

Further along the passage, another door began to open. Will whisked her into the room and closed the door before taking both her hands.

"Hester, what is it? What is wrong?"

She clung to his fingers. "I have behaved ill to you. I have not been honest. And now you will think I didn't tell you before because I was trying to trick you into marriage."

Amusement lit his eyes. "Were you? I admit I can't see the

point."

"No, I wasn't. I wanted to marry you because I love you. Please believe that, whatever else I tell you."

The spark of amusement faded. He handed her onto the settle and sat beside her, still holding one hand. "I'm not going to like this, am I?"

She shook her head. "No. No, you're not." She drew in a deep breath. "But we must at least begin with honesty between us, or what hope do we have? If you wish to end our engagement, I will understand."

"Hester, of course I shall not end it," he exclaimed. "And neither will you!"

"The truth is, I am not all that you think me. I am a silly, deceived woman."

Cairney's lip began to curl. "By Irving?"

"Goodness, no. He has never deceived me for a moment. I thought only that he and I might make use of each other."

"Why?" he asked blankly.

"Because I need a husband," she whispered. "Three months ago, I believed the foolish lies of a certain nobleman and...and granted him favors I should not."

Cairney whitened a little, but she hung on to the hope that his anger was not with her.

"I found out the next day—I overheard him and a friend, in fact, for we were staying at the same party—that he merely wanted my fortune. I don't know if you can imagine that kind of hurt... But anger and pride saved me. I turned my back on him and sent him away."

"Good."

She clung to his hand. "It is now. But some weeks later, I began to suspect there were...consequences to my folly." She swallowed. "I *need a husband*, Will."

She watched the understanding seep into his face, the realization of the extent of the favors she had granted. He did not withdraw his hand, but it no longer held hers. It felt limp. And though she searched desperately, she could find no warmth in his eyes. None at all.

"You are with child." His voice was cold, too.

She nodded miserably. "That is why I considered Harold Irving, let him escort us here. I did not feel remotely guilty because he was lying to me about his devotion. I don't know whether or not I would ever have told him. Or whether he would have cared. I know you care—in an entirely different way—which is why I have to tell you and hope you can forgive me."

His hand slid free of hers entirely, and he stood so abruptly that the old settle rocked on its legs.

"Can you?" she whispered. But she thought she already knew the answer, and it broke her heart.

"I don't know," he said hoarsely. "As God is my witness, I do not know. You must give me time to…to absorb this, to think what it means for us. For you."

She closed her eyes for an instant and reached for the courage she had always had. She even smiled brightly as she rose to her feet. "I understand. Don't worry. I shall manage. Goodbye, Will."

She sailed out of the door before he could even turn and see her face. She didn't know how she got out of the inn before the tears started. Outside, she was lucky enough to find it raining, which almost made her laugh, because no one would notice a wet face. And by the time she returned to the hotel, she had a new plan.

She managed to smile wryly at her next stroke of good luck, when she saw Harold Irving lounging on one of the foyer sofas, idly turning the pages of a London newspaper. He might have been waiting for her. Certainly, his face lit up and he jumped immediately to his feet, though she could not flatter herself that his eagerness was caused by affection or any genuine desire for her company.

"You may escort me to my door," she told him. She suspected he bit his tongue on some disparaging remark about Mr. Cairney. She wondered if she would have hit him. But he said nothing, even when she walked past her mother's door.

"Perhaps I might have a word," she said, opening her own door and waiting until he followed her before closing it again. "I believe you would like to marry my fortune," she began without preamble.

Harold's mouth fell open, and he hastily closed it again. "I wouldn't put it in quite such vulgar terms. I assure you—"

"Yes, yes," she interrupted. "I am not foolish, Mr. Irving, nor am I naïve any longer. My fortune is one of the two things I possess. The other is my family honor. I am prepared to marry you if you agree to acknowledge my unborn child as yours."

He blinked. His eyes flickered to her belly, but he didn't even need to think about it. She had known he would not. He thrust out his hand. "Deal," he said.

THE FOLLOWING MORNING, Lucy was going down to breakfast when Lord Braithwaite walked into the house asking for Cornelius. Guessing at once that this was to do with Luke Farmer, she hurried down the rest of the stairs, calling to the servant, "Don't worry, John, I'll take his lordship, since I am on the same errand."

Lord Braithwaite bowed, looking surprised, but if he was also put out, he hid it well. She led him through the hall to the back of the house to the office used for estate business.

"I've brought Lord Braithwaite," she announced, walking into the room.

Cornelius sprang up from behind his desk like a jack-in-the-box, looking somehow like a schoolboy determined to tell the truth to his angry headmaster. This was so far out of character as to intrigue Lucy.

She turned to Braithwaite, who held out his hand to Cornelius. "So sorry to interrupt you," he said ruefully. "I have come with a confession and can only beg your forgiveness."

Cornelius blinked. "You have? I mean, you do? Why?"

"Please, sit down," Lucy intervened, since Cornelius seemed to have forgotten the basic courtesies. She stuck her head back out the door. "Coffee, if you please, John."

The men were seated in the chairs by the fireplace. Lucy placed herself inconspicuously on the edge of the smaller desk, but neither man seemed to be aware of her.

"You took on one Rob Smith to oblige me," Braithwaite said.

"I was glad of him. And he is a good worker. It is I who am obliged."

"The thing is," Braithwaite said with difficulty, "I was not entirely truthful. I changed his name to protect him as well as you. In fact, he is Luke Farmer, the son of one of my own tenants, and he escaped from the town gaol."

Cornelius was not easily disconcerted. "Where he had been accused of…what?"

"Highway robbery," Braithwaite said. "I wanted to hide him until I could prove the identification was false. Which it clearly is. The witnesses did not know him from my groom, and both described a different man altogether. I've promised to take him back to Winslow and have the matter cleared up before he's locked up again, if necessary."

Cornelius was staring at him in bewilderment. "You want a character reference?"

"No, I want your permission to take him into Blackhaven to stand before Winslow and the witnesses to clear the matter up. I'd have done it before, only Winslow was being recalcitrant and insisting Farmer must return to gaol. Now that he has finally consented to see Farmer at the hotel with constables present, I want to stick to my part in proceedings before he changes his mind."

John appeared with the coffee at that point, and Lucy hastily dismissed him while she poured the coffee instead.

"Will you send him back to us again?" Cornelius asked evenly.

"God willing," Braithwaite replied.

Lucy handed him a cup of coffee. She knew the Earl of Eddleston stood behind them all, including Mr. Winslow, pulling the strings. He was far too good at it.

"I'll fetch Smith," Cornelius said with resignation. "Though I'm sure he would rather work his father's land than mine."

Lucy went off to breakfast wondering whom she could persuade to drive into Blackhaven with her. She wasn't sure why, but she felt a personal responsibility for Farmer, even though he was irrevocably tied in her mind to Eddleston.

IN THE END, she entered the hotel with Julius, who was calling on Antonia. "Are you coming to pay your respects?" he asked Lucy.

"I'll just drop in on Miss Poole first, and join you later, if I may? If you go out, I'm sure I'll find you! By teatime at the latest." No matter how much she liked and approved of Antonia, she had no desire to play gooseberry with them all day.

In fact, while Julius hurried ahead to his beloved, Lucy wandered more slowly past the coffee room door. She was sure she heard Farmer's voice, and crossed her fingers for him. Even if he was associated with Eddleston.

As she approached Hester's room, she had to steel herself to face her friend's happiness. She refused to allow her own sense of desolation to spoil that. But nothing prepared her for the listlessness with which her friend greeted her.

Hester did not even rise from her chair, merely cast Lucy a distracted smile. The middle-aged maid with her gave a helpless shrug in Lucy's direction, a silent plea, and then went out.

Lucy crouched at Hester's feet and took her hands. "Hester, what is it? What has happened? Has Mr. Cairney behaved ill?"

"Oh, no," Hester said at once. "He is the best of men. It is I who behaved ill. I thought only of my own feelings…" She blinked several times and straightened her back. "But it does not matter now. It is all over with Mr. Cairney, and I have agreed to marry Harold Irving."

"*What?*" Lucy sat back on her heels. "You can't!"

Hester's distant gaze refocused on Lucy's face. "I have to."

"No, you don't, Hester. You must not! He was once married to Lord Eddleston's sister, who died under circumstances that—at their very best—reflect badly on him! Hester—"

"Then we deserve each other, perhaps," Hester said with a sad smile that did not touch her eyes.

"You absolutely do not!"

Hester withdrew her hands. "It is all arranged, Lucy. Please do not interfere."

HAROLD HAD DONE his very best to arrange everything he could think of. He had explained to the nasty old Poole woman exactly what rumors he would spread about Hester should she try to stand in his way, and sworn her to silence. He did not want any of this getting back to Lord Eddleston before the knot was well and truly tied—just in case Eddleston really did have some kind of proof or a witness prepared to testify against him about Anne. Though he doubted it.

Now all was set in motion. He had ordered the post-chaise and accompanied his intended to the bank to withdraw funds enough for some luxurious traveling.

And now he was shuffling off the last of his Blackhaven business—not because he cared but because wished to give the impression of proceeding as normal. Which encompassed being helpful in the tedious matter of the highwaymen who had held them up what seemed a lifetime ago.

"Really, how often do we need to identify this same man?"

Harold said irritably, when he had politely handed Mrs. Poole into the most comfortable chair.

"The problem is," the magistrate said apologetically, "so far you appear to have identified several different men between you."

As well as Winslow, the Earl of Braithwaite was present, as was his brother-in-law, the local member of Parliament. Four lesser men stood to sharp attention behind Winslow. Harold barely noticed them.

"Nonsense," Mrs. Poole said roundly. "We identified him before his arrest, and to Lord Braithwaite."

"Actually," Winslow said, "you identified *this* man to Lord Braithwaite."

One of the men behind him stepped forward to stand beside Winslow's table.

"And this man to me," Winslow added, and another of the lesser men, who looked like a farm laborer, moved to the other side of the table. "On the other hand, neither of these gentlemen resemble the descriptions you gave, either to me or to Lord Braithwaite."

"We barely saw the man," Irving said impatiently. "We were judging by his voice."

"You never heard this man speak," Braithwaite pointed out, indicating the first man who had stepped forward. "In fact, he is my groom and could not possibly have been holding up carriages on the Carlisle road at the time of your bad experience."

Harold blushed furiously and resorted to bluster. "Then let him speak now! Let them all say, 'Stand and deliver!'"

Obligingly, each of the four lesser men recited the words required, with varying degrees of embarrassment. Harold recognized none of them. It could have been any of them, but he was pretty sure the truth lay in the fact that Winslow had clearly ruled out the two they had already identified.

Mrs. Poole obviously had the same idea, for at exactly the same time as he said, "That one," the old lady said it, too. Only while Harold pointed at the auburn-haired man, she pointed at the other.

Braithwaite and Winslow exchanged glances that were not entirely free of amusement. Harold began to feel hot under the collar.

"I am afraid," said the magistrate, "that you have just identified my constable and one of the town gaolers."

At that moment, the door opened and Hester swept in, followed, Harold was annoyed to see, by Lucy Vale. Braithwaite and Winslow both rose to their feet in some surprise.

"Ladies." Winslow bowed. "I am afraid we are holding important business at the moment, but I expect to be finished—"

"I know," Hester interrupted. "Mama told me she and Mr. Irving were identifying the supposed highwayman. Again." She walked past all of the four lesser men. "I could have saved you a great deal of time and effort if I had been allowed to speak to you in the first place. It was none of these men."

The old lady clicked her tongue in irritation. Harold scowled at her—his first attempt at intimidation where she was concerned—but she did not even glance at him.

Winslow said, "May I ask how it is you are so sure?"

"The eyes are wrong, the brows are wrong. Their whole posture is wrong. And the faces are not the right shape. They are all innocent of the crime against us, whatever else they may be accused of."

Winslow sighed. "I am inclined to agree with you. Especially since, between them, my other witnesses have now identified each man present. Except Lord Braithwaite and Mr. Hanson. Mrs. Poole, Mr. Irving, I commend you for your efforts. It is not easy to recall precise details after a traumatic event. Miss Poole, I am grateful for your intervention. Farmer, despite fleeing from justice, I am releasing you. You are free to go, once you make a statement. Ladies, gentlemen, thank you and good day."

Despite feeling dismissed like a naughty schoolboy, Harold was glad to get out of the room. He had more important business to attend to.

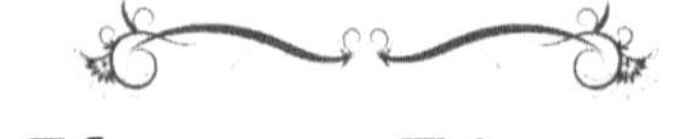

# Chapter Sixteen

"HESTER!" MR. IRVING said sharply behind them.

To Lucy's relief, Hester neither turned nor acknowledged him. Instead, she sailed upstairs at Lucy's side and straight to her sitting room.

At last, after she closed the sitting room door, a genuine smile broke out on Hester's face. "I believe I enjoyed that."

"Good," Lucy said. "And thank you."

"I am glad to do you this small favor. I doubt we shall meet again."

"Quite the contrary, Hester! You cannot—"

A knock on the door interrupted her. Without waiting for an answer, Harold Irving walked in. Lucy glared at him in outrage, but he did not even glance at her.

"Are you ready?" he said coldly to Hester.

"I am." Hester walked through the inner door to her bed-chamber. She emerged almost immediately carrying a large leather bag, which she dropped at his feet. "You may carry it and at least look like a gentleman. Goodbye, Lucy. I wish we could have become proper friends."

Lucy's jaw dropped. "Wait!" she said desperately, trying to pull herself together, to think how to prevent this terrible mistake. "Hester, wait! Where are you going?"

Hester did not stop, but Irving did, turning in the doorway to block her pursuit. His face was unveiled, ugly, and threatening.

"Never make the mistake of trying to thwart me, madam. For once, take your dismissal like a lady." And he shut the door in her face.

At least he did not lock it.

Lucy's mind spun. What to do? How to avert this impending disaster? How could she even keep track of them when she did not know what he intended? It made no difference to her whatever that Hester had clearly agreed to it. Hester was under some kind of duress, or she would never have spoken to Irving as she had. And she would *never* have given up Mr. Cairney, whom she genuinely loved.

Desperately trying to think, Lucy paced to the window. In the street below, a bright yellow hired post-chaise and four stood directly before the hotel's front door, the postilions already mounted and ready to go.

*Of course!* They were eloping to Gretna Green, or somewhere else equally unsuitable across the Scottish border, where they could be married immediately.

Lucy bolted across the room, threw the door wide, and flew along the passage to the stairs. She emerged panting, so relieved to see the chaise door still open that she hurled herself toward it and grabbed for Hester's hand.

Hester's fingers gripped hers hard. "Lucy! Bless you, Lucy, please go. There is nothing else you can do. Everything is better this way."

Irving had just taken his seat opposite and was glowering with impatience. "Begone, Miss Vale," he commanded. "You are drawing unwelcome attention. If you cannot think of Miss Poole, at least think of yourself."

"I *am* thinking of her," Lucy snapped. "And I have no intention of letting her go. Hester, you must stay with us. Whatever threat—"

With an exclamation of impatience, Irving caught her wrist in both hands, and when she still didn't let go—or even stop talking—he simply yanked her inside the coach and slammed the door shut. The postilions called out, and they were off.

EDD SAT AT the desk in his inn bedchamber, trying to write a speech in favor of worker combinations. But he could not concentrate. His mind kept wandering off on its own to Lucy and how to win her back. And when he tried to exert some self-discipline, he wondered instead if Farmer was released. He hoped Lucy's family would not hate him for that too.

He groaned and forced his attention back to his writing. He had just decided the speech was not too bad after all when a knock sounded on his door.

"Come in," he called, and glanced up to see not the chambermaid but Lord Braithwaite.

The earl did not look pleased.

Edd's heart sank. He replaced the pen in the stand and waved Braithwaite to the other chair. "What happened?" he asked with resignation. "Did they not release him?"

"Oh, yes. It all went swimmingly. Irving and Mrs. Poole tried to identify the constable and the gaoler as their highwayman, and then Miss Poole appeared out of nowhere—in company with your Miss Vale—and declared none of them were the highwayman. After which, Winslow really had no choice but to dismiss the charges against Farmer and release him."

Edd grinned with relief—and with gratitude to Lucy, who must have persuaded Hester to intervene. "Then why have you got a face like a smacked arse?"

"Because Winslow kept Farmer back to make his statement and then lectured him on fleeing justice for any reason. After which, Winslow made him swear he would stay within the environs of the town and surrounding countryside for the next month.

"Farmer said yes and nodded to everything. And then, without any warning at all, he bolted. Winslow and I called after him to stop—he didn't—so we went after him, just in time to see him riding off up the road, hell for leather. On Winslow's horse."

It wasn't remotely funny, but Edd's lips twitched with the urge to laugh.

"What the devil, Edd?" Braithwaite demanded. "What got into the fool? Winslow is absolutely hopping mad, fit to hang Farmer from the nearest tree!"

Edd groaned and tugged at his hair. "Well, at least he won't do that—too proper, thank God." He let his hands fall. "What set him off? Farmer, I mean. What was he doing immediately before he bolted?"

"Listening and agreeing with Winslow. Though his attention seemed to have wandered out the window."

Edd sat up. "Then he saw something in the street that set him off. What did *you* see there? Apart from Farmer galloping off on the magistrate's horse." Another inappropriate breath of laughter shook him, and this time Braithwaite reluctantly smiled back.

"Nothing out of the ordinary," he said. "The doorman had no idea either. Farmer just came bounding out of the alley that leads to the stables and took off up the road. He certainly did not pause to make his plans known to the doorman."

Edd shook his head. "It doesn't make sense. Why would Farmer do that? He had just won everything he wanted… Did the doorman see anything unusual in the street before Farmer's mad gallop?"

"No. He had been helping a couple of elderly ladies into one of the hired cabs for their daily watering, while a post-chaise set off in perfect order. Otherwise, the street was quite quiet. I'll tell you what, though, Edd—it's the last time I involve myself in your affairs."

"It was your affair to start with," Edd protested. "I only interfered to oblige you and Hanson."

"Ha," Braithwaite said derisively. "I knew nothing about the wretched business until you showed up. Well, I am going home to relative sanity. Let me know if you hear from our fugitive."

At first Lucy was only glad that she was not separated from Hester. As long as they were together, surely, neither reputation would be harmed by this mad start.

"You are eloping," Lucy stated.

"Yes," Hester said hoarsely.

"So you see why your presence is unwelcome," Irving said. "We will let you down at the first stage, and you may make your own way back to Blackhaven."

"I have no means to return to Blackhaven," Lucy snapped.

"I shall give you the means, of course," Hester said before Irving could speak again. "But he is right, Lucy—you cannot come with us."

"Not even as your bridesmaid?" Lucy said innocently.

"No, Lucy, you will then be part of my ruin. Border weddings are not at all the thing, even though we can probably be in Scotland before dark—"

"All the more reason for me to chaperone you."

"You are the one who won't have a husband!" Hester retorted. "I will not put you in that situation."

Lucy took her arm. "Then don't. Come back with me. We shall stay at Black Hill while my brothers deal with *him.*"

Hester uttered a sound halfway between a laugh and a sob. "Oh, Lucy, you are so innocent! Your brothers cannot solve this for me, nor can you or Mr. Cairney or anyone else."

"But Mr. Irving can?" Lucy said slowly. An idea had begun to form, one that she probably should not even have thought of, as an unmarried girl. Only she had known Tyler's kisses and the melting of her body into his, with the strange and wonderful desires that came with such closeness. And she had been only too aware of the trials and tribulations of Felicia's marriage.

Had Hester also yielded to passion, only with an unscrupulous man? Had someone taken advantage of her and left her to bear the consequences? It was the only solution that made sense. Cairney must have balked at bringing up another man's child, and now there was only Irving.

Her gaze met Hester's, and she knew she was right.

"I need this," Hester said with difficulty. "You must not stand in my way."

Lucy drew in a deep, shuddering breath. Everything Tyler—*Eddleston*, damn him—had said about Irving came rushing back to her. She could not leave Hester to become the victim of such a man, whatever her mistakes. Surely there was a way to avoid Hester's ruin? Or at least not to give in to it immediately.

And besides, every moment spent in Irving's company was a moment in which she could bring about his downfall.

"Let me stay with you," she begged Hester, while offering up silent apologies to her entire family. "I have nothing and no one to go home for."

EDD HAD ALMOST finished writing his speech when there came another furious pounding on the door.

Hoping it was Farmer returned to face the music, he yelled, "Come in!" over the thunderous knocking and twisted around to face the idiot with a scowl.

The door flew open, and Sir Julius Vale stormed into the room. Kicking the door shut with the back of his heel, he glared around the room until he found Edd frozen with astonishment at his desk.

"Where is she?" Vale demanded.

Pulling himself together, Edd stuck the pen in its stand and rose to his feet. A twinge of unease began to curl in his stomach.

"Lucy?"

"Of course, Lucy! Unless you have trifled with any more of my sisters."

"I am sure it would be a pleasure, sir, but I would not dare. Why do you imagine Lucy is here?"

"Because she is not at the hotel or anywhere else in town. She was to join us for tea and did not."

"She is not here," Edd said, all levity vanishing. He reached for his coat. "Have you tried Miss Poole?"

"She is not with the Pooles," Vale snapped. "Nor any other of her favorite haunts, including the ice parlor."

Edd paused. For no reason, Farmer's inexplicable mad dash on Winslow's horse came back to him. "According to the doorman at the hotel, via Braithwaite, a post-chaise set off from the hotel."

Vale stared at him. "Why would Lucy be in a post-chaise?"

"Why would Farmer steal Winslow's horse and flee immediately after being freed, unless he saw something he *had* to act on?"

"Either you are insane," Vale said, opening the door and accompanying him from the room, "or you know a great deal that I do not. Either way, you are scaring me."

"I'm scaring myself," Edd admitted. "We need to go to the hotel."

"I've just *come* from the hotel!"

"Who did you see?" Edd asked urgently. "With your own eyes. Did you speak to Miss Poole?"

The door just beside them flew open, and William Cairney blocked their path, glowering. He looked terrible, his hair unbrushed, his face unshaven, his eyes shadowed and unrested. "Why do you speak of Miss Poole?" he barked.

"Because we are looking for her friend," Edd said with slightly more discretion, as he realized they were speaking far too loudly not to be overheard. "Come with us, by all means."

"What use is he?" Vale muttered, charging for the stairs.

"Miss Poole's recently dismissed betrothed," Edd murmured

back, but clearly not quietly enough.

"The shortest engagement in history," Cairney snarled behind them. "Where are we going?"

"To call on Miss Poole," Edd said, offering him the comb from his coat pocket while his mind whirled with fears and possibilities and plans, instantly discarded.

As they strode up the road, he was vaguely aware of Vale and Cairney introducing themselves to each other with incongruous civility, and Vale explaining his concern over Lucy's whereabouts. But their voices were like the vague buzzing of distant bees. He had never been so afraid in his life.

He strode into the hotel ahead of the others and straight up to the desk. "Is Mr. Irving still staying here?"

"Irving?" Vale muttered behind him in disbelief.

"Yes, sir," the clerk said at once.

Edd, not remotely comforted, nodded curtly and headed for the stairs.

"Sir, he is not here at the moment," the clerk called after him. "He went out some time ago."

It did not surprise Edd, but still the fear clawed harder at his stomach. Briefly, he contemplated breaking into Irving's room, just to be sure the weasel had not paid the clerk to lie. But that was his less likely theory. He led the way straight to Mrs. Poole's room.

"You only spoke to Mrs. Poole?" he asked, rounding suddenly on Vale. "You did not see Miss Poole, too?"

"No," Vale admitted. "I didn't see her, but Mrs. Poole maintained Lucy was not with her daughter, that she had called earlier but left."

Edd nodded and knocked on the door.

"A moment of Mrs. Poole's time, if you please," he said peremptorily to the maid who answered the door. "It is a matter of some importance and concerns Miss Poole."

Without a word, the maid opened the door wide.

"Wilkins!" exclaimed Mrs. Poole in some outrage. Clearly the maid had disobeyed orders in admitting them.

Mrs. Poole sat in a chair by the glow of the fire. Despite her fury, she did not look her usual confident self. In fact she looked sick with worry. Which did not stop her glaring with loathing at Cairney.

"*You,*" she uttered. "I wonder you dare show your face to me."

"Where is she, ma'am?" Cairney asked evenly.

"That is none of your business."

"I'm afraid it is *my* business," Vale said, with the briefest of bows. "I have every reason to believe that my sister is with your daughter. And if you do not tell me the truth, I shall have to involve the magistrate and every resource of the law to find her."

"No, no, think of the scandal," Mrs. Poole said feebly.

"Why?" Edd pounced before Vale could retort. "*You* are not, are you, ma'am? The fear in your eyes is of more than scandal. What did Irving threaten you with?"

"What *is* this about Irving?" Vale exploded.

Edd ignored him, relentlessly holding Mrs. Poole's gaze.

"Tell him, ma'am," the maid begged. "These are good gentlemen, and they're our only hope."

To Edd's horror, a tear trickled out of the old lady's eye. But she still came out fighting. "It is *your* fault!" she flung at Cairney. "If you had not seduced her away from him, this crisis would never have happened!"

"What crisis?" Edd asked, outwardly calm, while inside, he wanted to shake her. "Has Irving abducted her?"

Cairney gnashed his teeth.

"No," Mrs. Poole whispered. "She went willingly, to marry him in Scotland."

"He's only after her fortune!" Cairney burst out.

"We all know that!" Mrs. Poole snapped. "And so does she. He has some hold on her that I don't understand, and when I threatened him with the law, *he* threatened *me* not only with her ruin but a promise to hurt her physically if I spoke a word to anyone about her going. You don't understand! I am afraid he will *kill* her now I have broken my word and told you!"

She buried her face in her hands, prompting Cairney, unexpectedly, to place his hand on her shoulder in comfort while he gazed helplessly at Edd.

"So he is a blackguard," Vale said. "I am more than happy to help retrieve her from his clutches, but what the devil has this to do with my little sister?"

"Nothing." Mrs. Poole dropped her hands to look at him. "Miss Vale called only briefly. He told me she had not stayed."

"*He* told you," Cairney repeated.

"He probably meant it at the time," Edd said slowly. "But if I know Lucy, she won't have let go. That is what Farmer saw from the window—Lucy getting into the post-chaise with Irving. He's gone after them." He spun around, throwing words back over his shoulder as he strode for the door. "You did the right thing, Mrs. Poole. Lucy will look after her, and we shall look after them both. Where's your carriage, Vale?"

"In the hotel yard. Wait, Eddleston! Why the devil would Irving take Lucy on his elopement?"

"Probably because she gave him little choice. And possibly because he has no objection to doing me a bad turn by ruining Lucy's reputation."

"What does he have against you?" Cairney demanded. "Aside from the fact you can be damned annoying."

"That is a whole other story." Edd halted so suddenly that Vale walked into him. "We need respectability. We need… Mrs. Poole!" He pushed back into the room to find Mrs. Poole tying on her bonnet. He smiled at her. "Good girl. Coming for a drive?"

He was not even thinking about his words, and he doubted she was either. Certainly she did not look as outraged as she probably should. The maid threw a fine traveling cloak around her mistress's shoulders, beaming at her with encouragement, and they all trooped together out to the stable yard.

The Vale carriage was a rather fine vehicle—no doubt Sir

Julius had taken his betrothed for a pleasant drive in it earlier on. But the horses harnessed to it still looked fresh.

Vale swore beneath his breath. "The coachman! I sent him off to scour the town for Lucy—again—and he's clearly not back."

Edd threw open the door, then leapt for the coachman's box. "Who needs a coachman? All aboard, ladies and gentlemen."

As he gathered the reins and the whip, he heard Vale murmur, "I might be beginning to like that fellow."

And because Edd's fear dissipated with action, he was able to smile.

# Chapter Seventeen

L UCY COULD NOT speak alone to Hester until they stopped to change horses. And Irving had made the postilions go two stages in order to get further from Blackhaven before halting.

"Unless you mean your bride to die of starvation before you can marry her, we shall dine here," Lucy told him, as he handed her down with reluctance. "And if you are too frightened, I shall give you my word not to call for help."

Although he eyed her with considerable dislike, he made no demur. Instead, he obtained them a private parlor and ordered dinner, while the ladies managed to escape to the cloakroom alone together.

"I understand why you are doing this," Lucy said as soon as she had ascertained there was no one else within earshot. "But you would not choose him if you truly knew what kind of man he is."

"That is my decision, not yours," Hester said wearily.

"Exactly," Lucy said. "And you have to make the right one in full knowledge of the circumstances. Promise me only that you will not stop me provoking him? Except to save my life."

"Lucy, don't be so dramatic," Hester protested. "There are no lives at risk here. Only reputations, and since you will not let me send you back—"

"Yes, yes, I know it is my own fault," Lucy interrupted. "But I also know things you do not, from Lord Eddleston. And we should both hear Irving's view of them."

Hester shook her head but argued no further. Although Lucy watched her quite closely for signs of ill health, her malaise seemed to be entirely of the spirit. So they returned to the private parlor together to find the table set and Irving pouring himself a generous glass of claret.

"Wine, ladies?" he offered, presumably at Hester's expense.

Hester shook her head, and Lucy declined civilly. He did not hold either of their chairs for them, which might have been a relief but still exposed his disrespect for Hester. Was this how he had broken the spirit of Lord Eddleston's sister? By constant neglect and disparagement until she felt worthless and unloved?

With shock, Lucy realized she still believed Eddleston about his sister.

Why?

She disbelieved everything else he had said to her! Or did she? Was she just being angry and childish because she had not guessed Tyler was the earl? And because her idea of the wealthy Eddleston did not fit with her romantic view of the penniless radical Tyler, traveling the world for adventure and the righting of wrongs? What was it she had loved? An illusion? Or was she now refusing to see the reality?

She sipped the small beer from the glass in front of her. She could only rule out the possibility of Irving poisoning Hester until they were married, with the proof in his hands. And then he would gain full control of Hester. And her child, his gateway to wealth for the rest of his life.

"Satisfy my curiosity," she said to him. "If you would be so good."

He smiled thinly. "I might, if your question is remotely sensible."

"Why have you agreed to take me with you on your elopement?"

"I have not yet decided that I will. I shall probably leave you here."

She studied him, and let a faint smile curve her lips. "You could, but I don't believe you will. If you were going to, you would have pushed me *away* from the chaise in Blackhaven, not pulled me in."

If she surprised him, he gave no sign, merely began to eat his soup. Hester served Lucy and herself, ladling only a tiny amount into her own dish.

"Are you imagining this is some kind of revenge on Lord Eddleston?" Lucy asked. "Because I very much doubt that he will notice I have gone."

"I don't believe that for a moment," Irving replied. "But even if it were true, I am sure it won't be long before your numerous large and imposing brothers inform him of the fact. Clandestine assignations are never wise. Are they, Hester?"

"No," Hester agreed. She sipped the soup from her spoon, then laid it down.

Lucy, more furious at the insult to Hester than anything else, had to force herself to keep to the plan.

"You don't like each other, you and Eddleston," she said. "And yet you are brothers-in-law, are you not?"

"My beloved first wife was his sister," Irving said.

"Beloved?" Lucy repeated in surprise. "I did not know you loved her."

"Of course I did. Whatever Eddleston might have told you."

"Why would he tell me anything?"

Irving shrugged, still very much in command of the situation. "Because he never liked me. He was jealous of his sister's affection for me."

"Are you sure you were not jealous of her affection for him?"

"Don't be ridiculous," he scoffed. "He was a mere child when she died."

"So you are not a jealous man? You will not be jealous, for example, of Hester's friendship with me? Or with her other friends? Mr. Cairney, perhaps. And Lord Eddleston."

"Neither of those cretins will be welcome in my house," Irving snapped.

"Whose house?" Lucy taunted him.

His smile was not remotely hesitant. "Mine, when I am Hester's husband."

The admission hurt nobody, since everyone, including Hester, knew he was marrying her for her fortune.

"Then you will forbid Hester's friends from calling on her?" Lucy said with entirely false astonishment.

"Unsuitable friends, of course. It is a husband's duty."

"What of her mother?" Lucy asked. "Will she be invited?"

"No," Irving said with unconcealed relish.

Hester set down her cup.

"No, of course not," Lucy said. "Nor the rest of the family, I suspect. That is what you did to Lady Anne, is it not? Separated her from her family while you spent her money and made her ill."

Malevolence flashed in his eyes, but still he was not worried.

Hester said flatly, "It will not arise in our marriage. My mother will live with us if she chooses. If she does not so choose, she will visit whenever she wishes."

"She will *not* choose," Irving stated. "And neither will you."

"How will you make Hester obey?" Lucy asked. "Take her to court? Will that not make you look weak and foolish beyond recovery? The *ton* will laugh at you."

"Did they laugh at me when I was married to Anne Gore?" he retorted.

"Poor Lady Anne. Do you plan to keep Hester obedient in the same way?"

Irving threw down his spoon and reached for his wine. "She is here, isn't she?" He tipped half the glass down his throat.

"And you think it will work on Hester for the rest of her life?" Lucy said dubiously. "Hester is a lady of considerable spirit."

"Are you, Hester?" Irving mocked. He finished his glass and poured himself some more wine.

Hester pushed her soup bowl away. "I have agreed to marry

you. I have not agreed to cut my family or my friends."

Irving met her gaze. "I have finished my soup. I'll have whatever is edible in the next dish now."

Without a word, Hester rose and removed the soup tureen to the worn sideboard. She took the cover from the next dish, while Lucy removed the soup plates. Hester served some delicious-smelling stew to Irving before sitting and serving herself and Lucy.

"You see what a delightful wife she will make me," Irving said.

"But she will still invite her mother to live with you," Lucy argued.

"No," Irving said, clearly amused, "she will not."

Lucy allowed herself to sound worried. "I don't really see how you would stop her."

"But Hester sees. Don't you, Hester?"

Hester laid down her knife and fork. "I shall not inflict my mother's company on you more than is necessary. I know she is difficult. We can set her up in a separate wing of the house or let her live in a different establishment. But I shall not cut her off."

"You see?" Lucy said with obvious delight. "Spirited!"

"My sainted Anne was spirited too," Irving said with his first hint of irritation.

"Then how did you make her obey? Neglect her, deprive her of every courtesy that was her due? Insult her to her face and before your servants and your friends? Show her how mean you could be to her little brother?"

Irving laughed. More to the point, Hester was staring at him. She had known and accepted that he was a bully—there had probably been threats to keep Mrs. Poole quiet about the elopement until it was too late. But giving in once to a bully, because it suited your own needs at the time, was not the same as facing a lifetime of cruel repression, and Hester, clearly, was beginning to suspect it.

"Don't look at me like that," Irving said soothingly. "I am not a monster. You shall have everything you want, provided you are an obedient wife. And you will swear to be so tomorrow before God. If the barbaric Scottish rites even include God. I anticipate another very happy marriage."

"I doubt Lady Anne was happy," Lucy remarked, playing with a forkful of beef in her stew. "But I expect you kept her compliant with laudanum."

"On the orders of a physician. For her nerves. I do hope you do not suffer from your nerves, Hester."

"I do not." Hester took a deep breath. "Nor do I normally suffer from idiocy. Have I made a mistake in agreeing to marry you, Harold?"

He laughed. "My dear, your mistake was made much earlier than that. At least three months earlier, from what you told me. Now you need me to rectify the matter."

"Nonsense," Lucy said. "She may need a husband, but frankly, there is no shortage of fortune hunters. There is, however, a shortage of fortunes."

Irving frowned at her impatiently.

Lucy gave him her most dazzling smile. "You need her more than she needs you. Shall we go, Hester?"

Hester half rose to her feet, and Lucy almost panicked that it was too soon. She had not yet learned everything she needed to.

"Yes, do let us proceed, Hester," Irving said at once, rising and going quickly to Hester's side. Only by the jerkiness of his movements did he betray his anger. "But let us leave this foul-mouthed little trollop, whom I find entirely inappropriate company." He took Hester's hand as though assisting her the rest of the way to her feet.

Hester shook him off. "No. This has gone far enough. I have made a mistake, and I am returning to Blackhaven with Miss Vale. It would be best if you found another means of transport to wherever you wish to go."

"Hester, Hester, no it would not," Irving said silkily while his face turned ugly. He leaned closer, digging his fingers hard into

Hester's arm while he began to whisper into her ear.

Lucy could not hear the words, but she saw her friend's face whiten. "Are you whispering the same words you said to Lady Anne?" she asked, jumping to her feet. "Threatening her with violence? Did you strike Anne, too?"

"Many times," Irving said without even looking at her. "She learned as quickly as I know Hester will to obey me. It is a husband's duty to beat his wife into obedience, you know. The law says so."

"Does it say you can drive her to suicide, too?"

"Suicide is a crime. Even the Gores were not foolish enough to accuse her of that."

"No, but then, you could not wait, could you? You had spent her money, so now that she was no use to you, you helped her on her way, didn't you? An overdose of laudanum?"

"Very simple to achieve," he sneered.

"You won't find Hester so easy to persuade. She would never swallow it."

Irving laughed.

"Afraid of him yet?" Lucy asked Hester.

"No," Hester said between her teeth.

"You see? How on earth did you persuade poor Anne to swallow her medicine?"

"I didn't," Irving said, smiling viciously down into Hester's face. "I forced it down her throat and held her nose. You see, my dearest wife, I am stronger, and the law is on my side. You will always obey me, just as Anne—"

Having heard all she needed, Lucy, temporarily ignored, jumped up onto the nearest chair, seized the large stew bowl, and brought it crashing down on Irving's head.

She let it go and jumped down, reaching for the soup tureen on the sideboard. Hester used the moment to drag herself out of his suddenly loosened hold. Irving's face bore an expression of surprised incomprehension, just for a moment, before he slid to the floor.

Unwilling to release the soup tureen just yet, Lucy tucked it under her arm and slid her free hand into Hester's. "Is he dead?"

Hester swallowed, regarding the beef and carrot sliding down his hair and cheek. He was half propped up by the table leg. "I don't think so. Which is a pity, in some ways."

"Let's go before he wakes up."

Only when Hester had gathered their cloaks and hats did Lucy set down the tureen. At the last moment, she knelt and extracted the purse from Irving's pocket. She presented it to Hester, who gave a shaky breath of laughter. Then they left the room.

Hester gave a handful of coins to the innkeeper on their way out, and he bowed low.

"Our friend is asleep," Lucy said. "Pray, don't disturb him. In fact…best lock him in until he sleeps it off." She lowered her voice. "Too much claret, you know. The man cannot hold his wine. Goodbye!"

Hysteria was threatening by the time they all but fell out the door together. The chaise and fresh horses were waiting, and at the sight of them, the postilions hurried to their horses.

"A change of plan," Hester told them. "Be so good as to return to Blackhaven."

The nearest postilion scratched his head. "Is that what the gentleman wants to do?"

"The gentleman will not be accompanying us."

"I'd best speak to him, then."

Hester drew herself up. "My good man, are you failing to understand my simple instructions?"

"No, ma'am, I understand perfectly, but it was the gentleman who instructed us and who—"

"I do not wish to be obliged," Hester interrupted, "to write letters of complaint to your employers."

The postilions looked at each other in dismay.

"You will be paid for the whole journey, as agreed," Lucy added, by way of incentive.

The first postilion said, "I'll just step into the inn and clear it with the gentleman—"

"What's the trouble here, then?" asked a different voice entirely.

Lucy swung around—and beheld Luke Farmer, dressed more smartly than she had ever seen him. A lifetime ago, he had been going to claim his innocence with Mr. Winslow. "Luke? What…?"

"Where is he?" Farmer asked grimly.

"Irving? In there. Miss Poole and I are going home to Blackhaven, only the postilions seem to think they can only take orders from other men."

"Then I'd better do," Farmer said, turning a suddenly fearsome gaze on the postilions. "I'm Sergeant Farmer. And for your information, that so-called gentleman in there is under arrest. Flim-flam man. And these ladies require to be returned to their families as soon as possible. If you ain't up to the job, I'll find someone who is."

"No, no, happy to oblige," the first postilion insisted.

"Good. Where are the outriders?"

The postilions began to look hunted. "He never hired no outriders."

"Well, it'll be dark before we get back to Blackhaven, and there are highwaymen about."

"*Really?*" Lucy marveled.

"No need to worry, miss," Farmer said. "I'll act as your outrider. Still got my trusty firearm here." He opened the chaise door and let down the steps, offering his hand to help the ladies inside. "Mount up, men!" he flung at the postilions.

Lucy didn't know whether to be furious or grateful that they obeyed him at once.

# Chapter Eighteen

E DD WAS SLIGHTLY worried at the first posting house, where they stopped to change horses, to discover that the ostlers had seen no post-chaise carrying a man of Irving's description and two young ladies.

He had been so sure that Irving would make for the border, and that Lucy and Hester were with him. What if he was wrong? What if he was wasting precious time on an unforgivably foolish wild goose chase? Mrs. Poole believed Irving was taking Hester to Scotland to be married, but he could have lied and fooled them all. God knew what he intended, especially if Lucy was with them, spoiling his plans…

He decided to go on to the next stage at least. And since it would be dark before then—it was already dusk—he lit the outside lanterns.

Vale stuck his head out of the window. "Do you know the road well enough to drive in the dark?"

"Soon find out," Edd said, and climbed back on the box.

Five minutes later, he saw the lights of another vehicle approaching at speed. Not quite reckless enough to risk overturning Vale's carriage, Edd slowed the horses. He could make out that the other vehicle was a hired post-chaise and four, with two postilions and what looked like a solitary outrider ahead of it.

Rather to his surprise, the outrider slowed, forcing the other horses to do so, while the man grinned at him like an old friend.

Edd pulled up his horses. "Farmer?"

"Very glad to see you, sir. Got the ladies safe and sound. They dealt with his nibs at the posting inn back there and are ready to come home."

*Thank God.* Relief poured off him in waves.

"Well done, Farmer," he said shakily. "I definitely owe you."

Farmer grimaced. "I might need to take you up on it. Can you turn that coach?"

"We'll be right behind you," Edd said.

It went against the grain, knowing she was in there, to let it go past without a word, but surely it was best both ladies return to Blackhaven without further delay. Besides, he doubted she would be pleased to see him at this precise point. Or any point.

He watched Farmer and the chaise pass Vale's carriage and pick up speed, then dismounted, told the others the good news, and got Vale to help him turn the horses and carriages around.

They caught up with the chaise within a mile.

HAROLD WOKE TO cold, slimy wetness and an acute pain in his head. He stared groggily down at his lap, where a perfectly round pool of gravy seemed to have formed, with pieces of what looked like onion, beef, and carrot poking out.

"What the—" He sat up and let out a yell as his sore head bumped against the table.

He was sitting partially under the table, his back against a stout leg, and was covered in stew from his hair to his thighs.

Dear God, one of them had hit him on the head with the stew bowl. It had to have been Lucy Vale—no true lady would behave in such a way, and he'd always known there must be bad blood in her—for he had been holding Hester at the time, bending her to his will, just as he had always bent Anne.

Cautiously, he dragged himself out from under the edge of the table, which he used to help him to his feet. Both women had gone. And he had a lump on his head the size of an egg.

*She will pay for that, too,* he thought viciously. Both of them would pay. Staggering to the window, he peered out into the yard. Dusk was falling. There was no sign of the post-chaise. But perhaps it was just out of sight at the front of the house. He might still be in time.

Wincing, he strode across the room and yanked at the door. Nothing happened. His ears began to sing with fury and his head throbbed more violently. They had locked him in!

He crashed his fists against the door. "Ho there! Unlock this damned door!"

It took five minutes of knocking and shouting to elicit more than whispering on the other side of the door. Then a male voice said cautiously, "Sir? Perhaps you should just sit in the armchair and have a little nap."

"Nap?" Harold exploded. "My good man, I am injured! Assaulted! I need medical attention!" The last words were barely out of his mouth when he regretted them.

"I'll just send for the doctor, then, sir. He'll be with you shortly."

"No, no, wait!" Harold said hastily, reduced to pleading. "One moment, please. Are you the innkeeper?"

"Yes, sir, I am."

"The two ladies who arrived with me—you must stop them leaving the inn… If you would be so good," he added between his teeth.

"I can't do that, sir. The ladies have gone already. Took the post-chaise. They explained as how you'd had a little too much libation and needed to sleep…"

"Do I sound drunk to you!" Harold shouted furiously through the still-locked door.

"No, sir," the innkeeper admitted. "But you do sound very angry."

Desperately, Harold bit down on his tongue and counted to ten. "You would be angry too had two harpies thrown a bowl of stew at you and knocked you unconscious."

A stifled giggle came from the other side of the door, and the innkeeper's voice was not quite steady as he said, "Well, perhaps I ought to let you out, sir. But I must ask for your word not to take your anger out on my staff."

"I got another bowl of stew here," said a merry female voice, followed by a giggle as, presumably, she was sent away.

Harold suspected half the inn had been listening in and laughing at his misfortune. Well, there was nothing he could do about that. Except seize the cloths with which the hot dishes had been brought in and hastily wipe down his head, face, and front.

He made a grab for his traveling cloak just as the key turned in the lock and the innkeeper entered somewhat warily.

"How long ago did they leave?" Harold barked, feeling in his pocket for his purse.

"About a quarter hour ago, maybe."

"I shall need a fast horse," Harold said, but his fingers remained empty and another realization hit him. "Damn them, they stole my purse!"

"I don't know nothing about that, sir, but the ladies paid the shot. Handsomely, as it happens."

Harold eyed him threateningly. "Handsomely enough to pay for the hire of a horse?"

"Not quite, sir. And definitely not when I got no guarantees the animal will come back."

Harold had never wanted to gnash his teeth before. "I am happy to give you my direction." A happy thought came to him. "Lord Eddleston, care of the King's Head in Blackhaven."

IT WAS ALMOST midnight when the chaise finally came to a halt outside the front door of the Blackhaven Hotel. Lucy and Hester had spent most of the time discussing what to do about Irving.

"He won't have the gall to come back to Blackhaven," Hester had said. "My concern is to see justice done, for what he tried to do to me, and for what he clearly already did to the poor lady who was married to him."

"He can't be allowed to go on," Lucy agreed. "But I think we can leave it to Lord Eddleston now. There will be no need to drag your name into it."

Hester cast her a sardonic look. "I think my reputation is unsalvageable, don't you? I don't much care whether it happens now or in a couple of months, when my pregnancy begins to show."

"Hester, you don't have to stay here! Go to the country. Go abroad. Your baby can be adopted, cared for—"

"I know," Hester said, lying back against the squabs, her forearm over her eyes, probably to hide the tears. "It is time I thought differently. I have been depending too much on men, whether good men like Mr. Cairney, or bad men like Mr. Irving, whom I so foolishly thought I could manipulate."

"Whatever you decide, I can come with you," Lucy said recklessly.

But Hester, clearly, was too emotionally and physically exhausted to make plans tonight.

When the carriage stopped, Farmer was there to open the door and let down the steps. He handed her out, and then Hester. While Hester paid the postilions, Lucy moved toward the door and realized the hotel was unusually busy and very brightly lit for so late in the evening. She wondered uneasily if her brothers were inside, causing trouble on her behalf. Julius at least would have been worried sick when she had not even appeared for tea with Antonia. Too late, she realized she should have retained the post-chaise and got it to take her up to Black Hill.

"We can send a messenger to your family," Hester said, taking her arm and drawing her to the front door, where two gentlemen in evening dress stood aside to let the ladies enter first.

"No need," Farmer said, following. "I'll just see you inside and then ride up to Black Hill."

"Are you sure?" Lucy said to him. "You must be exhausted."

Farmer grinned. "Haven't had so much fun since Spain."

"What in the world is going on?" Lucy exclaimed. For the foyer was full of milling, well-dressed gentlemen and extremely glamorous ladies, thronging to and from the back of the building, where double doors opened to reveal a hall blazing with light and noise and people.

"Gaming club night, miss," the doorman said. "Here's Ralph to show you to the staircase. The noise shouldn't trouble you above stairs."

The boy in livery bowed and walked with them protectively to the foot of the stairs. Farmer followed, looking suspiciously about him. Lucy's insatiable curiosity caused her to look once more toward the double doors, through which emerged a handsome young man with a very familiar lady on his arm. The lady was elegantly, yet daringly, dressed in a low-cut gown that displayed her lovely figure to perfection, and she was laughing up at her escort with just a shade too much boldness.

Lucy gripped the banister as her jaw dropped. "Felicia?"

Her sister's head snapped around. "Lucy? Oh, the *devil!*"

Lucy stepped back from the staircase. Hester looked unsure whether she should remain with her or not. Felicia, abandoning her escort, stalked straight to Lucy. "What on earth are you doing here at this hour?"

"I might ask the same of you," Lucy replied in the same accusatory tone, even though the cases were quite different. Felicia, as a widow, had much more latitude in Society than an unmarried girl.

To Lucy's surprise, color seeped into her sister's face. "Where is Julius?" Felicia demanded.

"Here I am," came Julius's unmistakable voice, which had carried across ship's decks in storms and had no difficulty whatsoever penetrating the racket from the back room. Of course, it drew rather more attention than anyone wanted, but at least it made Felicia relax. "Our excursion was somewhat delayed by an accident. But I had forgotten it was the gaming club night, or we would not have allowed the young ladies to enter ahead of us. Felicia," he greeted his other sister without expression. "Very stylish."

As he moved aside, Lucy was stunned to see Mrs. Poole on the arm of William Cairney. And then Tyler—*Eddleston*—seemed to materialize among them, almost beside her.

"No surprise," he warned beneath his breath. "None at all."

Lucy could only smile. She did not even know why, but she seemed incapable of any other movement.

"I'm tired, Hester," Mrs. Poole announced. "Let us go up and allow Sir Julius and Miss Vale to get home at last."

The considerable attention they had garnered from those milling around had already dissipated. There was clearly nothing for them to speculate or even gossip about. The incomprehensible presence of Julius and Mrs. Poole had saved the day.

Until a disheveled figure pushed past the doorman and charged across the foyer.

Lucy's blood ran cold. After all that, it seemed scandal would catch them up anyway.

"Halt this instant!" Harold Irving commanded. "Where is the magistrate fellow? I wish to report a theft and an assault!"

"Another one?" Mr. Winslow, clearly bored, strolled over from the direction of the gaming room.

Harold raised a shaking hand, one finger already pointing. Cairney stepped in front of Hester. Eddleston and Julius already separated Lucy from him, but neither was much protection against his tongue.

"Anyway," Farmer said aggressively, "*you* are under arrest!"

It was what had made the postilions obey him, and it probably seemed a good idea to use the ploy again. But as soon as he spoke, Lucy knew he had played right into Irving's hands.

Irving relaxed visibly and smiled, gloating like a miser who had dropped a farthing and found a guinea. "Under arrest?" he repeated gently. "For what?"

There was nothing Farmer could say, not in this company, with so many avidly listening ears. Irving's abducting Hester and Lucy would only damage them, especially when Julius had already announced they had all been on an excursion together.

And then a blinding light flashed in Lucy's brain. She stepped between Eddleston and Julius without looking at them. "For the murder of your wife, Lady Anne, which you admitted before witnesses. Mr. Winslow, do you have a constable nearby?"

Everyone else was staring at her. But Winslow nodded. "I do," he said dryly. "I meant to arrest *him*"—he jerked a thumb at Farmer—"but Mr. Irving will do just as well."

Irving began to stammer. "Outrageous slander. You have no witnesses that dare testify to such lies."

"Oh, she does," Hester said from the stairs.

"You? Who eloped to be my wife?"

"Oh please, Harold," Eddleston said wearily. "With her mother? And Miss Vale and her brother? To say nothing of her betrothed! I'm happy not to wait for the constable."

Eddleston advanced with clear intent. Irving stared at him, but whatever he saw in his enemy's eyes clearly convinced him he was in genuine and highly dangerous trouble.

He spun on his heel and bolted.

Eddleston flew after him, but he only got halfway across the room before Julius and Cairney grabbed an arm each and hauled him to a straining standstill.

"Enough, my lord," Winslow said curtly. "I do not want a murder committed in this town. And besides," he added with a flash of a smile, "he has nowhere to go."

Eddleston stopped straining, and warily, Julius and Cairney let him go.

"Fellow's insane," Julius remarked, though whether he referred to Irving or Eddleston was unclear to Lucy. Or to

Eddleston, judging by the wry smile that flickered across his lips.

Cairney straightened his cuffs. "Now," he said. "Might I have peace to escort my betrothed and her mother to their room?" With commendable ease of manner, he strolled back to the staircase and offered Mrs. Poole his arm.

"Lucy?" Julius said amiably. "Felicia? Shall we go?"

As Lucy crossed the hall toward Julius and everyone else went back to their talking, drinking, and gambling, Eddleston looked up from his deep contemplation of his own mud-splashed boots. His intense gaze locked with hers.

"Did he?" he asked.

"Admit it? Oh yes." She took Julius's arm blindly.

At the last moment, Eddleston remembered to bow, and then she was past him. She didn't know why she wanted to cry.

"THANK YOU FOR that," Hester said at the door to her sitting room. Her voice felt a little hoarse. "For calling me your betrothed in public. You know I shall not hold you to it, but I appreciate the help. I am so sorry for everything."

Cairney drew in his breath. "It is I who am sorry," he blurted. "I did not even listen. I was so concerned for my own hurt I did not even consider what you must be suffering."

She thrust out her hand impulsively, and he seized it, drawing nearer to speak so low that no one else could have heard, even her mother waiting impatiently inside.

"Forgive me, Hester. I love you. I didn't even realize how much until I thought of you in the power of that blackguard."

"And I love you," Hester whispered, as tears came to her eyes. "But I know I come with too much—"

"I will love the child as my own, because it is yours. Whoever the father was, he will not come between us. Tomorrow, we shall talk."

At last, it seemed, the world was coming right for her, for her family, and even for Will Cairney.

She touched his hair. "We will," she promised, smiling, then fled inside to her mother and closed the door.

She and her mother stared at each other.

"What a day," Hester said, and began to laugh.

"HOW DID YOU know?" Lucy asked when she and Julius were alone in the coach, driving at last to Black Hill. Felicia, clearly exerting her independence, had chosen to stay and enjoy the rest of her evening.

"I spoke to Eddleston," Julius said.

Lucy frowned. "How did *he* know?"

"I'm not sure. He took a couple of bizarre pieces of information, linked them with a third, and somehow solved the puzzle."

That sounded like Eddleston. Well, like Tyler. She rubbed her forehead. "But what made you go to him in the first place? I'd already told you I did not want to marry him."

"And I had a good idea why. When you failed to turn up for tea, Antonia and I scoured the town for you, without success. Then Antonia went back to her room in case you were there, and I barged in on Eddleston, convinced by then that either he was hiding you or you were up to something that involved him. Apparently, a post-chaise had been seen leaving the hotel around the same time that Luke Farmer took off from his hearing with Winslow—on Winslow's own horse."

Lucy let out a surprised snort of laughter.

"Yes, it affected Eddleston much the same way. Anyway, we went and interrogated Mrs. Poole. Well, he interrogated her. I had just accepted everything she had previously told me. I began to get the measure of the inestimable Mr. Irving, though

Eddleston seemed already to know it. He certainly drove the carriage as if all the fiends of hell were after us."

"*Eddleston* drove the coach?"

"We had no time to waste. But it seems Farmer rescued you first."

"Well, he was undeniably useful in forcing the stupid postilions to bring us back to Blackhaven without Irving, but actually, we rescued ourselves."

Julius's eyes bored into hers. "How did you do that?"

"By riling him. Which served the double purpose of convincing Hester what sort of a monster he was, and forcing him to threaten Hester into submission. Which is when I hit him with the stew pot."

Julius's lips twitched, and then he began to laugh, which made Lucy laugh too, only there were too many tears in her tightened throat and she ended by sobbing helplessly in her brother's arms.

# Chapter Nineteen

THE MORNING BROUGHT Antonia and her son for breakfast. Felicia had apparently taken her the news that Lucy was found. She did not ask questions, though no doubt Julius would tell her the story of the stew, but gave Lucy a smile of understanding and friendship. Lucy looked forward to the day they would be sisters.

The twins, of course, were not so reticent, though at least they were distracted by the presence of young Edward, whom they took away with them after breakfast. Lucy claimed to have gardening duties, and left Julius and Antonia alone together.

The weather was not promising, but Lucy donned her oldest dress and, with spade and shears, set to digging up the substantial weeds and thorns from the untamed side of the formal garden. It was hard work, but she needed it to release her excessive energy and to prevent her thinking of Lord Eddleston.

He had come to rescue her and Hester, in alliance with Julius and Mr. Cairney. She hoped Mr. Cairney would see past Hester's mistake and marry her anyway, but there were no guarantees. Gentlemen were so hypocritical over their wives' behavior. Nick Maitland, for example, would never have tolerated infidelity in Felicia.

*Who was that man she was with last night? I'm sure I know him.* The thought distracted her, but only for a moment before

Eddleston intruded again. Had he really looked proud of her? There had certainly been deep and painful gratitude in his eyes when she accused Irving of Lady Anne's murder. A glow that even she was at a loss to account for. Surprise because she had remembered? Pleasure that she had done this for him?

And she had. Yes, she had needed Hester to know Irving's true nature and walk away, but even after that, she had continued pressing, and she had done it for Tyler because his face when he spoke of his sister still haunted her.

Drat the man—he haunted her anyway. She had never liked anyone as much, never had such fun with anyone, never melted so sweetly as she did into his kiss. She had sensed a soul mate, and that was why his betrayal hurt so badly.

He had made her believe all sorts of things that were not true, about his feelings for her, about their future together. Under the skin, he was little different from Felicia's cheating husband, making women believe whatever he wanted them to.

*Is he?* No one had ever called the Earl of Eddleston a rake. Felicia would have known about such a reputation. Probably Julius, too. And definitely the twins! She smiled in spite of herself and realized it was beginning to rain.

Ignoring it, she bent and hauled on a weed until it came out by the root. She flung it in the barrow and bent to get the smaller grasses beneath. As she hauled out yards of bindweed, the few spots of rain turned into a proper shower, and then something a bit more torrential, but she didn't stop. She was making quite a bit of progress. It would be pleasant for Antonia, she thought, to move into a house with an entire formal garden rather than the mere half that they had now. It looked a bit ridiculous, in fact.

Besides, she was sure the rain would go away soon. By the time it did, water rolled off her hair and face as she worked, and she was soaked to the skin. She didn't feel cold, though, as she worked on. She was even beginning to dry out when she felt the first spots of a renewed shower and heard the sounds of a carriage coming up the drive.

She straightened to regard it, pushing her damp hair off her face. It was a hired carriage from the town, such as waited outside the hotel. Surely it was not Felicia coming home at this hour!

Certainly, Felicia had not been at breakfast. Lucy hoped her sister had not done anything she would regret…

Instead of going on to the house, the coachman pulled his horse to a standstill in the drive and a single occupant alighted—a tall, lean gentleman in perfect morning dress consisting of buff pantaloons, dark blue coat, white necktie, and high-crowned beaver hat.

Her heart lurched. *Surely that is…*

The carriage rumbled on toward the house. The passenger began to walk in Lucy's direction, and God help her, it *was* Lord Eddleston. She could tell by the way he walked, all quick, hurried, quite unconscious grace. In a panic, she pretended not to see him, and bent to throw the pile of weeds at her feet into the barrow. A large spot of rain landed on the back of her head.

"Good morning," he said behind her, forcing her to stop and straighten. He had taken off his hat and looked very young and handsome and uncertain.

She affected surprise. "What are you doing here?"

He gestured to his perfectly tailored clothing. "Making a morning call."

"I'm sure John will find—"

"To see you," he interrupted.

Too late, she remembered the state of her sodden person, her damp, tangled hair falling from its pins, her ancient, mud-spattered gown with bits of bindweed sticking to it. She flushed, unable to think of anything to say.

"Shall we go inside?" he suggested. "I think it is about to rain. Again."

"I am not dressed for callers," she replied with a tilt of her chin. "But Julius and Antonia are around somewhere. And your friends, the twins."

"Not sure they are talking to me either," he said. He offered his arm. "Shall we?"

She gazed at his arm with curious helplessness and could only shake her head.

"Lucy," he said softly. "Don't hate me for one mistake. Be honest, would you not have done the same?"

She glared at him. "What, lied my way into someone's…good graces?" She had almost said *affections*, but it would be total folly to admit that.

"No," he said. "If you had been given the opportunity to meet me, observe me, without my knowing who you were, would you not have taken it? To find out what sort of a man I was without my being on my best betrothed behavior? To see if we could be friends or not without all the formality and awkwardness our first meeting would have entailed? Where we didn't have to look each other up and down as though we were inspecting suitable horses?"

Annoyingly, a snort of laughter escaped her. She covered it with a cough, but he wasn't fooled. His eyes gleamed and her heart ached.

"I thought you *were* Tyler," she got out.

"I am. I might not be a very good peer, but I'm an excellent troublemaker. So are you." The smile faded in his eyes. "Thank you for Irving. For believing me about Anne, at least."

She swung away from him. There was a positive patter of rain on her head now. "I wanted to believe everything. Oh, why did you come, Tyler?"

She didn't mean to use that name, but it slipped out and he didn't seem to mind. Though he didn't touch her, he moved around to stand facing her once more.

He didn't seem to notice the rain either. "I came to see if you would let me speak to your brother."

Her lips parted in shock. He could not mean what she was imagining. "You may speak to whomever you please," she got out. "It is nothing to me."

"Isn't it?" he said softly. His gloved hand game up, catching a raindrop on her cheek with one finger. "Just a little? I tried to court you on my own terms, and it didn't work out too well. I am happy to do it correctly now, if it will help."

"Help what?" she threw at him. "Help whom?"

"Me," he admitted. "And you. I do love you, Lucy Vale, and I wish you would love me."

Fresh shock held her paralyzed an instant too long. He bent his head, and his mouth found hers. She wanted to pound his shoulders until he freed her and then stalk away with her pride intact. She wanted to melt into his arms and give in to the undeniable sweetness. Conflicting emotions overwhelmed her, and her mouth opened on a sob.

He took advantage, immediately deepening the kiss, but then so did she, throwing her arms around his neck and kissing him back with all her passion, all her anger, all her loss and desperate love. Rain and tears trickled over their faces, their lips, and even that was part of the joy.

It was he who gentled the kiss, whispering against her mouth, "No deceit, no tricks, only love. It's all I have, all I will ever have."

She drew back a mere inch. "And when you kissed me before?"

"Love."

"I am afraid to believe you."

"Why?" he asked.

"Because I want to, too much." She stood on tiptoe to kiss him again, and the rain began to pelt down harder.

With a breath of laughter, he broke free and took her hand, beginning to run toward the house for shelter.

But Lucy didn't want to be in the house with other people—she wanted to be alone with *him*, to explore this heady mixture of emotion, need, and knowledge. It was instinct that made her pull him away in the other direction, toward the old summer house instead. But as they ran, she began to understand, and laughed with sheer gladness.

He threw open the door, casting his arm around her shoulders to tug her inside.

"You are soaking wet!" he exclaimed.

"So are you." She pushed the door shut behind them, shot the bolt home, and reached for the buttons of his coat. "You had better take this off."

He stood still, gazing down at her as she unbuttoned the coat, and then he shrugged it off into her hands. She hung it on the back of a chair, while he looked around their shelter. Roderick and Aubrey had repaired the roof in the spring, so it no longer leaked. Delilah had found some furniture in the attic to clean and place here—a settle, a round table and two chairs, together with an array of Felicia's cushions and others Lucy had found in cupboards at Black Hill. They were still waiting for summer weather in which to enjoy the fruits of their labor. But it worked as a shelter, too.

Lucy came back to him and began on his waistcoat buttons. He caught her hands.

"What are you about?" he asked softly. "You are much wetter than I am."

"I know." She held his gaze, feeling her heart pound and her stomach twist with nerves and desire. "You may undress me, if you like."

He did not move, though his eyes darkened. "Lucy Vale, are you seducing me?" he asked softly.

"Could I?"

He swallowed. "No," he said with patent untruth. "Not as long as I remember I am a gentleman."

"Would it help if I said you are quite right? That I probably would have done exactly the same as you if I had had the opportunity to meet you without being known?"

"It helps something."

"If I said I love you?"

His eyes closed. "If you meant it."

She slipped her hands free of his to slide them over his shoulder and tuck herself against him. "I mean it, Tyler," she whispered into his neck. "I love you. I have always loved you, from the moment that silly hat landed on your head at the assembly ball—*Tyler!*" Her exclamation almost squeaked out as he wrapped his arms around her and spun her around, and then, as she slipped to the floor and she felt the hardness of his desire, his mouth took hers in a kiss of such tenderness that she was enchanted all over again.

It went on a long time, exploring and loving, growing deeper and more passionate, while his hands moved over the curves of her breasts and waist and hips, light and achingly gentle.

"Will you let me speak to your brother?" he asked, just a little breathlessly. "Will you marry me?"

"I'll marry you whether you speak to my brother or not."

This time he smiled as he kissed her, and his fingers were busy at the back of her gown, caressing the damp, sensitive flesh of her back and shoulders as he unfastened everything, swept it to the floor, and lifted her naked in his arms.

With his elbows and feet, he nudged all the cushions to the floor and laid her among their softness, his caresses now gloriously intimate, creating a havoc of pleasure and desire until she seemed to be throbbing with it.

Although she did not remember removing it, his waistcoat was gone. Now he paused to drag his shirt off over his head. She marveled at the smooth heat of his skin beneath her fingers, her lips. She arched her body against him, gasping as he kissed her breasts and stroked her hip and thigh.

She almost sobbed when his fingers slid between her legs, understanding at last that here was the core of her desire. He knew exactly how to assuage it, making her gasp and moan at the myriad pleasures he drew from her body, until she cried out with astonished wonder as her whole being seemed to shatter with bliss.

"There, my love," he whispered into her mouth. "That is enough for now…"

She gasped, her nerves still convulsing with delight. "No, it is not," she said clearly. Now she understood why he still wore his pantaloons, and she could not allow it. "I want everything, Tyler. I want *you*."

Something that wasn't quite a laugh broke from him. "God help me, I hoped you would say that."

He sat up to wrench open his buttons and kick off the rest of his garments, and then, allowing her only an intriguing glimpse of his astonishing male organ, he covered her with his whole, naked body. Any doubts she might have had vanished as he nudged against the sensitive places between her legs, which were still tingling with delight and yet greedy for more.

He buried his fingers in her hair and kissed her mouth as he began to enter her body with slow, sensual strokes that banished initial discomfort and reignited the fire within her. She had not thought she could know more joy this way, but she did. She did.

IT STRUCK EDDLESTON, as he lay in Lucy's arms, still stunned with the bliss he had found there, that he should probably berate himself for his conduct. But he could not regret the sweetness of their intimacy, nor the pleasure he had so clearly given her.

And as for what she had given him…!

She was eager and passionate and tender, nearly undoing the iron self-discipline he had exerted *almost* to the end. It had made the final release all the more overwhelming, second only in his heart to the trust she had given him. He vowed, silently, always to live up to that.

In the meantime, once he could move… Folding her closer into his arms and kissing her proved that he could.

"When shall we be married?" he asked.

"Hmm. Perhaps we should make Julius feel in control by asking him. It's only a couple of days since I told him I did not want to marry you under any circumstances."

"You won't change your mind again, will you?" he asked uneasily.

The mischief in her eyes gave him warning of teasing to come, but in the end, she only smiled and shook her head. "I was hurt."

"I know. I am sorry for that, if for nothing else."

She kissed his earlobe, and fresh desire began to stir. "It seems our mothers were wiser than we thought. I always believed mine must have been a rather silly creature—I don't remember her at all. But perhaps she understood that her child and her friend's would be bound to suit."

"Perhaps," Edd said doubtfully. "More likely, it is pure luck, but either way, I'll take it."

He kissed her lingeringly. During the embrace, he realized the rain no longer pattered on the roof. The birds were singing again. And, tempting as it was, he would not risk hurting her with further physical love.

"Time to put on your damp clothes and face the music," he said, releasing her and rising to find his scattered clothes. He was very aware of her gaze following his naked person as he walked, bent, and stretched. He liked that too, though not as much as watching Lucy's naked beauty in similar pursuits.

"Julius is with Antonia," she volunteered as he helped refasten her damp gown. "And Edward, her little boy, although I think the twins have him. I don't know who else is in the house. Cornelius is always out on the land, but he may have been driven back by the rain."

"It is past time I met them all. Lucy?"

She turned her head to look at him, no doubt sensing his sudden seriousness.

"When would *you* like to be married?"

He saw several thoughts and emotions flit across her face and turned her, tilting up her chin.

"Lucy. I would marry you tomorrow if I could. *Now*, in fact. I shall not change my mind—not because of what we have just done, but because I love you. At the same time, there could be consequences of that, so we should not leave it *too* long."

Her eyes widened. "You mean I could have a baby?"

"*We* could have a baby," he corrected her, feeling a sudden stab of guilt. "Did you not know?"

"Actually, yes, I did. But it went out of my mind."

"I should have taken better care of you."

"You took excellent care of me," she said smugly, and he couldn't help laughing and kissing her because she was so wonderful.

# Chapter Twenty

I N THE END, Edd saw Sir Julius alone in the library, as was proper, while Lucy hurried upstairs to changed out of her uncomfortably wet clothes. He hoped she wouldn't catch a chill.

"You're looking a trifle damp, Eddleston," Sir Julius remarked, shaking hands amiably enough.

"I stopped the carriage in the drive because I saw Lucy in the garden and went to speak to her. Got caught in the rain." He held Sir Julius's gaze. "We sheltered in the summer house for a little and talked." Among other things, but he was damned sure Sir Julius didn't want to know about those, though he might well suspect them.

"And?" Sir Julius asked, gesturing to the brandy decanter.

Edd inclined his head gratefully. "And we have agreed we would like to be married after all. I hope you are agreeable."

Sir Julius poured two glasses and presented one to Edd. "I will speak to Lucy. After which, you may or may not be allowed to speak to her."

"I understand," Edd said meekly.

Sir Julius eyed him with the gimlet stare that must have terrified ships full of wild, rough sailors in the past. A smile glimmered. "I expect you do, and you are not remotely worried, are you?"

"We have reached an understanding. I hope you approve."

"As it happens, I do. I could tell by your behavior yesterday that you truly care for her. And if we are talking material possessions, I am well aware that she—and our family—are the gainers in the alliance. Because of your rank and because of the settlements already agreed by our apparently not-quite-so-misguided parents. Black Hill is not yet on its feet, and the harvest here, as elsewhere, will not be great this year. But we have high hopes for the future."

Edd raised his glass. "As do I."

"You'll join us for luncheon?" Sir Julius raised his glass in return. "Unless Lucy sends you away in tears."

"I will. Thank you."

Luncheon, which Edd fully expected to be awkward, turned out to be unexpectedly fun. He saw a softer side of the imposing Sir Julius, in his interactions with his betrothed and her lively son. Cornelius, the land steward, turned out to be not so serious as he looked, and even Major Vale—Roderick—who glowered at him at first meeting, thawed under Lucy's obviously happy chatter.

Pretty and charming in a becoming morning gown of palest sea green, she managed her brothers with a deftness that left Edd in awe. Her sisters wore expressions of almost identical appreciation, though he was aware he was under scrutiny. The twins looked almost smug, as if the engagement was all their doing. And perhaps it was.

"What of the unspeakable Irving?" Sir Julius asked at last. "Is he in custody yet?"

"They hadn't found him when I left this morning," Edd replied. "But he cannot have gone far, and I believe they are watching the docks and the roads out of the town."

"And Hester?" Lucy asked anxiously. "Have you seen her?"

"No, but I met Mr. Cairney over breakfast at the King's Head. He and Miss Poole are once more engaged."

"Oh, thank goodness."

"You want everyone to be engaged now that you are?" Aubrey teased.

"Only to the right people," Lucy replied with dignity.

Edd had only begun to guess the truth about Hester and her desperation to be married to someone, even Irving, when, toward the end of luncheon, a note was delivered to Sir Julius from Mrs. Poole.

"Miss Poole and Mr. Cairney will be married by special license tomorrow," he said with raised brows. "Apparently your presence, Lucy, and mine will be appreciated at the vicarage at eleven of the clock."

"What a dark horse," Edd said, amused. "Cairney must have had a special license in his pocket all along."

"Do you have one too?" Felicia—Mrs. Maitland—asked with a hint of challenge.

"No," Lucy answered for him. "We had no intention of marrying when he first came to Blackhaven. We are going to have the banns read, like Julius and Antonia."

"When Mama marries Captain Julius," Edward announced, "he's going to be my papa!"

"I'm looking forward to that," Roderick murmured with relish, and raised his wine glass to his brother.

"Only two weeks to go," Leona said.

"With the Braithwaite masked ball between," Felicia said. "Will you be there, my lord?"

"I expect so," Edd replied. An amusing idea was forming in his mind, to do with masquerades and dressing up. But no, he probably should not embarrass his bride's family. Not just yet.

Harold Irving seethed with rage. Even in the years spent abroad—largely to appease Anne's family—he had never been reduced to such squalor. He had never been forced to hide from the law, to stay in such a mean little room as the guest of a tavern whore who happened to have a soft spot for him.

Of course, he had promised to pay her, but that would never happen now he was separated from Hester's funds. It might still be possible to get her back, he argued with himself. A speedy abduction—he could threaten and drug her into obedience if they were alone—followed by a swift marriage in Scotland and passage on a fast ship to Europe. *Oh yes.*

But he would have to act quickly. He had sent Molly, who rented this miserable room in the Blackhaven back streets that visitors never saw, to report on Hester's movements. Of course, he would have to catch her with a full purse or the venture was doomed to failure.

He straightened at the sound of footsteps on the stairs. A moment later, the door opened and Molly swept in.

"She just got married," Molly said with infuriating relish. "At the vicarage."

Blood sang in Harold's ears. "Who did? Lucy Vale?"

"Course not! Though she were there, and Sir Julius and the handsome young nob, too."

"Molly," he uttered between his teeth.

"Your Miss Poole," Molly said. "Married Mr. Cairney—Scottish gent, apparently—by special license. Mr. Grant married 'em this morning, all right and tight."

Harold dropped his head in his hands. He had been fooling himself. It had been over the moment that termagant Vale girl hit him. Only he had hated to admit it, even to himself, because he had no other plan, no other heiress to pursue. He had tied his flag too obviously to Hester to switch allegiance without at least some lapse of time.

"I blame Eddleston for this," he whispered.

"Who's he, then?" Molly asked without much interest. "Want a cup of tea?"

"St. John Gore, Earl of bloody Eddleston. My snot-nosed brother-in-law. And no, I do *not* want a cup of tea." He glared at her. "I want a pistol."

At that, she paled, throwing herself to the floor at his feet.

"No, no, Harold, it's not that bad. You can't kill yourself over a woman…"

"I have no intention of killing myself," Harold snarled. "I want a large, accurate, double-barreled pistol. Can you get it for me?"

"You taking to the high toby?" she asked in awe.

He laughed, so furious that he did not even care how hysterical he sounded. "That's right. The high toby. Can you get it for me?"

LUKE FARMER, ALTHOUGH reunited at last with his family, returned to Black Hill the following day. In company with Lucy, he told Cornelius the whole story.

"If you'll have me, I'd like to return to work here until the spring at least," he said.

Cornelius frowned at him, which Lucy knew meant he was thinking. "You've been honest with me at last," he said. "I appreciate that, so I'll grant you the same favor. You don't seem terribly reliable, and I need reliable men."

"I *need* to be reliable," Farmer said intensely. "I want to marry Betsy the parlor maid. I want to be considered for one of your vacant tenancies next year. And I'll work all the hours God sends to make these things happen, if only you'll give me another chance."

"You have a lot of people speaking for you," Cornelius allowed. "Mr. Hanson, Lord Eddleston, Lord Braithwaite himself."

"And me," Lucy chimed in.

Cornelius turned his gaze on her and blinked. A hint of a smile dawned. "And you," he said. "Which actually means more than the rest put together. Since my sister recommends you, you can stay until spring, on condition of good behavior. If you impress me, I might even speak to my brother on your behalf about a tenancy."

Farmer grinned. He did not tug his forelock—such was not his nature or his belief—but he did ask immediately, "What can I do?"

Lucy left them to it, delighted for Farmer, but also with a pleasant glow of pride inside her. Because Cornelius valued her opinion. At least one of her siblings had noticed and trusted her reading of character.

Which was not always flawless, she recalled, feeling the glow fading slightly, not when it came to those closest to her.

That foolish passage between herself and Nick… She had kept it from Felicia so as not to taint what was left of her husband's memory. She had thought that more important than honesty. But that decision also shielded Lucy from Felicia's contempt. Was it not more for herself she had held her tongue?

She came to a halt in the middle of the hall and let out a slow breath. It was time.

She turned and went in search of Felicia.

She found her in her bedchamber, looking over masks and dominos for the Braithwaite ball.

"What about costumes?" Felicia said, frowning. "Will you wear a costume, Lucy, or just a ball gown?"

"Oh, a costume, if I can get it ready on time. I was going to ask for your help because it's quite complicated. If you are still prepared to help me, that is."

"Of course I'll help you, goose," Felicia said, setting aside a matching domino and mask in a charming shade of dusky pink. "Why would I not?"

Lucy sat down on the bed, fingering the mask nearest her. "Fliss…"

"Yes?"

Lucy bit her lip. "I want to tell you something that will make you angry with me, but please believe you could never be as angry as I am with myself. And I am not telling you because of Nick. This is for you and me."

"Oh dear." Felicia swirled off the pink cloak she had been trying on and dropped it on the bed. She sat down beside Lucy. "That sounds ominous."

"Fliss…" Lucy forced herself to keep looking at her sister, though she wanted to shut her eyes in shame. She could not bear to see Felicia's fresh hurt. But Nick was gone, and she could no longer dance around Felicia, keeping her distance, harming their relationship because of him.

She stumbled into speech before she could plan the words. "I let Nick kiss me once. Not because I was in love with him, because I wasn't. He was just familiar and handsome, and I was curious. I knew it meant nothing to him. He was foxed and neither of us cared, so I thought you would not care either. You knew what he was like. But *everything* still hurt you, didn't it? *I* hurt you, even if you didn't know, and I am so sorry."

"Oh, Lucy," Felicia said, and there was such sadness in her voice that Lucy wanted to curl up with shame. Stunningly, Felicia took her hand. "All that time… Did you think I did not know?"

Lucy's lips parted in shock. "You…knew? How? Did you see?"

"No. He told me the next day. Even Nick was ashamed of kissing my sister, though he tried to pass it off as a joke. I was furious."

"I'm so sorry, Fliss—"

"Not with you!" Felicia exclaimed. "With him! You were fifteen years old, living in our care. That was why I tried to get you to live with Aunt Diana in Bath, because I could not trust him when he was foxed. It was for your safety."

"M-my safety?" Lucy stammered. "Not because you sensed something about me that was awful?"

"Oh, Lucy, of course not. You were a child, and I was trying to look after you. And this has bothered you for *three years*?"

Lucy nodded dumbly.

Felicia put her arms around her. "Silly girl. I wish you had spoken to me before." She let out a hiccup. "But then, I should have spoken to you. I was too ashamed of the husband I was supposed to love, honor, and obey."

Lucy clung to her for a moment, then pulled back with a sniff.

Felicia smiled a little tremulously. "For what it is worth, Eddleston is a very different kind of man. I doubt you will have trouble with the loving and honoring, or even obeying."

"The obeying might be a problem," Lucy allowed. "But he isn't very inclined to lay down the law. Oh, I do love him, Fliss. So much it *hurts*. Is that how you felt about Nick?"

Felicia shrugged. "Not really. Maybe at first. But it was really just...excitement. Flattery because he noticed me above all others." She smiled with a hint of sadness. "The funny thing is, I believe he genuinely loved me—more, in the end, than I ever loved him. But we never had the time to find out."

"Will you ever love somebody else?"

A secretive little smile curved Felicia's lips. "Perhaps."

HAROLD STILL HAD the key to his hotel room. He doubted it had been cleared out yet, and the Pooles could stand the bill. However, as a wanted man, he could hardly allow himself to be recognized by entering through the front door.

Yet again, Molly came to the rescue, cajoling a man delivering bread to give one of the trays to her. "Just for a wager," she said, batting her eyelashes.

Harold, already dressed in borrowed apron and cap, shambled into the kitchen with his tray, ditched it, and bolted up the service stairs to his own room.

He had picked a time when the passages were quiet, but even so, he wasn't completely sure he would not find a constable waiting for him in his old bedchamber. He pressed his ear to the door, listening for a long time before the sound of approaching footsteps forced him to shove his key in the lock, turn it, and dive inside.

The room was empty. It looked as if nothing had been touched, although he would have wagered Winslow had been through his pockets. Even his bag from the ill-fated jaunt to Scotland lay on his bed, still packed. Not that there was anything to find there. Harold went straight to the mantelpiece and took from it his once treasured invitation to the Countess of Braithwaite's masked ball. He shoved it inside his pocket.

He was stuffing his clothes from the smart leather bag into a less conspicuous bundle when, glancing out of the window, he saw the Earl of Braithwaite himself, walking up the street with two of his sisters. With a jolt, he remembered that all the Braithwaite girls were heiresses. And that two of them were still unmarried. That one in the street to begin with, and she was a fetching little thing. As were all her sisters.

Harold sat down abruptly on the window seat.

Was it possible that all was not yet over after all? Could he not have one more throw of the dice? Make one more plan that would encompass both revenge and his own comfortable life? The wheels of his mind began to turn.

*Beat this, St. John bloody Eddleston.*

THE SUMMER BALL at the castle was a major event in Blackhaven. All the local gentry were invited, along with the army officers stationed nearby and the townspeople with any pretensions to gentility. A few favored visitors to the town were generally included, for the Braithwaites were a sociable family, and on top of that, they frequently had smart friends from London staying at the castle, too.

"That was how the vicar met his wife," Felicia informed them at the dinner table. "If indirectly. And how Miss Muir's niece became Lady Wickenden."

"You mean it's a more successful Marriage Mart?" Aubrey

mocked, his gaze darting from Julius to Lucy. "More even than the assembly ball?"

"Well, there's another of those coming up, too," Cornelius said, "so you might as well give up your bachelorhood now."

Lucy had the feeling that her brothers were only pretending annoyance at having to attend the castle ball. But her own costume and a few snatched moments with Eddleston kept her too busy to find out.

"Lucy and I will need to travel separately," Felicia said when it came to organizing vehicles to the castle, "so send the first carriage back for us immediately."

"You are up to something," Roderick said, staring at Lucy.

"My costume is too big," she said. "But Felicia is helping."

"You're not smuggling the twins in under massive, hooped skirts, are you?"

"No," Leona said with some regret. "Though maybe we could try for that next time."

"Don't be too outrageous," Delilah said, a hint of anxiety in her eyes. "Lord and Lady Braithwaite might be tolerant and easygoing, but the dowager countess is most assuredly not!"

"It will only be for a few moments," Lucy said, "and no one will know who I am, thanks to my mask!" And possibly a change of domino if it all went wrong.

# Chapter Twenty-One

APPARENTLY MASKED BALLS had been all the rage at the late Congress of Vienna. Edd could see the enormous possibilities for amusement and mistakes. It might have been fun to first appear to Lucy in such a mysterious guise, but he would not have given up the last two weeks for the world—not even the days in the middle when she would not speak to him.

Still, he imagined as he strolled around the castle ballroom, there would be opportunities for more outrageous flirting than usual. Especially encouraged by the alcoves cleverly disguised into the mural of a moonlit garden, which had been painted all along one wall by Braithwaite's artist brother-in-law, Lord Tamar. The painting looked almost like a reflection of the real one lit up outside by a hundred lanterns.

"We used to just use the great hall as the ballroom," the young countess explained to Edd, after sending him to admire it, while she stood near the grand entrance to welcome her guests. "But it was a little dark and cramped, so we made a few adjustments, and now we can extend it whenever necessary into this newer part of the castle, where we put in the new French windows you can see onto the terrace."

"It looks magnificent," Edd said, returning to stand just a little behind her. Conversing with her gave him a reason to lurk by the door and inspect all the arrivals. Mostly, he was looking out for

Lucy, but also for anyone who might be Irving.

Irving was a vindictive swine, and since he had not yet been caught, Edd was more than half convinced that he would mask himself and come to the ball just to cause trouble for those he would see as the architects of his downfall—Braithwaite, Cairney, and Eddleston himself.

He spotted Cairney—with the new Mrs. Cairney—at once. But then, even masked, they were easily recognized by their happy smiles.

"I expect you disapprove of such frivolous expenditure," Lady Braithwaite said, harking back to the ballroom alterations and startling him so that his gaze flew to hers.

"Whatever gave you that idea?" he asked.

"You are a radical, are you not? We have so much, while too many have too little."

Edd smiled slightly. "Such a state of affairs has existed for hundreds of years and can hardly be improved by denying oneself a new window or two. It is education and attitudes that have to change across the whole country, so that we value people. All people."

"Even the Romanies?" she said, and he recalled that she had been separated from her family as a small child and brought up largely by Romany people—a frequently distrusted race, unjustly despised by many.

"*All* people," he said firmly. "Treated fairly and paid fairly."

"And who decides what is fair?" she asked. "Those who pay the wages!"

"Or those who earn them," he said at once, "who are vastly more numerous."

"You let your own people decide their salaries?" she challenged. "Their own rents?"

"Well, we have agreed on those things."

She smiled with unexpected warmth. "Michael is right. You are an unusual man."

They were both distracted then by the arrival of Sir Julius and

Major Vale, escorting their sister Delilah. Despite his mask, Sir Julius was easily spotted by the eye patch bulking one side of the mask and tied around his head. And by the fact that he went straight across the ballroom to Antonia Macy, who had arrived only moments before with her friends Miss Talbot and Lord Linfield.

Where was Lucy? Edd spotted her other brothers stalking in shortly afterward. Cornelius, in a dark green domino and matching mask, looked as if he would rather be anywhere else in the world. The even more handsome Aubrey appeared vaguely predatory in black.

"Are you expecting all the Vales?" he asked the countess.

"Yes, apart from the twins, which is a shame in some ways."

"Only think of the havoc they could cause," Edd mused, already planning a party of his own when he was married.

The countess laughed and tapped her fan against his wrist. "Go and choose your first partner. We are about to open the ball."

Edd moved away, concerned that he still had not found Lucy. Could she really have disguised herself beyond his ability to recognize? Those beautiful, expressive green eyes, the upward-curving mouth, so prone to smiling, the vital way she moved as if dancing instead of merely walking. Even masked and costumed, or enveloped in a domino cloak, surely he would have recognized her?

As discreetly as he could, he strolled around the ballroom, looking afresh at everyone in their jewels and masks, costumes and dominos. Hailed by a couple of London friends, he paused to talk to them. Lord Wickenden dangled his mask from one finger, while Lord Daxton wore his across his forehead.

"You make me feel so conventional," Edd complained, which at least made everyone laugh.

Then, just as the orchestra began the introduction to the first dance—a waltz—one of the ladies said, "Oh, Dax, look! Costume of the night!"

Edd followed Lady Dax's gaze to two late arrivals being rather hastily welcomed by Lady Braithwaite. Two ladies had arrived, one in a jeweled, dusky pink mask and matching domino, the other in a massive, hooped gown of the previous century, with a scarlet domino cloak spread around it. Her mask was black, trimmed with scarlet lace. But it was this second lady's stunning headgear that drew all eyes.

Part towering, powdered wig, it was decorated with jewels, and with a square patch of silk the same color as her gown. It might have been what held the massive contraption together, but somehow it resembled a window.

Edd's lips twitched. "Oh, my," he murmured to his companions, already walking away from them toward this magnificent vision. "I am entranced."

The orchestra extended its introduction. The two ladies walked into the ballroom arm in arm. She of the massive headdress bore a smile that looked almost as stiff as the way she walked, as though she was frightened the massive edifice on her head would collapse. Edd wished intensely that Lucy was here to see it before it fell.

He was quite close to her before the idea even entered his head. And then he was awash with so much love and laughter that he wondered why he did not explode. Instead, he halted in front of the two ladies and bowed.

"Madam, I am in awe," he said. "Grant me, if you will, the favor of this dance."

Edd held out his hand. The lady detached her fingers from her friend's arm and turned her whole body in order to see and take his hand.

Her companion giggled.

The lady herself did not, although her voice shook slightly as she said, "Thank you, sir, I will try."

Very carefully he guided her toward the dance floor. By tradition, the countess opened the ball by dancing with Mr. Winslow, the local squire as well as the magistrate, and Braithwaite danced with Mrs. Winslow, but they were only allowed a few turns before everyone else began spilling onto the floor.

Afraid she would be jostled, Edd took his partner very loosely and carefully into his arms. "Lucy, you are magnificent," he breathed.

Lucy let out a giggle that was part snort. "Drat, you do know me!"

"Oh, it took me some time. Whatever that contraption is, it changes your every move."

He glanced at it admiringly and was sure it moved. In fact, it made a sound alarmingly like a whine. He brought his widened gaze back to her. "Oh, Lucy," he said in wonder. "You haven't, have you?"

Slowly she slid her hand free and raised it to the silk square in her wig. As soon as she moved it, a small canine snout appeared. Another whine, a violent wobble of the wig, as a whole puppy burst out of it and landed ecstatically on Eddleston's chest.

A buzz of astonishment hummed around the ballroom, sprinkled with spurts of laughter. Edd, clutching the wriggling pup with one hand, swept Lucy off the floor with the other. Almost helpless with mirth, Lucy raised one hand to the applause breaking out around her. She even managed a quick curtesy before Edd pulled her into a run, straight out of Lady Braithwaite's newly installed French windows.

"Put him down," she gasped. "Luke's waiting below."

Edd obeyed, and the fickle pup immediately deserted him, dashing off down the steps to find his beloved Luke in the garden.

"Thanks, Luke," Lucy hissed after him, and received a Farmer-like grunt in response.

But people were beginning to follow them outside. Lucy, dragging Edd by the hand, dashed inside again by the other door and straight out of the ballroom, through a short passage and into a darkened room, where, somehow, he managed to howl with laughter and kiss her at the same time.

"How did you achieve that?" he got out at last as she began

untying the wig, which was actually fastened under her chin.

"Oh, I made the little frame on three sides and covered it with an old wig I found in the attic and restyled around it. Can you feel a lamp and a flint on the table there? Your Lady Maria agreed to help me out when she came to call yesterday, and told me about this room."

Obligingly, Eddleston found his way to the lamp and lit it, adjusting the glow. Maria Hanson had indeed aided and abetted. There was even a mirror here.

"Anyway," Lucy continued, removing the legion of pins very carefully from the wig while her betrothed watched in fascination, "I borrowed Toby and got him used to staying in the little cage with the silk over the opening. Luke came with us in the carriage, and Felicia put Toby inside just before we entered the ballroom. Balancing the whole thing was the hardest part. To be honest, I didn't think it would last as long. I certainly didn't think I could dance!"

"You'd probably have made it to the end if the pup hadn't picked up my scent. Well, now we know it can be done!"

"Still, I didn't want to embarrass my family *too* much, so..." She dropped the wig on the table, revealing an almost perfect coiffure beneath.

He smiled.

She said demurely, "Would you mind unlacing me?"

In the glass, their eyes met, and she must have heard the change in his breathing, for her eyes twinkled at him. "I am not so improper," she said severely. "Beneath this massive gown is one rather prettier."

He pretended to sigh as he unlaced her, although he did kiss the back of her neck. The scent of her skin, the sight of her partially naked back, caused even more havoc. Her own quickened breathing aroused him further. But in time, the over-gown and the hoops were removed, leaving the narrow, flowing evening gown only slightly crushed beneath.

He picked up the discarded things and placed them neatly on

a chair. "The scarlet domino will give you away. Do you mind?"

"No. Look." Proudly, she swept up the domino from the floor where it had fallen and revealed its ivory silk lining. Then she swung it around her shoulders and smiled at him.

Behind the laughter in her eyes was a spark he wanted to hold on to forever. He brushed aside her fingers, fastened the domino at her throat, then softly kissed her lips.

"I cannot wait to be married to you," he said.

"Nor I to you," she whispered, and his happiness was complete.

HAROLD WAS NOT foolish enough to arrive with everyone else. In the press of people, the danger of being recognized, even masked, was too great. He certainly did not wish to be welcomed by Lord Braithwaite, who knew him far too well by this time.

He walked up to the castle alone and spent some time familiarizing himself with the gardens and terraces, and the quickest way to the gates where the post-chaise would await him. He could hear the music coming from the ballroom, and the pleasant hum of talk and laughter. For a moment, resentment soared back to the surface. *He* should have been there as an honored guest, with his wealthy new wife on his arm. Instead, she was with the Scotsman while Harold was sneaking in like an uninvited troublemaker.

Well, he certainly meant to cause a considerable amount of trouble, but he damned well *was* invited, as he proved sometime later when he sauntered alone and masked through the front door and dropped his card of invitation into the footman's hands before strolling onward and into the ballroom.

He found it remarkably easy to recognize people he knew behind the masks—which gave him a rather sharp jolt of fear when he contemplated how they might recognize *him* so easily.

But then, surely no one would expect him to *dare* to come here.

He saw Hester Poole at once—so unfashionable as to be dancing with her own husband. Braithwaite was easily spotted, although his bevy of pretty sisters gave Harold a little more trouble. One was pregnant, so he ruled her out immediately. Eventually, by process of elimination, he found the youngest two and memorized their dress and masks and the precise color of their domino cloaks. After all, he needed to be able to pick at least one of them out of a crowd very quickly.

By then, he had also located Lucy Vale, dancing with some local clodhopper and looking unexpectedly demure in an ivory domino cloak. He wondered if Eddleston had rejected her because of her jaunt with Harold. Oh, he hoped so. Providing it did not spoil the rest of his plan.

He put the next phase into operation just as the dance ended. He approached the maid scuttling in to remove used glasses from the ballroom and, before she could begin, pressed one of the two small, folded notes into her hand.

She stared up at him in astonishment.

"For the lady in the ivory domino." A coin—purloined from poor Molly—followed the note. He smiled at her. "You will be assisting true love."

The silly girl's eyes went misty, and she gave him a fatuous smile. "I will, sir," she promised.

Thank God for the unquestioning obedience of the servant class. He thanked her gravely and sauntered off to intercept the nearest footman, into whose pocket he slipped the other note.

"For the gentleman with the burgundy domino," he murmured when the footman cast him something close to a glower. "From his ladylove."

"Which burgundy domino, sir?" the footman asked in long-suffering tones, and to his annoyance, Harold saw at least three other cloaks of the same color whirling about the room.

"The one barely wearing it all. Falling off his right shoulder. With the matching mask embroidered in black. Can you distinguish him, or shall I give the note and coin to one of your sharper-eyed fellows?"

The footman's expression did not change. "I'll do it, sir," he said, and another of Molly's hard-earned coins slid into the footman's pocket.

Harold sauntered on, and by good fortune found himself beside one of the Braithwaite girls he had earmarked as his bride. His luck was clearly changing at last. What a pity he had no money left for cards.

LUCY WAS STILL euphoric about the effect of her headdress jest on her betrothed. For some reason, its importance went far beyond the joke for her. She had wanted to entertain him, to prove that she could. And somehow, as she had, producing all the effects she had wanted to and more, she realized she had nothing to prove, that he loved her far more deeply than mere surface fun.

In their marriage, there would be bad times as well as good. Sadness as well as laughter. It was inevitable. But it was the love, and the friendship, that would hold them together through both, and all the shades between.

She re-entered the ballroom discreetly with Maria Hanson and, by several different people, was told the hilarious tale of the lady with the puppy in her wig. Across the room, Lord Eddleston was telling it too—with, apparently, no idea who she had been. When she saw him dancing with Felicia shortly afterward, she wondered if her sister thanked him for that discretion.

Truthfully, she should not have risked drawing such ridicule to her family. Society was unkind, particularly to women like Delilah who were known to be illegitimate, however acknowledged by family. Leona would face the same prejudices. Lucy making herself a figure of fun would not have helped them. So, she was on her best behavior for the rest of the evening.

She partnered her betrothed for a country dance and promised him the supper waltz, which she looked forward to immensely, but otherwise they did not cling to each other.

So she was slightly surprised when, just as she was parting from a black-masked gentleman after their waltz, one of the Braithwaite maids sidled up to her and presented her with a glass in a slightly awkward manner that entailed Lucy taking it by the base and feeling the folded note beneath.

The girl curtseyed, as though Lucy had requested the lemonade—which was, in fact, welcome. Excusing herself from both Delilah and the gentleman in black, Lucy hurried away to one of the alcoves to read her note.

She knew it could only be from Lord Eddleston. *Ballroom terrace, eleven of the clock. Terse,* she thought with some amusement, although at least the flourish at the end was heart-shaped. And he hardly had the time—or the paper—to compose love poetry. She was just delighted he could not wait another half-hour until the supper dance to see her.

Another Tyler kiss…if the terrace was empty. And they *were* betrothed. No one would judge them too harshly, even if they were seen. Until then, she was happy to come across Julius and Antonia and sit quietly with them until the end of the current dance. Then, since it approached eleven o'clock, she excused herself and sauntered toward the terrace. Julius was probably watching her. Like her, he may even have seen Lord Eddleston step onto the terrace some yards ahead of her.

The night-scented breeze from the French window was welcome on her cheeks as she approached the other open door. The garden beyond, the fountain and the spreading branches of the chestnut tree—all seemed curiously magical in the moonlight, like a fairytale scene, somehow all blending with her elated happiness.

The terrace was deserted, apart from the man in the burgundy domino who turned from the shadows to see her.

His eyes widened, his lips parted, but in shock rather than

pleasure. "Lucy, go back," he said hoarsely. "Go!"

She could not help the hurt, but as usual, sheer curiosity ensured she kept coming. "Don't be ridiculous. You invited me."

He moved then, with unexpected speed, all but hurling himself at her, just as a deafening crack rent the air. He grasped her shoulders and cried out, "Now! *Now*, damn you!" And pulled her to the ground.

# Chapter Twenty-Two

ON HIS PREVIOUS reconnaissance, Harold had found the perfect place among the branches of the chestnut tree. From there, he had a perfect view of the terrace. And from the terrace, he knew he should be invisible among the shadows.

Arriving in place only a minute or two before the assignation time, he shrugged the domino behind his back, tore his mask away, and took the heavy pistol from his coat pocket. Only just in time. Eddleston, it seemed, was pathetically eager to meet his fate.

Both barrels were already loaded, though fortunately the pistol had not the hair-trigger mechanism of a dueling pistol. It was hard to squeeze this trigger by accident. Harold raised it to the correct gap between branches and took careful aim.

*Come on,* he urged his enemy impatiently. *Come out of the shadows.*

But that, it seemed, Eddleston was reluctant to do. At least until Lucy in her ivory cloak stepped through the middle door, a perfect target. Harold waited, because he wanted Eddleston to see her die, if possible.

He thought he heard the low, urgent sound of Eddleston's voice, and whatever was said urged Lucy to go faster. Damn, Harold was going to have to shoot her first. It didn't really matter. The shot would bring Eddleston out of the shadows quickly enough, and then Harold would have to move swiftly.

The post-chaise had better be in place, waiting for him…

He adjusted his aim to the region of Lucy's breast and pulled the trigger. At almost the same moment, Eddleston flew out of the shadows, hurling himself in front of her.

*Perfect.* The explosion of his pistol rent the air, and both bodies fell to the ground.

It must have been a damned lucky shot! Had the ball passed through Eddleston's body into hers? Either way, he had no time to celebrate.

Eddleston was not yet dead but shouting something. It sounded like "Now! Now, damn you!"

*Idiot,* Harold thought, stuffing the pistol back in his pocket— he still had one shot to use if necessary. Eddleston didn't know that noise and chaos worked in Harold's favor. People were bursting through the terrace doors just as they should. Loud voices, shouting, screaming… *Oh yes!*

But as he began to run toward the terrace, the garden seemed to be alive too. Figures rushed at him from all sides, seizing him by the arms.

"Let me go, you fools!" he yelled. "A man is dying up there! A lady!"

"They had better not be," said a coldly furious voice right in front of him. A tall man in a red military coat, one of the Vale brothers. "Or you will suffer before you hang."

Harold's blood ran cold. There was promise in that icy voice, so much worse than mere threat. He barely noticed as Major Vale took the pistol from his pocket.

His one consolation was the cry from the terrace: "No! Tyler, no, you can't die!"

EDD HAD NOT believed in the note for a moment. He had been

expecting something like this, and the handwriting was hardly the feminine script he imagined would flow from Lucy's hand. He, Winslow, and Braithwaite already had men stationed all around the gardens as well as inside the castle, waiting for trouble. From them, he knew of the post-chaise waiting at the gates for Irving's post-vengeance flight.

So he strolled onto the terrace to await the attack, from whichever direction it would come. Irving was vicious and violent. Edd was neither, but he had been to school. He knew how to look after himself, and he doubted Irving expected that.

Edd kept to the shadows, drawing him in, but when he turned to face the person stepping outside from the ballroom, it was not Irving but Lucy.

For an instant, shock cleaved his tongue to the roof of his mouth. He tried to tell her to go back, and he saw the hurt flicker in her face. It felt like kicking a puppy, only there was no time for such niceties. Some slight movement, the faintest of sounds, drew his attention toward the chestnut tree, and that was when he realized his stupid, unforgivable error.

He had expected a personal attack. But it had never entered his head that Irving would have a *gun*. He had taken no weapons on his elopement, and there had been none in his hotel room. With no time to lash himself, Edd threw himself in front of Lucy just as the shot was fired.

He felt the impact in his shoulder and thanked God for it. But he still had to drag her down, away from the gun's sights. And somehow, he shouted for the men before pain hit him in waves.

Beneath him, Lucy's beautiful face was blurry, but he could still see the terror in her eyes. "No! Tyler, no, you can't die!"

"I won't," he mumbled, and then the world went dark.

WHEN LIGHT BEGAN to worm its way back into consciousness, he was lying on his side. He felt as if someone was sticking needles into the agonized flesh of his shoulder. Blearily, he opened his eyes.

An unknown man came into focus, sitting beside him, frowning over whatever he was doing behind Edd. The man could only have been a few years older than Eddleston, but he had a vast air of competence. Then Edd saw his fingers and what they were holding. He really was sticking needles into his flesh.

With a gasp, he recalled the events on the terrace and jerked upward. "Lucy!"

The doctor—Edd hoped he was a doctor—pushed him back onto the pillow with one hand on his chest.

"I'm here, Tyler!" said Lucy. She appeared in front of him, kneeling on the floor to clasp his hand. Her face was wet, and she was frightened, but no less beautiful for that.

"Thank God," he whispered. "Thank God."

"And you," said a male voice grimly behind her.

Edd looked up and saw Major Roderick Vale. He had never been terribly sure that the major approved of him, but there was definite favor in the harsh eyes glaring at him now.

"If you hadn't dived in front of her, it's Lucy who would have been shot, and most probably through the heart."

Edd licked his dry lips. "Did the ball go through me?" he asked hoarsely. "Did it hit her?"

Major Vale smiled. He had an unexpectedly sweet smile for so grim a man. "Not in the slightest. Lampton's just dug the ball out of you. Lucy is entirely unmarked. Apart from weeping over you."

Enchanted, Edd smiled at Lucy. He managed to free his hand from her grip and touched the damp skin of her face. "There is no need to weep. I'll still insist on the supper waltz."

"Actually, you've missed it," the doctor said. He was smoothing something over the wound now. He reached for the bandage, which Lucy passed to him. "Which is just as well, because I would have forbidden it. If you don't want to tear the stitches and encourage infection, you'll keep that shoulder still for several weeks."

He eased Edd into a sitting position and began to wrap a bandage around his chest to hold the dressing in place.

"You're going to be in pain for some time," the doctor told him cheerfully, "but the ball came out whole, and providing no infection gets in, you should heal very well, as good as new in time."

"Irving?" Edd asked Major Vale.

"Disarmed, charged, and in the town gaol." His voice softened very slightly. "You have done your bit, my lord, never doubt it."

"It was I who dragged her into Irving's orbit in the first place," Edd confessed. "Looking for vengeance, if not justice, for my sister."

"I believe you will have it," Major Vale said, and then Lucy dropped what looked like a nightshirt over Edd's head.

"You'll stay here at the castle until at least tomorrow," the doctor ordered him. "I'll come back and look at you again then." Unexpectedly, he held out his hand, a sardonic smile on his face. "Welcome to Blackhaven. Most people seem to come here to be shot."

"Just as well," said Lady Maria, Hanson's wife, appearing suddenly in the doorway. "Or they would not have you to care for them, doctor."

"Ha," said Dr. Lampton. "My lord, I'll leave something for the pain. Mainly, you'll need rest, so sleep. Out, everyone."

Major Vale turned to his sister and scowled. "Ten minutes, Lucy."

As everyone left—except Lucy, who made herself more comfortable on the bed beside him—Edd could have sworn he heard distant music.

"Is the ball still going on?"

"Do you mind? Mr. Hanson said you would prefer it."

"I do." He smiled. "Especially since it means everyone else is in the ballroom and you can kiss me undisturbed. If you choose to."

"I do," she whispered. Her lips trembled as they kissed his. "Oh, Tyler, I was so afraid…"

"So was I," he admitted. "So stupid! I never imagined he would have a gun. And then I was terrified I would not reach you in time. It was like one of those dreams where you never reach where you need to be…"

She kissed him again to stop the words. "I couldn't have borne it if you had died."

"I won't. I'll be on my feet in no time. I have a wedding to attend in three weeks."

"Actually, there will be Julius's in a little over one week. And then ours."

"That sounds good." He closed his eyes and savored her closeness, her scent, her being. Despite the pain, and despite how close he had come to losing her, if not his own life, he felt a sense of peace creep over him. Peace and gratitude and sheer rightness. And a love he had never imagined.

"It *is* good," she said softly, resting her head against his on the pillow. "Very, very good." He felt her smile against his cheek. "I wonder which of us will be next?"

# Epilogue

*Three years later, December 1819*

"HE'S COMING!"

The cry went up first outside, somewhere on the white, frosty landscape beyond the windows, and quickly spread indoors—an excited cheer from the depths of the kitchen, an exclamation from the stairs and whispers in the passage outside the drawing room door.

The Countess of Eddleston smiled—quite inappropriately in the midst of so serious a meeting with the charitable ladies—for around Eddleston there was only one *he* referred to without name. The earl, St. John Gore, who would always be Tyler to Lucy, was coming home.

A day earlier than she had expected. But then, Tyler rarely did the expected.

"Our funds have dwindled, my lady," Mrs. Harper, the vicar's wife, stated with something close to outrage. "Running the school is expensive!"

"Indeed it is," Lucy replied, barely listening. "But educating our young people is a worthy achievement indeed, one we can all take pride in…"

The door burst open, and two very small, almost identical children gamboled in, grinning with mischief and excitement.

"Mama! Papa is coming."

The twins were only two years old, but they could get up a fair speed that ran their poor nurse ragged. Not in the least put out by the august company, they charged straight to Lucy, pursued now by Rosemary, their long-suffering nurse.

"I'm so sorry, my lady," Rosemary panted. "As soon as they heard Fred tell Tom, they were off, quick as lightning!"

By then, the twins had hold of one hand each, attempting to tug Lucy from her chair. Lucy's every desire was to jump up and run with them, so powerful was her need to see Tyler after his fortnight's absence. Especially when she saw the supercilious outrage on the faces of one or two of her charitable visitors. However, basic good manners—and the desire to instill them into her sons—forced her to frown at them.

"Do you not see we have visitors?" she asked.

"Yes, but *Papa*…" Walter began.

Oliver nudged him, and together they turned and bowed to the company. "Good morning!" they said in unison, although in fact it was afternoon. However, they smiled so sweetly that even the vicar's wife softened enough to smile back.

"Now go and apologize to Rosemary for obliging her to run after you, and then you may go and wait for Papa at the front door."

"Yes, Mama!"

She yearned to go with them, but at that moment someone else strode into the room, somewhat rumpled and travel-stained, and sweeping in with him something of the cold, fresh outdoors and a strong hint of horse.

"Papa!" the boys yelled, and hurled themselves past Rosemary to grab one of their father's legs each.

No convention in the world could have prevented Lucy springing out of her chair and rushing to be embraced between the boys. And Tyler, his face already alight with affection for his sons, turned to her with delighted surprise.

She didn't know why he always found her welcome so unexpected. There was still something in him of the unassuming young man she had first met, still mixed so beguilingly with the impulsive, fun-loving creature. These days, with the responsibilities of fatherhood and his continued work for the vulnerable, he had grown another, graver layer that gave him a dominating presence when he needed it. But she still loved to see the wonder and gratitude in his eyes when she welcomed him home with unaffected joy.

He must have known they had company, but still he swooped in and kissed her full on the lips. "All well?" he murmured with a shade of anxiety, for she was again with child.

"Very well. Especially now." She gave him another quick kiss and drew back, allowing him to bend and scoop up a boy in each arm.

Thus encumbered, he marched up to the ladies and managed to bow, grinning. "Forgive my interruption, ladies. But it is a pleasure to see you, as always."

"Oh, I believe we had finished, my lord—had we not, Lady Eddleston?" said the vicar's wife. And among much twittering and sidelong glances at the earl, the ladies departed.

Tyler collapsed on the sofa with Lucy, throwing his arm around her shoulders while the twins crawled over him like puppies. Lucy let the moment of pure happiness wash over her. Sometimes she could not believe her luck in having somehow won such a joyous life.

Of course, nothing was perfect. Tyler was not always an easy man to love. When his plans went wrong and tragedy occurred— such as the riots in Manchester that summer, now known as the Peterloo Massacre—he took it appallingly to heart, accepting blame and responsibility that was not his.

For weeks, he had been sunk into melancholy, until she had been able to remind him of the good he had won, and the risks he had always known were there. He was not responsible for the poor decisions that led to the tragedy of Peterloo. But he was still responsible for leading the fight on behalf of the powerless. And finally, he had picked himself up, recalled the happiness of what he had, and carried on.

One of Lucy's pleasures in life was helping his cause too, not just in charities but in her conversations with other women. Some of them thought she was mad, of course, or dabbling in matters that did not concern her, but she liked to believe she had made *some* others think differently, and that they might have some influence on their husbands or sons…

"It's good to be home," he said, stretching out his legs so that the boys slid down them with much hilarity. "And it's almost Christmas Eve. Would you rather have gone to Blackhaven for Christmas?"

"It would have been fun," she said. "But too much rushing around. I was thinking we could go in the spring instead, if you have the time." She touched her slightly swollen belly. "Perhaps this little creature will be born there."

To her relief, Tyler nodded. "You would like Dr. Lampton to attend you? Actually, I would be happier if he were there."

The twins had been a long and difficult birth, and neither the local midwife nor physician had filled her with confidence. And yet the boys—and Lucy—had not only survived but thrived. And perhaps it was right that the earl's heirs should have been born at the earl's family seat. But this time, she had a longing to be among her own people.

She loved her life here at Eddleston and was proud of her growing reputation as London's most amusing political hostess. But occasionally, she felt the urge to be home. Julius was right. Black Hill and Blackhaven would always be that, and she wanted her children to know it too.

"I'll write to Julius," Tyler said.

"I'll write to everyone, and see who will be there," Lucy said with satisfaction. "And before then, there is much to enjoy."

"Christmas," Walter said, bouncing on his father's co-operative foot.

"And before that, tea," Lucy said. "Go with Rosemary, wash

and brush your hair, and you may have tea with Papa and me."

"Hurray!" they cried, springing up and dashing for Rosemary. They seized her by the hands, all but hauling her from the room while she tried not to laugh.

"They are a handful," Tyler said proudly.

Smiling, Lucy laid her head on his shoulder. "I expect your nurse thanked heaven, fasting, that there was only one of you."

"Probably," he admitted.

He was silent, and she wondered if he was thinking of his sister. Now that Harold Irving had paid for his crime, Tyler seemed to speak of Anne without the same heavy shadow of pain. It was the lighter memories he dwelled upon and shared, and she was glad of that.

"It will be good to see everyone else again too," Lucy said, her mind drifting back to Blackhaven. "We must visit the Farmers, especially now that Betsy has a baby of her own. Apparently, Toby guards the child from all but its parents!"

"Knowing the Gaffneys, that is probably sensible. Are you tired, Lucy?"

She looked up at him in surprise. "Tired? I'm not the one who has ridden a hundred miles! No, I am not remotely tired."

His gaze dropped to her lips. "Are you sure? I thought you might like a nap before tea."

She caught the faint huskiness of his voice and the glint in his eyes, and her body began to melt. She had missed him in every way. He lowered his head and took her mouth, leaving her in no doubt of his own desires.

"Perhaps I could do with a short rest," she said breathlessly.

He smiled with more than a hint of wickedness and rose, drawing her to her feet. "Allow me to escort you, my lady."

"In case I have forgotten the way, my lord?"

"The way to what?" he whispered in her ear. "Pleasure?"

She remembered that very well indeed, as she went on to show him with considerable enthusiasm for a lady in need of a rest. And she was certainly rewarded with a delicious reminder of her own. After which, they went sedately downstairs to have tea with their children.

"Tonight, we will have longer," he promised.

And Lucy smiled, just because life really was wonderful.

# About the Author

Mary Lancaster lives in Scotland with her husband, three mostly grown-up kids and a small, crazy dog.

Her first literary love was historical fiction, a genre which she relishes mixing up with romance and adventure in her own writing. Her most recent books are light, fun Regency romances written for Dragonblade Publishing: *The Imperial Season* series set at the Congress of Vienna; and the popular *Blackhaven Brides* series, which is set in a fashionable English spa town frequented by the great and the bad of Regency society.

Connect with Mary on-line – she loves to hear from readers:

Email Mary:
Mary@MaryLancaster.com

Website:
www.MaryLancaster.com

Newsletter sign-up:
http://eepurl.com/b4Xoif

Facebook:
facebook.com/mary.lancaster.1656

Facebook Author Page:
facebook.com/MaryLancasterNovelist

Twitter:
@MaryLancNovels

Amazon Author Page:
amazon.com/Mary-Lancaster/e/B00DJ5IACI

Bookbub:
bookbub.com/profile/mary-lancaster